*"Will you do it, Matt?" Princess Adele asked anxiously. "Will you marry me?"*

Matt leaned back into his chair and closed his eyes. "I'll probably regret it, but...yeah, I'll marry you."

"Thank you," she whispered. "I'll be in your debt forever."

"Yeah, yeah." He opened his eyes just a fraction. "Six months after the annulment, you'll barely remember my name."

"That's not true. I'll always—" She stopped abruptly.

From across the room, Matt kept watching her. He simply couldn't take his eyes off her. And the more he tried to push aside thoughts of her, the more vivid those thoughts became. He could taste her lips, feel her body, hear her soft whimpers.

She kept telling him no, but the look in her eyes said something else. That look said, *I want you. Even though I know we're all wrong for each other, I want you....*

Dear Reader,

Once again, Silhouette Intimate Moments starts its month off with a bang, thanks to Beverly Barton's *The Princess's Bodyguard,* another in this author's enormously popular miniseries THE PROTECTORS. A princess used to royal suitors has to "settle" for an in-name-only marriage to her commoner bodyguard. Or maybe she isn't settling at all? Look for more Protectors in *On Her Guard,* Beverly Barton's Single Title, coming next month.

ROMANCING THE CROWN continues with *Sarah's Knight* by Mary McBride. An arrogant palace doctor finds he needs help himself when his little boy stops speaking. To the rescue: a beautiful nanny sent to work with the child—but who winds up falling for the good doctor himself. And in Candace Irvin's *Crossing the Line,* an army pilot crash-lands, and she and her surviving passenger—a handsome captain—deal simultaneously with their attraction to each other and the ongoing crash investigation. Virginia Kantra begins her TROUBLE IN EDEN miniseries with *All a Man Can Do,* in which a police chief finds himself drawn to the reporter who is the sister of a prime murder suspect. In *The Cop Next Door* by Jenna Mills, a woman back in town to unlock the secrets of her past runs smack into the stubborn town sheriff. And Melissa James makes her debut with *Her Galahad,* in which a woman who thought her first husband was dead finds herself on the run from her abusive *second* husband. And who should come to her rescue but Husband Number One—not so dead after all!

Enjoy, and be sure to come back next month for more of the excitement and passion, right here in Intimate Moments.

Leslie J. Wainger
Executive Senior Editor

Please address questions and book requests to:
Silhouette Reader Service
U.S.: 3010 Walden Ave., P.O. Box 1325, Buffalo, NY 14269
Canadian: P.O. Box 609, Fort Erie, Ont. L2A 5X3

# BEVERLY BARTON
# The Princess's Bodyguard

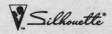

**INTIMATE MOMENTS**™

Published by Silhouette Books

**America's Publisher of Contemporary Romance**

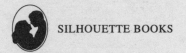 SILHOUETTE BOOKS

ISBN 0-373-27247-2

THE PRINCESS'S BODYGUARD

# BEVERLY BARTON

has been in love with romance since her grandfather gave her an illustrated book of *Beauty and the Beast*. An avid reader since childhood, Beverly wrote her first book at the age of nine. After marriage to her own "hero" and the births of her daughter and son, Beverly chose to be a full-time homemaker, aka wife, mother, friend and volunteer. The author of over thirty-five books, Beverly is a member of Romance Writers of America and helped found the Heart of Dixie chapter in Alabama. She has won numerous awards and has made the Waldenbooks and *USA TODAY* bestseller lists.

To LJ, Linda, Gayle and Leslie,
thanks for all the fun and laughter,
all the shared moments,
the shared confidences and the friendships I treasure.

# Prologue

What he needed was some fun, Matt O'Brien decided.
A week of wine, women and song. And what better place
to enjoy himself than here in Paris. He'd checked into the
hotel the night before, arriving from Switzerland on an
evening flight. His latest assignment had left him in bad
need of a vacation, so he hoped to spend a week in France,
seeing the sights and enjoying the company of at least one
or two lovely mademoiselles. When he opened the door to
allow room service to roll in the breakfast cart, he lifted
his index finger to his lips in a silent request for the waiter
to enter quietly. Matt nodded toward the man sleeping in
one of the double beds. The waiter bobbed his head up
and down and smiled. Matt signed for the meal. As soon
as the waiter left, Matt poured himself a cup of coffee and
sat down to take a look at the latest edition of *Le Monde*,
the Paris newspaper he'd requested.

Being able to speak several languages—adequately if
not fluently—was a plus in his business. He'd been an

agent for the Dundee Security and Investigation Agency, based in Atlanta, Georgia, for several years now, after serving his country in the Air Force for more than ten years. Since the agency's reputation as "the best in the U.S." had become known worldwide, more and more requests were coming in from foreign countries. That's how he and Worth Cordell, his fellow Dundee agent, had wound up in Switzerland investigating the disappearance of a wealthy Swiss banker. They'd been hired by the man's daughter, who hadn't been satisfied with the way the local authorities had dealt with her father's case. In the end, Matt had risked his life to protect Maura Ottokar, whose stepmother had arranged the murder of her husband and had intended to kill Maura, too, as she was the only other heir to the man's fortune.

Matt propped his feet on the ottoman, flipped open the newspaper and scanned the headlines. He had discovered that reading foreign newspapers was a great way to practice his language skills. As he sipped the coffee and indulged in a delicious pastry, a headline caught his eye. The engagement of Princess Adele of Orlantha to Dedrick Vardan, Duke of Roswald, was announced by King Leopold. Matt chuckled. Why any modern-thinking people would allow themselves to be ruled by a monarchy seemed implausible to him. It was one thing for the monarchy to be a figurehead and another if they were part of the governing power, as they were in the Rhode-Island-size country of Orlantha. In the equally small neighboring principality of Balanchine, the monarchy was the absolute governing body. From time to time news about these two little squabbling countries that had been one country two hundred years ago became a front-page item.

"What's so damn funny?" Worth Cordell rolled over in bed, opened his eyes and glared at Matt.

"Sorry. I didn't mean to wake you."

Matt grinned. Worth didn't. The Switzerland assignment had been the first the two men had shared, and Matt had found out rather quickly that his comrade-in-arms wasn't the friendly good-ol'-boy type like Jack Parker, a former Dundee agent who'd been a hell of a lot of fun when they'd shared assignments. Worth was a quiet, withdrawn man, with a deadly stare that could destroy an opponent a good twenty feet away. He didn't drink, didn't smoke, didn't gamble and, as far as Matt could tell, didn't womanize. And he didn't share war stories or personal confidences with his co-workers. All Matt knew about the big, rugged loner was that he stood six-four, had originally come from Arkansas and had once been a Green Beret Ranger.

Worth rolled out of bed wearing only a pair of cotton boxers, but quickly slipped into the faded jeans he'd hung across the back of a nearby chair.

"Hey, are you sure you don't want to stay on in Paris with me?" Matt called as Worth disappeared into the bathroom. "Couldn't you use some R & R before your next assignment?"

Worth didn't respond. Matt shrugged. The guy could be downright unfriendly. After finishing off the pastry and coffee, Matt refilled his cup and returned his interest to the newspaper. He glanced at the picture of the princess and her betrothed. The guy was gangly, with a long, narrow face and a bored expression. A real toad. He had the appearance of a guy whose gene pool included a little inbreeding. On the other hand the princess looked like...well, like a princess. Petite, small-boned, fragile. And lovely.

But there was something else about her. She didn't look happy. In fact, she looked more like a condemned woman than a bride-to-be.

Worth emerged from the bathroom, his auburn hair damp and his dark eyes wide open. "How's the coffee?"

"Not bad."

Worth poured himself a cup and sat across from Matt in the chair at the desk. "Are you about finished with the paper?"

"Just started looking," Matt said. "This—" he held up the page to show Worth "—caught my eye."

"I didn't know you were a royal watcher." Worth brought the cup to his lips.

Matt chuckled. "I'm not. I just happened to notice the headline." Matt folded the paper in two and tossed it to Worth, who caught it midair.

"My French isn't too good," Worth admitted.

"Why don't you call the front desk and have them bring up a copy of the—"

"Nah." Worth flopped the paper down on the desk, opened it and scanned the page. "Am I reading this right? These two have been engaged since they were kids?"

"Politics," Matt said. "Makes you wonder what century those people are living in, doesn't it?"

Worth turned the page. "I'm catching the next flight back to Atlanta," he said, abruptly changing the subject. "While you were down in the bar last night, I called Ellen and she already has my next assignment lined up."

What was it with this guy? Matt wondered. Ever since he'd joined the Dundee Agency over a year ago, he'd gone from one assignment to the next, without a break. Didn't he ever rest? Ever have any fun?

"Have you got something against taking a day off?" Matt asked. "You're making the rest of us look bad."

Worth didn't glance up from the paper. "I prefer working."

"Yeah, well, to each his own. I for one plan to whoop and holler a little while I'm in Paris."

Worth continued glancing through the paper, for all intents and purposes ignoring Matt. Hell, with an attitude like that, Matt was glad Worth wasn't going to stay on. The guy was a real stick-in-the-mud. Matt leaned back, folded his hands behind his head and slowly closed his eyelids. Instantly a pair of dark eyes set in a sad little face appeared in his mind. The unhappy princess. Maybe here in Paris he'd meet someone half as pretty as Princess Adele. But a tempting little tidbit of Parisian fluff wouldn't be able to compare to the princess. Her full, pouting mouth materialized in his mind. Damn, he could almost taste her.

Matt's eyelids flew open. What was the matter with him, daydreaming about a rich, snobbish woman who would never give a guy like him the time of day? But there was something about her that made her unforgettable. Was it the beauty or the sadness? Or a combination of the two?

Matt grunted. He knew two things. One, no woman was unforgettable. Two, if he was the princess's fiancé, she'd be smiling.


Adele Reynard, heir to the throne of Orlantha, packed quickly, intending to take only the bare necessities and one change of clothes. She could buy whatever she needed once she and Yves were safely across the border. Ordinarily Adele wasn't the type to run away; she believed in standing up against tyranny and fighting to the finish. But in this case her father had taken away all other options. If she remained in Orlantha, she would be forced to marry Dedrick—which was a fate worse than death. Not only did she personally dislike the pompous ass, she had recently come to distrust him. And even to fear him.

"Yves is here," Lisa Mercer said. "He is parked at the back entrance. He told the guards that he's here to pick me up for our date."

Lisa, Adele's secretary for the past seven years, handed

her the red wig styled in an identical fashion to Lisa's short, stylish hairdo. "Here, put this on. It's the finishing touch." Adele took the wig, slipped it over her short, curly locks that she'd dampened slightly and combed as flat as possible against her scalp. Lisa surveyed Adele from wig to chunky sandals. "Perfect. With my clothes, shoes and now the wig, you could easily pass for me. Well, at least from a distance. You're not quite as tall and your eyes are brown where mine are green, but—"

"Once I'm gone, do not give away anything about where I've gone or with whom. Swear to my father and to Lord Burhardt that you have no idea where I went," Adele said. "Give my father this." Adele picked up the envelope off her bed and handed it to Lisa. "I've written him a very brief letter telling him that I refuse to marry Dedrick and that I will not return home until he agrees to call off the wedding."

"If King Leopold suspects that I helped you—that I'm the one who contacted Yves for you—then when you return you may find me exiled or in prison." Lisa's lips curved into a smile.

Adele hugged Lisa. "If Father finds out that you helped me, you have my permission to assure him that you had no idea what I planned to do and you were simply following my instructions."

"Please, Your Highness, be careful." Lisa followed Adele out into the hallway. "If what you suspect about the duke is true, your life could be in danger."

Clutching her small suitcase, Adele paused, glanced over her shoulder and said, "I won't be able to contact you for a while, but please tell Pippin that I can be contacted through Dia Constantine in Golnar. Any important messages can be sent through her. I hope he is able to unearth some solid evidence against Dedrick that I can take to my father."

Lisa nodded. "I'll send a message to him as soon as I can."

Adele hurried up the hallway and down the back stairs. At this time of night the entire kitchen staff would be in bed, so she felt relatively safe going through the kitchen and out the back way. Her heart beat erratically as she made her way outside to the service lane behind the castle. A black Ferrari waited, the lights off, the motor running. A tall, lanky blond jumped out of the sports car, grabbed Adele's small case, tossed it into the trunk, then opened the passenger door for her. Once inside, Yves Jurgen leaned across the console and kissed Adele's cheek.

"*Chère,* what a marvelous disguise," Yves said. "Who would ever suspect that underneath those funky clothes and boyish hairdo is the ultrachic and very traditional princess?"

"Did the guards buy your story?"

"But of course." Yves revved the motor. "I am a consummate actor, am I not?"

"You're what the Americans call a big ham." Adele fastened her seat belt.

Yves clutched his shirt where it lay over his heart. "You wound me, my dear princess."

"Enough of this," she told him. "We must leave now. If my father finds out that I'm trying to escape, he'll lock me away and put guards at my door until the wedding."

Yves changed gears and headed the Ferrari toward the long drive that took them to the tall, imperial gates that separated the royal grounds from the city of Erembourg.

"Your papa will be furious when he discovers you have fled," Yves said. "It is a good thing for me that there is nothing he can do to harm me or ruin my good reputation."

"What good reputation?" Adele said teasingly. Yves Jurgen was known internationally as "The Playboy of Europe." Impossibly arrogant and a heartbreaker extraordinaire, Yves had tried unsuccessfully to woo her when she was twenty. But once he'd realized she was one woman he would never bed, he graciously accepted her friendship. If he had been her lover, Yves would have moved on to other women long ago, but as a friend, oddly enough, he was steadfast and loyal.

"You do have a point, my sweet Adele."

When the guards glanced into the car, Adele slunk lower in the seat and pretended to be engrossed in straightening her short, leather skirt. Yves smiled, waved and spoke to the uniformed guards. When the gates opened, Adele breathed a sigh of relief.

"The first hurdle passed," Yves said as the gates closed behind them. "And once we're over the border, we should be safe. I'll have you in Vienna before dawn."

Adele laid her head back and closed her eyes, wondering how long she would be safe at Yves's estate outside Vienna. A week, two at the most? Sooner or later someone would leak the information to the press. One of his servants or an acquaintance. She needed to call Dia in a few days to let her know what was going on, that if necessary she might have to seek sanctuary in Golnar, where not even her father's powerful influence could touch her.

Come morning, her disappearance would disrupt the palace. The king would be outraged, and no one, not even his wife or his chief advisor, Lord Burhardt, would be able to calm him. She wasn't sure exactly what her father would do, but she knew one thing for certain—he would do whatever necessary to bring her home in time for the wedding. But she was equally determined to elude her father's search and find a way to prove to him not only how unsuitable Dedrick was for her but how dangerous Dedrick was to Orlantha.

# *Chapter 1*

**K**ing Leopold crushed the letter in his meaty hand as he paced back and forth in his private chambers. With a mane of steel-gray hair and hypnotizing dark eyes, the ruler of Orlantha was still a handsome man at sixty. Six feet tall, with wide shoulders and thick chest, he emitted an aura of regal power. The willowy blond Queen Muriel, the king's second wife and twenty years his junior, wrung her hands as she watched her husband and kept repeating the same caution. "Now, dear, don't upset yourself." Lisa waited, as she'd been instructed, her back ramrod straight and her chin tilted upward. Princess Adele had trusted her to keep her whereabouts a secret, and she intended to do just that. But considering how upset His Majesty was she wished that she had not been the one to deliver the letter.

The king's health had been failing for the past several years, after his heart attack and bypass surgery. Only last year he had made a monumental decision—to abdicate the throne in favor of Princess Adele, upon her marriage to the duke. This decision was made when his doctors advised the king to reduce the stress in his life, and when it became apparent that the queen, after ten years of marriage, would not be giving the king a son to rule the kingdom.

Princess Adele was greatly admired and loved by the citizens of Orlantha. Poised, graceful, intelligent and charming, she was seen by her people as the ideal princess. A reformer and progressive thinker at heart, Adele worked diligently to help improve conditions in Orlantha, and her participation in social and charity organizations was legendary. Lisa knew that Orlantha would welcome Adele as queen with great celebration. The elected members of the council, who coruled the country with the monarch, also respected the princess, who supported the continuation of joint leadership. Pippin Ritter, vice chancellor of the council, had come to Princess Adele months ago with the information that Dedrick Vardan, Duke of Roswald, was a suspected member of a secret society called the Royalists, with ties to Balanchine. The Royalists' objective was to reunite Orlantha and Balanchine under one monarch, who would be the supreme ruler after abolishing the elected council. Balanchine's King Eduard was nearly eighty and had no heir. By a suspicious coincidence, Dedrick Vardan's mother was King Eduard's cousin.

"How dare Adele make such a demand! She says that she will not return home unless I call off her wedding to Dedrick. The very idea. I will not allow her to get away with blackmail." King Leopold stopped, glared at Lisa and asked, "Do you have any idea where she went?"

Lisa swallowed hard. "No, Your Majesty. She simply commanded me to give you the letter."

"Why didn't you try to stop her?" the king asked.

"Sire, you must know that once the princess makes up her mind, no one can persuade her otherwise."

Attired in a tailored navy-blue suit, Lord Sidney Burhardt, the king's chief advisor—and some said second only in power to the king—clicked his heels after entering the room. All eyes turned to Lord Burhardt. He had the bearing of a soldier, which he had once been, and an air of superiority that immediately put others in their place. Add to those qualities his white-blond hair, cut conservatively short, and icy-blue eyes, and the chief advisor had the appearance of a Nazi SS officer as depicted in American films about World War II.

"Miss Mercer," Lord Burhardt said. Lisa trembled. "Why did you not come directly to the king…or to me…before the princess left? If you had warned us, we could have prevented her from leaving."

"As you well know, my first loyalty is to the princess." Lisa looked directly at the king, judiciously avoiding eye contact with the chief advisor.

"Yes, yes, of course your loyalty is to the princess, as it should be." The king looked at Lord Burhardt. "Just as your first loyalty is to me. So, do not badger poor Lisa. I'm thankful that Adele at least left a letter. Otherwise I might have continued thinking she had been kidnapped."

"Yes, of course. We're all thankful that the princess left the palace of her own accord," Lord Burhardt replied. "But if the news is leaked to the press…if the people discover that she has fled only weeks before her wedding… I do wish Miss Mercer had tried to persuade the princess to stay—"

"How could we expect Adele's secretary to be able to control her when I, her father, am unable to do anything with her? She's a stubborn, willful girl. But in this matter she will comply with my wishes. She will marry Dedrick one month from this Saturday!"

"Then, Your Majesty, I suggest we—" Lord Burhardt said, but was quickly cut short by the king.

"Send for Colonel Rickard immediately," the king commanded.

"My dear, why send for the chief of security now that Adele has already slipped past his guards?" Muriel asked.

King Leopold glared at his wife, who shrank away from him and cast her gaze to the floor.

"I'll call for Colonel Rickard," Lord Burhardt said.

King Leopold walked over, placed his arm around his wife's shoulders and hugged her affectionately. She lifted her face and smiled at him.

Lisa's stomach knotted painfully. Would Colonel Rickard question her? Would he figure out that the princess had left the palace disguised as her?

Within five minutes the tall, slender chief of palace security stood before the king, an embarrassed flush on his pale face. Lisa felt sorry for Colonel Rickard. After all, it had been on his watch, so to speak, that the princess had managed to leave the palace grounds without detection—and without her palace guards.

"The princess has not been kidnapped," the king said.

Colonel Rickard sighed; his lips twitched with a grateful half smile. "Then you've heard from her, Your Majesty?"

King Leopold held up the crushed letter and pointed it at Colonel Rickard as if it were a weapon. "The damn fool girl has run off and says in this message—" he shook his clenched fist "—that she will not return until I call off her wedding to Dedrick."

"This information is strictly confidential." Lord Burhardt offered first the colonel and then Lisa a deadly, warning glare. "It is to go no further than the people in this room."

"Quite right," the king said. "Colonel, I want the princess found and brought home as soon as possible. How do you suggest we go about accomplishing this without alerting the press in any way? Things must be handled discreetly. A scandal must be averted!''

"I understand, Your Majesty," the colonel said. "I suggest hiring a private firm to track down the princess and, with your permission, bring her home even if it means taking her against her will."

"A private firm? Hmm." The king rubbed his chin. "A firm outside of Orlantha? Yes, yes. A trusted firm with operatives who know how to keep their mouths shut."

"I will make some discreet inquiries, sire, and have suggestions for you within the hour." The colonel bowed.

King Leopold waved a dismissive hand. "Yes, go. Now. And hurry. We have no time to lose." The minute the colonel bowed again and then exited the chambers, the king turned to Lord Burhardt. "Issue a statement that the princess has the flu and is confined to her quarters. Contact Dr. Latimer and instruct him to come to the palace this morning."

Lord Burhardt bowed, clicked his heels and left. Lisa waited, praying the king would dismiss her. She needed to contact Pippin Ritter as soon as possible to tell him where the princess was and to pass along the information she'd left for him.

The king slumped down on a huge, ornate chair by the fireplace. The queen came to him, leaned over the chair and placed her hands on his shoulders.

"Please rest, my dear." Queen Muriel patted her husband tenderly. "Adele will be found and returned home. All will be well."

The king glanced at Lisa. "She told me that she didn't love Dedrick. That's what this is all about, isn't it? Some romantic nonsense. I assured her that she would grow to care for Dedrick. The man has several sterling qualities. He's intelligent, quick-witted, charming, and his bloodlines are pure. I refuse to believe that it's anything more than prewedding jitters with Adele.''

Lisa remained quiet, aware that she had no right to voice an opinion. She thought Dedrick was only fairly intelligent, and he was seldom charming except when in the king's presence. Those who knew him well were aware that he drank to excess, gambled and womanized. Hardly sterling qualities.

''Adele told me some ludicrous story about suspecting Dedrick of treason,'' the king said. ''She thinks he's one of those damn Royalists who wants us to reunite with Balanchine. I told her there was no point in her fabricating lies about him.''

''Sire, what if…what if they aren't lies?'' Lisa expected an outraged cry from the king, but instead he simply stared at her as if she were speaking in an alien tongue.

''You're dismissed,'' the king said. ''If you hear from Adele… Never mind. She won't telephone the palace.''

Lisa curtsied, then fled as quickly as possible. Once securely locked in her private quarters in the princess's wing of the palace, she used her cell phone to contact Vice Chancellor Ritter. He needed to know what had happened and that the princess would be sending and receiving messages through her friend, Dia Constantine.

Adele sipped at the pink champagne as she lounged in the drawing room of Chateau Gustel thirty kilometers outside Vienna. The house and grounds would be considered large by most people's standards, but in comparison to the palace and royal grounds in Erembourg, the estate was rather small. But it was quite comfortable, with an adequate staff. And Yves had been utterly charming these past three days. They'd had such fun flying off to Paris yesterday for a divine shopping spree. No one had had any idea that the kooky redhead on Yves's arm was actually the princess of Orlantha. Being incognito was proving to be amazingly exciting. But she couldn't hide out here with Yves indefinitely. It was only a matter of time before someone discovered her whereabouts. But for now she was safe. Living outside Orlantha, there wasn't much she could do to help Pippin and his trusted colleagues in their quest to find evidence against Dedrick. But she could buy them all some time by stopping the wedding or at least postponing it until she could show her father hard proof of Dedrick's disloyalty.

Yves breezed into the room, a newspaper under his arm and a quirky smile on his handsome face.

"What's wrong?" she asked. "You have a silly expression on your face."

"We've been found out," he replied.

"What?" Adele spilled a drop of champagne on her silk trousers as she rose from the settee.

Yves opened the paper and read to her, "Rumor has it that Princess Adele of Orlantha, reported to be in bed with the flu at the palace in Erembourg, is in actuality cavorting about Paris with none other than that bon vivant Yves Jurgen. Now, why would the engaged princess be traveling with a man other than her fiancé, Dedrick Vardan, Duke of Roswald?" Yves sighed dramatically. "The article goes on and on, but you get the idea. I'm afraid we've blown your cover, *chère*."

"That means it's only a matter of time before someone figures out I'm here in Vienna with you."

"We can pack our bags and head out for the Riviera whenever you say. This evening. Tomorrow."

Adele shook her head. "No, I'm afraid not. Everyone in Europe knows you. And apparently they recognize me, even in a red wig. I'm less likely to be recognized if I'm alone."

Yves *tsk-tsked.* "I hate the idea of your being out there alone. What will you do if—"

"I'll make arrangements to fly to Golnar in the morning," Adele said. "I'll phone Dia to let her know I'll need sanctuary with Theo and her a little sooner than I'd planned."

"I'll be sad to see you leave, dear heart. You're such an entertaining companion." Yves popped Adele gently on the nose. "I had made plans for us to meet some trusted friends for an intimate dinner tonight, but—"

"Don't change your plans," she told him. "I'll be busy packing and preparing for my trip to Golnar."

"Are you sure you don't mind? If you'd rather I stay here with you, I'll be more than glad to cancel."

"I'll be perfectly all right here," she told him. "At least for tonight. I doubt that anyone on my father's staff will be able to come up with the information about this estate in the next twenty-four hours. After all, the place still belongs to your cousin Jules, doesn't it?"

"Yes, but how did you know the chateau wasn't mine?"

"Because, Yves, my wicked friend, we both know that you have no money of your own and depend on relatives and wealthy older ladies to support you."

Yves clutched his chest and groaned. "I have shared too many of my secrets with you, *chère.*"

"And I with you."

Grinning, Yves lifted her hand and kissed it. "Then it is good that we trust each other, is it not?"

Dedrick rolled over in bed and stretched. The loud banging on the door had awakened him from a peaceful sleep. The voluptuous creature lying next to him roused, eased out of bed, slipped on a silk robe and headed for the door.

"Ask who it is," Dedrick told Vanda. "I can't have anyone finding me here."

"Don't worry," Vanda said, a devilish smile on her pretty face. "You can hide under the covers."

She cracked the door a fraction and peered through the opening. Before she could stop the man, he shoved the door open wide and knocked her aside as he entered her room at Madame Pellonia's, the most exclusive brothel in all of Orlantha.

"You fool!" the man shouted at Dedrick. "What if someone sees you here? Then the whole world will know why the princess doesn't want to marry you."

Dedrick rose from the bed leisurely, totally unconcerned with his friend's outrage. "You worry too much."

The intruder glowered at Vanda. "Leave us!"

Vanda frowned and looked to Dedrick for instructions.

He waved a dismissal. "Go. Go."

Vanda huffed, then stomped out of the room and slammed the door behind her.

Dedrick dressed, taking his time as his friend glared at him, his arms crossed over his chest.

"We must go to the palace immediately. The king has hired an American private detective to find the princess and return her to Orlantha. You should be at King Leopold's side, showing your support and concern. If he becomes the least bit suspicious—"

"Ah, but that's your job, isn't it? To waylay any suspicions."

"Princess Adele actually told her father that she believed you were a Royalist."

Dedrick laughed. "I'm sure dear papa didn't believe her. Why would anyone suspect me?"

"If your wedding to the princess is canceled, we will have no choice but to eliminate her and leave the king without an heir. We prefer to take over Orlantha by peaceful means. The Balanchine army is half the size of Orlantha's army. Once you become the prince consort, you will wield great power and can put many of our people in strategic positions within the government. And in time we will see to it that you become king of both Orlantha and Balanchine."

"I would hate to lose the chance for a wedding night with Adele. She's such a delicious little creature."

"Is that all you think about?"

"I think about many things," Dedrick said. "I think that once I am king of both Orlantha and Balanchine, you will not speak to me in such a manner."

"Once you are king, no, I will speak to you with due respect. But until that day—" the intruder grabbed Dedrick's lapels and glared directly into his eyes "—I am in charge. You will do as I say. Is that understood?"

Dedrick took a deep breath, clutched the other man's hands and removed them from his coat. "I understand perfectly."

"Good. Then go to the palace and assure King Leopold that you adore Adele and want nothing more than to be her husband."

Dedrick grinned. "What if this American detective can't find Adele?"

"My sources tell me that his firm is the best in the business. He will find her. It seems the princess was spotted with Yves Jurgen in Paris yesterday. This detective's agency is tracking her down as we speak. And when he leaves Orlantha to go after her, two of our men will follow him and make sure nothing goes wrong."


Matt's flight landed at the Vienna International Airport Holzbauer with only a twenty-minute delay. His rental car, a four-door silver Opel Omega, was ready and waiting for him. He'd spent enough time on airplanes these past few days to rack up quite a few frequent-flyer miles. Of course, Dundee picked up the tab for his flights, since all of them were work related. Ellen Denby, Dundee's CEO, had shot to hell his plans for a week of R&R in Paris. She'd phoned him only hours after Worth Cordell had taken a flight out of Roissy Charles de Gaulle, winging his way home to the good old U.S.A. Ellen had pointed out to Matt that he was already in Europe, only a short flight from Orlantha, so it would be foolish to send another agent to take the assignment. He'd tried to beg off. He should have known better. Ellen wasn't the type who could be persuaded or pressured; she was the type who expected her orders to be obeyed without question.

He had to admit that, even though he really hadn't wanted this assignment, he was curious as to why the lovely Princess Adele had flown the coop only a month before her wedding. During his interview with King Leopold, His Majesty had cited a case of premarital jitters as the reason his daughter had run away. But after sizing up the situation—and meeting the Duke of Roswald—Matt had drawn his own conclusions. Dedrick Vardan was a horse's ass. Pompous. Arrogant. Condescending. And come to think of it, the wannabe prince looked a bit like a horse. Or maybe more like a mule. But the guy sure knew how to play the king like a fiddle. And Lord Burhardt had sent cold chills up Matt's spine. His gut instincts warned him that the man would be dangerous if crossed. Then there was Colonel Rickard, who seemed to resent the fact that he hadn't been put in charge of returning the princess to the fold. The king had told Matt he wanted his daughter returned to the palace, and gave him permission to use whatever means necessary to bring her home.

After taking a look at faxed photos of Yves Jurgen that Dundee had sent, along with more information on the man than Matt actually needed, it was easy to see why the princess had run away from Dedrick and straight into Yves's waiting arms. Hell, Yves Jurgen was a damn pretty boy,

and from his "rap sheet" he knew everything there was
to know about women—how to please them and keep them
coming back for more. Matt's guess was that Princess
Adele had run away for one last fling with her former lover
before tying the knot with old mule face.

It really didn't matter to him why the princess had run
away. She was nothing more than an assignment to him.
Dundee contacts in Austria had tracked Yves and her to
an estate outside Vienna, so it was only a matter of time
before he knocked on the door, introduced himself and told
the princess that she'd been caught. He hoped she didn't
put up a fuss or that her lover didn't do something stupid.
He wanted to get this over with as soon as possible so he
could return to Paris and pick up where he'd left off with
a delectable blonde named Chantel.

Adele ate dinner alone at the chateau after making reservations to fly to Golnar in the morning. She had already
packed, except for toiletry items, her pajamas and the outfit
she'd wear tomorrow. When she'd phoned her best friend,
Dia Constantine, Dia had told Adele that she and Theo
would gladly provide a sanctuary for her. Dia was an old
boarding school classmate who had become her best friend
despite the differences in their backgrounds. Dia was the
product of a marriage between a stodgy English barrister
and his free-spirited Greek wife. A statuesque beauty with
jet-black hair and luminescent silver eyes, Dia had captured the attention and then the heart of Greek tycoon Theo
Constantine when they'd met at a party at the royal palace
in Erembourg. The two had been married for eight years
and had one child. Adele was Phila's godmother and she
adored the seven-year-old with a passion.

Adele would have gone straight to Golnar when she
escaped from the palace, but it would have been the first
place her father would have thought of when he discovered

her missing. If he'd caught her en route, he would have forced her to return to Orlantha, and no government would have dared offend the king. Of course, if she made it to Golnar, he would be powerless to force her to return. Golnar, a small island nation between Greece and Cyprus, had no diplomatic ties to Orlantha, and since Theo's wealth gave him unlimited power over local politics, the authorities would hardly allow a guest of his to be taken against her will.

No matter what, she simply had to give Pippin and his friends time to gather evidence against Dedrick. If that meant staying in Golnar for a year, then so be it.

As Adele listened to a tape of Tchaikovsky's concertos and drank her after-dinner demitasse, she heard a ruckus at the front door.

"Please, sir, no!" the butler called out in his native German language. "Stop right now, or I shall be forced to call the police."

"My German's a little rusty," a man's voice said. "But I understand that you're threatening to call the police. Go right ahead. Be my guest."

Adele tensed. The doors to the drawing room swung open. A tall, black-haired man wearing faded jeans and a weathered leather bomber jacket stormed into the room, the butler on his heels. Adele's heartbeat accelerated. Who was this stranger? Whoever he was he spoke English, not German or French.

Adele rose from the sofa and confronted the unwanted guest.

"I tried to stop him," the butler said. "Should I call the police?"

The last thing Adele wanted to deal with was the local authorities. If she involved the police, there was no telling what tomorrow's headlines would read. And she'd certainly be shipped home immediately once it was discovered that King Leopold expected her to return.

"No, don't telephone the police." She shook her head, then turned to her uninvited guest. "Who are you and what do you want?"

He stared at her, surveying her from head to toe. A shiver of uneasiness fluttered up Adele's spine. There was something sensual about the way he looked at her with those incredible blue eyes.

"I'm Matt O'Brien, with the Dundee Security and Investigation Agency."

Adele's stomach tightened. "What business do you have here at Chateau Gustel? If you want to see Yves, I'm afraid he's out for the evening. If you'll leave your card, I'll—"

"My business is with you, Princess."

He knew who she was. This didn't bode well for her. "And what business do you have with me, sir?"

"I'm here to escort you home to Orlantha."

"I see." So, who had hired this private investigator— her father or Dedrick? And how was she going to get herself out of this predicament? She'd been so sure that no one would find her here at the chateau, at least not for several days.

The butler cleared his throat. "Your Highness, is there anything I can do?"

"No, thank you. That will be all. I can take care of this matter."

Once the butler left, Adele smiled warmly at Matt O'Brien. "Won't you take a seat, Mr. O'Brien?"

"No, ma'am, thank you."

"For whom are you working, my father or—"

"King Leopold retained the Dundee Agency, and since I was the only agent already in Europe, I drew this assignment."

"I'm surprised that my father used an American firm. You are American, aren't you?"

"Yes, ma'am."

"And what will you do if I choose not to return to Orlantha with you?" *Show this hired henchman that you're not afraid of him,* she told herself. *Let him know that taking you back to your father will not be something easily accomplished.*

"I'm hoping you won't put up a fuss." The corners of his mouth lifted in a hint of a smile. "But my orders are to take you home, even if I have to hog-tie you, put you in a sack and toss you over my shoulder."

Adele gasped. Apparently, this American had not been taught the proper respect for someone in her position—a princess, the heir to the throne of Orlantha. "If you lay one hand on me, you...you brute, I shall see that you're—"

He laughed. A loud, boisterous laugh. Adele cringed. *Damn insolent cretin!* How dare he treat her in such a manner.

"Look, Little Miss Royal Runaway, we can do this the easy way or the hard way. It's up to you. But you can be sure of one thing—I'm taking your highfalutin fanny home to Daddy."

## Chapter 2

Matt had figured this wouldn't be an easy job and he'd been right. He should have known she would put up a fuss. Princess Adele stared at him, her big brown eyes glaring, and her full, pink lips clenched. With a defiant stance, her hands on her hips, and an I'm-not-going-anywhere-with-you expression on her face, she seemed to be daring him. Matt rubbed his jaw and chin. He wore two days' worth of beard stubble because he hadn't taken time to shave since he'd been rushed to Orlantha and put on this case. She probably thought he looked rather scruffy. He thought she looked incredible. Her shiny chestnut-brown hair curled about her ears in a soft, wavy bob. A pair of shimmery diamond studs—probably three carats each—glittered in her earlobes and a thin diamond-studded watch graced her wrist. Her petite body—he guessed she stood about five-two—was nicely rounded in all the right places. An hourglass shape, with a tiny waist. The outfit she wore—red cashmere sweater and gray wool slacks—had probably been purchased on her recent shopping spree in Paris and no doubt had cost a month's salary for the average person. Oh, yeah, she was one gorgeous woman, but she had ''Spoiled Rotten'' written all over her.

''The way you're looking at me is quite insulting,'' she told him with an air of snobbery.

''Excuse me, ma'am,'' he replied. ''I was just appreciating the scenery.''

A slight flush stained her cheeks. ''Mr. O'Brien, I don't know how much my father is paying you, but I will match his offer and raise it by…let's say, five thousand American dollars.''

''Let me get this straight—you're willing to pay me five thousand more than your father if I don't take you back to Orlantha?''

''That's correct.'' The tension in her body drained away, and she relaxed a bit.

''It's my understanding that your father holds the purse strings, that you aren't independently wealthy.''

She huffed, then pursed her lips and glowered at Matt. ''I have some capital at my disposal, certainly enough to buy you off.''

Barely able to control his amusement, Matt grinned. ''Look, Ms. Reynard or Princess or whatever you prefer to be called, I work for the Dundee Agency. We've got rules and regulations we have to follow, and a solid reputation to uphold, not to mention the fact that I've got a boss who can put the fear of God into any of her agents if we even think of doing anything disreputable.''

''I take that to mean you're refusing my offer.''

''Yes, ma'am, you can take it that way.''

''Then we seem to be at an impasse, don't we?''

''How's that?''

''Well, you expect me to go back to Orlantha with you,

and I refuse to return to the palace tonight or anytime in the near future. Not until my father calls off the wedding."

"Look, I can't say that I blame you for not wanting to marry old mule face. If I were a lady, I'd sure run in the opposite direction to get away from him. But my job isn't couples counseling. I was hired to take you back to the palace in Erembourg and that's what I intend to do."

Adele tensed again, her small body stiffening and her chin tilting upward slightly. She was half his size, yet even her body language challenged him. "You do not intimidate me."

No doubt about it. She wasn't going to make this easy for him.

"My orders are to use whatever means necessary to secure your return."

"Use whatever means… Are you saying that my father really did give you permission to force me to come with you?"

"Yep, that's exactly what he did. And Lord Burhardt, Colonel Rickard and your ever-loving fiancé all went right along with the order. Looks like it's you against the world, or at least your little world in Orlantha. I'd say unless you can talk your daddy out of it, you, Princess Beauty, are going home to marry the beast."

"You're the beast, Mr. O'Brien!" Adele's eyes flashed. Her nostrils flared. "I'm not leaving with you, and that's final." She stomped her foot.

"I should have just walked in, chloroformed you and been done with it. But no, I had to give you a chance to be reasonable. Stupid of me, I know, but that's just the kind of guy I am."

Matt reached out to take her arm, but she sidestepped him and began backing slowly toward the double doors behind her. "If you touch me, I'll scream."

"Then start screaming now because I'm going to touch you."

Adele opened her mouth, but before she got out more than a mild screech, Matt dashed forward, grabbed her and slammed his hand over her mouth. She wriggled and squirmed, trying to free herself. He held fast.

"We're going to march out of the chateau and straight to my car that's parked outside," Matt told her. "If you're a good little girl, I won't have to handcuff and gag you."

Her movements became frantic as she struggled against him. When he tried to walk her out of the room, she kicked him several times. Damn, why him? Why had he been the lucky guy to draw this assignment?

"Stop that right now," he said. "Otherwise, I'll have to carry you out of here in a fireman's lift."

Somehow she managed to maneuver her mouth so that she could bite him. Ouch! He let out a yelp as her teeth chomped down into his hand. And within two seconds, her ear-splitting scream echoed through the chateau. Suddenly the butler ran into the drawing room, followed by a tall, blond man wearing evening attire.

"What is going on here?" Yves Jurgen demanded.

The butler jabbered ninety-to-nothing in German, while Adele continued struggling and calling out for help. Obviously confused, Yves glanced back and forth from the butler to Adele.

"Silence!" Yves called.

The butler hushed immediately.

With Matt's arm around her waist, holding her body in front of his, Adele looked pleadingly at her friend. "Yves, this man is a private detective my father hired to find me and return me to Orlantha. Will you please tell him that he cannot force me to leave the chateau with him."

"My God! Unhand the princess!" Yves stepped forward, bringing himself directly in front of Adele and Matt. "Do you hear me? I will not allow you to—"

Matt shoved Adele aside, then confronted the pretty boy. "I don't want to hurt you, Mr. Jurgen, but if I have to, I will."

"Hurt me?" Yves laughed. "I assure you that if you persist in this matter, you will be the one hurt."

"Look, buddy boy, I'm walking out of here in about a minute, and the princess is going with me. I advise you not to try to stop us."

"Do something, Yves," Adele said.

When Adele tried to rush toward Yves, Matt grabbed her arm. "Stay put."

When he tried to walk her toward the door, she balked. And if that wasn't enough trouble, Yves came barreling toward him and grasped his shoulder. Without releasing Adele, he turned to face Yves just in time to see the man's fist coming toward him. Matt adeptly avoided the blow, but when Yves came at him a second time, Matt drew back his fist and coldcocked Yves with one blow to his jaw. The minute Yves hit the floor, the butler yelled something about the *polizei.* Matt just ignored the man. Adele began fighting him again and calling him names, first in French and then in German and finally in English.

"My, my, Princess, where did you learn such filthy language?"

And as he'd threatened, Matt hoisted her up and over his shoulder. She let out a loud screech and wiggled.

"Put me down!"

Mumbling several obscenities under his breath, Matt marched out of the drawing room, through the marble-floored entrance hall and outside to his rental car. And all the while Adele threatened him with everything from a public flogging to a beheading.

Matt opened the front passenger door of the car, depos-

ited Adele inside and closed the door. She opened the door
and tried to get out. He shoved her back inside, held her
in place until he fastened her seatbelt, then pulled out a
pair of handcuffs—which he'd brought with him, just in
case. After manacling her wrist with one cuff, he pulled
her hands behind her back and snapped the second cuff on
her other wrist.

"Now, you sit there and behave yourself."

Adele screamed again, then said, "Please, don't do this.
I'll do anything, pay you anything, if you'll let me go. I
can't go back to Orlantha. You have no idea what you're
doing."

"Save your breath," he told her. "I'm just doing my
job. When you get home, you can work this out with your
father."

"My father is as unreasonable as you are. I hate him. I
hate you. I hate all men."

Just what he needed—to listen to her bellowing and
bellyaching all the way back to Orlantha. He jerked out a
handkerchief from his other pocket and effectively gagged
her. Adele's eyes widened in shock.

"Sorry, Princess, but I have no intention of listening to
you carrying on like that while I'm driving."

Matt got in on the driver's side, started the engine and
headed down the brick driveway toward the main road.
With a little luck, they'd cross the border in a few hours
and by morning he'd be on a plane headed back to Paris.
Occasionally he glanced at the princess. She didn't look
at him, didn't acknowledge his presence in any way. She
sat there, with her hands cuffed behind her and his handkerchief tied over her mouth, staring straight ahead into
the dark night, her entire demeanor regal and unflinching.
He knew she had to be uncomfortable, but no one would
ever guess by the way she acted.

An hour and forty minutes later they were halfway to

the Austrian border, traveling along a back road, just in case Yves Jurgen had been foolish enough to try to follow them. The weather quickly turned nasty. An autumn storm created heavy streaks of lighting and rolling booms of thunder. Then came the downpour. The rain became so heavy that Matt couldn't see two feet in front of the car, leaving him no choice but to pull off to the side of the road.

He killed the motor and turned to Adele. "Will you promise to behave yourself if I remove the gag?"

She didn't respond immediately, just glowered at him. Then finally she nodded.

Matt reached out to untie the handkerchief. "If you start up again, the gag goes back in place. Understand?"

She nodded. He undid the knot and removed the gag. She took a deep breath, then licked the sides of her mouth where the handkerchief had chafed her skin.

"Mr. O'Brien, I didn't run away simply because I find Dedrick personally offensive."

"Look, honey, it doesn't matter to me why you ran off. Can't you get it through that pretty little head of yours that I'm just doing my job?"

"And I'm trying to do mine!"

Realizing she was probably going to give him some sad sob story, Matt didn't respond. The wind beat against the car, whistling around them as the rain continued pouring. He wondered how long they'd be stuck here. The sooner he got this woman off his hands, the better.

"Mr. O'Brien?"

"Mmm-hmm?"

"Do you know anything about the politics in Orlantha and Balanchine?"

"Yeah, a little."

"Are you aware that there are factions in both countries that wish to see the two reunited as one country?"

"I think I heard something to that effect."

"Have you also heard about a group called the Royalists?"

"Can't say that I have, but something tells me that I'm about to." Matt turned in his seat so that he faced Adele. "If you promise not to do anything stupid, I'll undo the handcuffs."

"Do you want me to promise that I will not try to run from you?" she asked.

"Yeah."

"Then I promise."

Matt stared at her for a moment, trying to discern her credibility. What the hell, he'd take a chance. After all, how far could she go if she did try to run?

After taking the key from his pocket, he gave her back a gentle shove forward, then reached down and unlocked the handcuffs.

She brought her hands slowly around to the front and rubbed first one wrist and then the other. Repeating the process several times, she said, "Thank you."

Matt wasn't sure which princess he preferred. The quiet-spoken, accommodating lady or the other—the defiant, hostile spitfire. He definitely trusted the spitfire more. This sweet act she was putting on now worried him. Was she up to something? Or had she simply changed tactics thinking honey attracted more than vinegar?

"About the Royalists," she said. "They are a secret society that is active in both Orlantha and Balanchine. Their goals are to reunite the two countries under one king and for the combined nations to be ruled *solely* by the monarch. They want to turn back the clock two hundred years."

"What does this have to do with your marriage to the duke?"

"I believe that Dedrick is a Royalist."

"Got any proof?"

"Not yet, but soon, we hope."

"We?"

"I'm sorry, Mr. O'Brien, but I cannot explain further. I simply do not know how trustworthy you are. Considering the fact that you're working for my father, I—"

"How does Dedrick being a Royalist have any effect on your marriage? You're a princess. Your old man is the king. I'd say your whole family are Royalists."

"No, we are not!" Adele huffed. "You do not understand. My father rules Orlantha in conjunction with an elected council, headed by a chancellor and a vice chancellor and we do not want Orlantha reunited with Balanchine under any circumstances, and most definitely not as a monarch-ruled country. We suspect...I suspect that if Dedrick becomes the prince consort, he will try to usurp more and more power, especially in the event of my father's death someday. As my husband, he would have almost as much authority over the government as I do."

"Interesting story," Matt said. "Why don't you tell it to your father when you return to Orlantha?"

"I have told my father, but he refuses to believe me."

"Because you don't have any evidence against the duke."

Adele sighed. "No, I don't have any evidence, and my father won't postpone the wedding and give us...give me time to prove Dedrick is not only an unsuitable husband for me but an unsuitable prince for Orlantha."

"So you ran away to buy time for your unnamed cohorts in Orlantha to gather evidence against Dedrick?"

"That's right." Adele smiled. "So you see, I cannot go back, not yet. If I return to Orlantha, my father will force me to marry Dedrick next month."

"Why don't you marry someone else?" Matt gazed

through the Opel's side window. "Looks like the rain's letting up." He started the engine and shifted gears.

"Marry someone else... You mean marry another man before my father can force me to marry Dedrick?"

Matt pulled the car back onto the road and headed southwest. "Yeah, that's exactly what I mean. If you're already married to another guy, your father can't force you to marry Dedrick."

"It would have to be a marriage in name only," she said. "A marriage of convenience that could be easily annulled once we have the proof we need against Dedrick." She grasped Matt's arm. "Mr. O'Brien, that's a wonderful idea. Yves would probably marry me, but I'm not sure I could trust him 100 percent. He'd want to remain the prince consort. And I'm sure Pippin would marry me, but he'd have to leave Orlantha and meet me somewhere."

"Who's Pippin? Sounds like some cartoon character."

Adele laughed. "Vice chancellor Pippin Ritter is a fine man and rather handsome. And he's a good friend."

"Then when you get home, marry the vice chancellor. Problem solved."

"We'd never be allowed to marry in Orlantha. But if I could get a message to Pippin, he could meet me—"

"Princess, I'm taking you to Orlantha tonight." When she gasped and started to speak, he went on, "Once you're back in your own country, you and this Pippin can figure out a plan. But I'm finishing the job I started."

"I thought you understood. I thought I could reason with you."

"I'm sorry, okay? But the internal politics in Orlantha really aren't any of my business." Matt caught a glimpse of her in his peripheral vision. There was that sad little face again, the one he'd seen in the Paris newspaper announcing her engagement. What was it about this woman that made him want to wrap his arms around her and tell

her that everything would be all right? He didn't know
her. Didn't want to know her. She was an assignment. If
he were smart, he wouldn't get involved.

"You're right, of course," she said. "Why should you
care about me or my country?"

There was nothing else to be said, so Matt kept quiet.
For the next thirty minutes the only sounds were the car's
engine and the renewed strength of the storm. They
seemed to be heading directly into even more turbulent
weather. Once again it became impossible for Matt to see
more than a couple of feet past the hood of the car. When
he came to a crossroads, marked with a signpost, he
stopped so that the headlights hit the sign. Gerwalt Inn.
Not a town marker, but a welcome to the local hotel.

"We're going to have to stop," Matt said. "I'll see if
I can find Gerwalt Inn, and we'll stay there until this storm
passes."

He could tell that the princess was trying not to smile,
but it was obvious she was pleased with the brief reprieve.

"Whatever you say, Mr. O'Brien."

He didn't like the sound of that. She was being much
too accommodating, which meant she was up to something. He'd have to make sure he kept close watch over
her.

Adele said a silent prayer of thanks for sending such a
hostile storm on this very night when she needed it so
badly. Once they stopped at the inn, she would find a way
to escape from her American captor. There had to be a
way to get away from him or to persuade him to let her
go. Perhaps at the inn, she would find someone to help
her. After all, she was bound to be recognized as the princess of Orlantha.

While Matt O'Brien drove slowly, being extra careful
because of the rain, Adele studied the Dundee agent. The

man needed a shave and a haircut. His thick black hair was tousled, his jeans faded and his leather bomber jacket worn with age. He was rather good-looking, if you liked the big, macho type. When he had grabbed her at the chateau, she had surmised that he was nearly a foot taller than she and about twice her size. And, going by his surname, she assumed he was of Irish descent. She guessed his age to be somewhere around thirty-five, give or take a couple of years. There was no gray in his jet-black hair or his beard, but he had tiny wrinkles at the edges of his eyes and shallow furrows in his forehead.

When the car stopped, Adele looked out the window, but the downpour was so heavy that all she could make out were blurry lights. Matt turned off the engine, pocketed the keys and looked at Adele. The man had the bluest eyes she'd ever seen. Bright, summer-day sky blue.

"We'll have to make a run for it," he told her. "We'll get drenched, but there's nothing else to do."

She nodded. Matt flung open the door and jumped out. Adele did the same. Matt grabbed her arm and together they ran toward the two-story inn. By the time they made it inside to the reception area, they were both thoroughly wet to the skin.

The inn's proprietor came out from behind the front desk to greet them.

*"Güten abend,"* the man said in German. *"Willkommen zum gasthaus."*

*"Güten abend,"* Adele replied.

Although he understood that they'd said "good evening" to each other and the innkeeper had welcomed them, Matt's guess was that the princess's command of the German language was far better than his. He didn't want to take any chances that she might start rattling off a spiel in German and he wouldn't be able to keep up.

"Do you speak English?" Matt asked.

"Yes, I speak English," the man said. "You are Americans?"

"I'm an American," Matt replied.

"And I am Prin—"

Matt reached out, draped his arm around her shoulders and hauled her up against him. "This is my bride, Priscilla. We're honeymooning here in Austria."

"We are not—" Adele said, but was cut short when Matt kissed her.

How dare he kiss her! How dare he... Oh, heaven help her. His mouth was warm, moist and commanding. She didn't think she'd ever been kissed quite so thoroughly in her entire twenty-eight years. She gripped his shoulders to steady her wobbly legs, and when he thrust his tongue into her mouth, all thoughts of a protest vanished. The kiss ended as quickly as it had begun, and for a split second Adele felt oddly adrift.

When he eased his mouth from hers, she glared at him. He whispered softly against her lips, "Don't try to pull anything, or I'll be forced to play dirty."

Adele nodded, only now understanding just how devious her captor could be. Matt turned to the proprietor who stood waiting, a broad smile on his face, apparently delighted by the honeymooners' ardor.

"We'd like a room, please," Matt said. "We'll be staying until the storm passes."

Matt pulled out his wallet, removed his credit card and handed it to the innkeeper. The innkeeper scurried behind the front desk, scanned the credit card, then retrieved a key and handed the key and the card to Matt. "What about your luggage, Mr. O'Brien?"

"It's in the car, but considering the way it's raining, I think we'll do without it tonight."

The innkeeper nodded. "I will have Hilda bring robes for you and your wife. With my compliments. And if there is anything else I can do for you, just let me know. I am Franz Gerwalt.''

"Thanks,'' Matt replied. "We'll let you know if—''

"Herr Gerwalt?'' Adele spoke softly, a warm, friendly smile on her damp face.

"Yes?''

"We would also like some brandy brought to our room, and I require two extra pillows,'' Adele said. "I assume there's a fireplace in our room.'' Franz Gerwalt nodded. "If there isn't a fire in the fireplace, please, see that one is prepared immediately.''

Matt tugged on her arm. "You're being terribly demanding, dear. You're acting like a spoiled brat.''

"I'm doing no such thing,'' she replied. "I am simply requesting adequate treatment, nothing more.''

The innkeeper frowned as he looked back and forth from Adele to Matt. "A lovers' quarrel on your honeymoon? You must not argue. We will be happy to accommodate Mrs. O'Brien's requests.''

"Thank you,'' Adele said. "I have one more request.''

"Certainly,'' the innkeeper replied.

"Will you please call the police and tell them that this man has kidnapped me?''

# Chapter 3

Holy Moses! Matt thought. He'd have to do something and do it quickly, before Herr Gerwalt had a chance to comprehend and believe the princess's accusation.

Matt grabbed Adele, hauled her up close to him and grinned sheepishly at Franz Gerwalt. "Such a kidder." Matt forced laughter. "Always joking around about my kidnapping her because we ran off to get married and her father accused me of kidnapping his baby girl."

Herr Gerwalt offered Matt and Adele a weak smile. "You Americans. I do not understand your odd sense of humor."

"I'm not—" Adele said, but before she could complete her sentence, Matt kissed her again.

She bit his lip, then stomped on his foot. Huffing loudly, she turned to the innkeeper. "Don't you recognize me? I'm—"

Matt swept her off her feet. Literally. This assignment was turning into a royal pain in the butt. If he didn't have a sore foot, a stinging lip and wasn't pissed off as hell, he might find humor in the situation. But as it was, he was about two seconds away from strangling the princess of Orlantha.

Turning around so Herr Gerwalt couldn't see that he'd covered Adele's mouth with his hand, Matt said, "We'll just go on up to our room. Thanks for everything." With a wiggling Adele squirming in his arms, Matt headed for the stairs, then paused. "By the way, I can make a long-distance call from our room using my calling card, right?"

"Yes, yes. Of course."

"Okay."

"I'll see to the fire at once and have those robes brought up to you. And if you need anything else, please—"

"Yeah, thanks."

The minute Matt reached the second floor of the inn, he bent his head to whisper in Adele's ear. "Unless you want me to handcuff you to a chair and gag you again, then I suggest you behave yourself. Do I make myself clear?"

She glared at him, her big brown eyes narrowed to angry slits. She ceased squirming but didn't respond to his warning.

He made his way down the corridor, looking for room 204, which turned out to be the third door on the left. After readjusting Adele in his arms, he inserted the key in the lock and opened the door. He switched on the lights in a quaint room, filled with what he assumed were European antiques. The low ceiling, small windows and heavy, dark furniture exuded an old-world charm. After closing and locking the door, he set Adele on her feet but kept a tight rein on her and continued holding his hand over her mouth.

"What's it going to be, Your Highness? Are we doing this the easy way or the hard way?" He looked her right in the eyes. "Are you going to cooperate and act your part as the blushing bride? Are you going to be a good girl?"

She nodded agreement. Matt eased his hand away from her mouth.

They stared at each other. Matt grinned. Adele frowned.

Matt manacled her wrist and dragged her across the room with him, straight toward a door he figured was the bathroom. After opening the door and finding the light switch, he shoved her inside the tiny bath that had one small window above the old bathtub. Thick lace curtains blocked out the night sky.

"Take off your wet things, and as soon as the maid brings our robes, I'll throw one in here to you."

Adele nodded, but when she started to close the door, Matt stuck his foot in the narrow opening. "Leave it partially open," he told her, pushing it open halfway.

"If you think that I'm going to undress in front of you, then you had better think again."

"Get real, honey, you aren't my type," Matt said, then when he saw the serious expression on her face, he grinned. "I thought you royals were used to having people dress and undress you."

"I have a lady's maid. But I can assure you that I am not accustomed to undressing in front of men, certainly not a man who is a total stranger to me." She clicked off the light in the bathroom.

Matt turned around, putting his back to her. "I won't look. I promise. But do not close that door."

"Why? What do you think I'm going to do, escape through the drainpipes?"

"I wouldn't put it past you to give it a try." His shoulders quivered as he chuckled silently. He could barely keep from laughing out loud.

"Has anyone every told you that you're obnoxious?" Adele asked.

With his back still to her, he responded, "No, ma'am.

People usually tell me that I'm smart, good-looking, fun to be with, loyal, good-humored—''

Adele huffed loudly. ''Obnoxious and conceited!''

Matt chuckled. A loud knock at the door gained his attention. He glanced over his shoulder toward the half-open bathroom door and caught sight of a slender, naked shoulder, part of a naked back, a round hip covered with silk panties and a long naked leg. He sucked in a deep breath. Holy Moses! He snapped his head back around before the princess caught him spying on her.

''You behave yourself,'' he told her. ''That's probably the maid at the door with our robes.''

''Please, let her in,'' Adele said. ''And ask her to prepare a fire in the fireplace. Also, make sure she's remembered my extra pillows and—''

''I thought you were kidding. Damn, you really *are* a spoiled brat, aren't you?'' Matt muttered the last sentence under his breath as he opened the door.

*''Güten abend. Wie sind Sie?''* the maid said good evening and asked how they were, then she continued speaking to Matt in her native German, which he struggled to understand because the gray-haired, middle-aged woman spoke rapidly. He caught several words. Honeymoon. Robes. Pillows. Something about being wet. And he understood the word for fire.

She handed him the white terry cloth robes, then laid the two fluffy goose down pillows at the foot of the canopied four-poster bed. Matt eased sideways toward the bathroom and tossed one of the robes to Adele, who stood behind the door. She caught it in midair.

''Did she bring—''

''Two extra pillows. And she's building the fire now.''

''May I come out? I have on my robe.''

''Just wait until she leaves,'' he told Adele. ''No point

in being tempted to tell the maid—in German this time—
that I've kidnapped you.''

Adele pushed open the door and stood in the doorway.
Matt allowed himself a quick perusal. Why couldn't this
woman have been as homely as her fiancé? Why did she
have to be so damn pretty? And small, delicate and well-
rounded? He looked away hurriedly.

The maid rose from where she had knelt on the hearth,
smiled at Matt and said something about dinner. She must
have asked him if they wanted dinner served in their room.

''Want some dinner, honey?'' Matt asked.

''She didn't bring the brandy I requested, did she?''

''Do you or do you not want something to eat?''

''May I put in an order for both of us?'' Adele asked.
''That is if you trust me not to—''

''I understand enough German to figure out if you're
ordering dinner or asking for help, so go ahead, order
away.''

Adele took several tentative steps into the room, looked
directly at their maid and ordered dinner in German. The
maid replied. The best Matt could make out, they'd be
getting some kind of stew, homemade bread and the
brandy Adele wanted. The maid curtsied and left the room.

Why did the maid bow to them? Had the woman recognized Adele? Or was she so used to being a servant that
the bow came naturally to her?

''Before you accuse me of revealing my identity to that
woman, let me tell you that it's not unusual for servants
to bow like that to anyone they consider their superior.''

''You royals are big on superiority, aren't you?'' Matt
headed straight toward Adele, intending to go into the
bathroom. But for some reason she apparently thought he
planned to manhandle her again, so she inched along the
wall, moving away from him as he neared.

''If you try to go out that door while I'm taking off my

wet clothes, then you'll wind up tied to that chair—'' he glanced at the straight-back wooden chair near the fireplace ''—for the rest of the night. Understand?''

''Perfectly.'' She tilted her pert little nose haughtily and walked past him toward the fireplace.

He watched her for a couple of minutes as she bent over so her head was near the open fire. She speared her fingers through her short hair, fluffing it as the warmth began to dry the shiny, dark curls. One well-shaped calf peeked out from beneath her robe. Matt's body tightened. *Get a hold of yourself,* he thought. *Don't go getting all hot and bothered over that one. She thinks you're a beast, a brute and socially inferior.* He knew her type. Rich, pampered, snobbish. But he'd never come face-to-face with a real princess, not until this assignment had thrown him smack dab in the middle of a true-life episode of *Lifestyles of the Rich and Famous.* A good ol' boy from Louisville, Kentucky, was definitely out of his league with Her Highness.

Forcing himself to stop drooling, Matt went into the bathroom and, leaving the door partially open so he could keep an eye on his charge, he yanked off his shirt.

Adele tossed back her head, then shook her curls as she stretched her neck. She was in a fine mess, wasn't she? Captured and held captive by an American barbarian who couldn't be bribed. The big brute seemed to respond better when she didn't fight him, so perhaps charm might work where rebellion and chicanery had failed.

Taking a seat by the fire, she glanced toward the bathroom, and what she saw took her breath away. Matt O'Brien was drying himself off. The white towel moved over his muscular arms, his hairy chest and his lean belly. Thank heaven he'd left on his boxer shorts. Damp, short black hair curled over his chest, arms and legs. Adele stared at him, hypnotized by his beautiful, powerful body.

He certainly wasn't the first attractive man she'd seen in such a complete state of undress. After all, she'd grown up in Europe, had vacationed on the Riviera. Nudity wasn't the least bit shocking to her. But she wasn't accustomed to having a partially naked man in her bathroom. Well, technically, the bathroom was theirs since they were posing as newlyweds.

With Matt's back to her, he continued drying himself. Adele watched in utter fascination, unable to remove her gaze from his magnificent body. What was wrong with her? What was it about this man that mesmerized her so? *Oh, be honest with yourself, Adele. The man is very handsome and has a fantastic body. You would have to be dead not to notice.*

The maid knocked on the outer door and asked permission to enter. Reluctantly Adele took her eyes off Matt, stood and walked across the room to open the door. The maid carried a large tray laden with food. A bottle of brandy and two snifters graced the center of the tray.

With Matt preoccupied in the bathroom, now might be a good time for her to whisper something to the maid, to ask the woman for help. The maid busied herself placing the items from the tray on an antique table by the windows. Just as Adele approached the maid, Matt walked out of the bathroom. Adele jumped, as if she'd been caught doing something naughty. Damn, why hadn't she acted sooner? She'd let the moment—and that was all she'd had—pass. She'd been too engrossed in staring at Matt's body to think straight.

The maid took first one chair and then another and placed them on either side of the table where she'd set their evening meal. After laying his wet jeans, shirt and underwear out in front of the fireplace, Matt tossed his jacket on the sofa, then reached into the wide pocket of the white terry cloth robe, pulled out his wallet and handed the maid a sizable tip. Adele groaned. Having received such a generous tip, the maid would hardly be inclined to believe that Matt was a bad man, certainly not a kidnapper.

The maid thanked Matt, then glanced at Adele and said in German to Matt, "Your wife is very beautiful. She reminds me of Princess Adele of Orlantha. Herr Gerwalt mentioned that he, too, noticed the resemblance."

Adele opened her mouth to announce her true identity, but before she could speak, Matt rushed to her side, slid his arm around her waist and said in rather crude German, "Yes, we've heard that a lot lately, since we've been in Europe. But you know, I think my wife is prettier than the princess."

The maid giggled, then hurried out of the room, closing the door quietly behind her.

"I'm afraid we're stuck with lamb stew. The chef has gone home for the night." Adele jerked away from him and went over to their makeshift dinner table. "By the way, your German is terrible."

"Yeah, I know, but I do well enough to get by." Matt joined her, pulled out her chair and seated her. He sat across from her, poured hot tea from a carafe into her cup then his before sniffing the thick, dark lamb stew. "Your English is almost perfect. You barely have an accent. Why is that?"

Adele sipped on her tea. "English was taught as a second language at the boarding school I attended. And I perfected the language when I attended college in England."

"Which college?"

"Cambridge."

"You actually went to Cambridge?" Matt lifted his spoon and delved into the stew.

Adele tore off a couple of pieces from the crusty loaf of bread.

"Why do you find that so amazing? I will one day be

queen of Orlantha. My education was very important to my father. I must be prepared to lead my country.''

Matt shook his head.

''You don't approve of educating women, Mr. O'Brien?''

''Oh, honey, if you only knew. I was raised by a tough, hardworking, give-'em-hell woman. My aunt Velma. She wouldn't take kindly to your thinking I'm some sort of chauvinist. Women's rights is one of the many things she drilled into me. Actually Velma O'Brien believed strongly in human rights and equality for all. So you see, Ms. Reynard, I believe in educating everybody. Male and female, regardless of race, color, creed, national origin or socio-economic background.''

''How very democratic of you.''

''Something you apparently know very little about,'' he countered.

''On the contrary. Orlantha is quite progressive and in many ways we're similar to Great Britain. We have a governing council, with a chancellor and vice chancellor.''

''Yeah, but unlike the Brits, y'all still have a ruling monarch who possesses a great deal of power. If your old man said 'Off with their heads,' then heads would roll.''

Adele's lips twitched. Although she found his statement humorous, she didn't dare laugh. The very thought of her father ordering people's deaths was ludicrous. She didn't know Mr. O'Brien's feminist Aunt Velma, but he didn't know King Leopold, whose bark was much worse than his bite.

Adele leaned slightly forward, smiled sweetly and looked soulfully into Matt O'Brien's spellbinding blue eyes. ''Is there anything—'' she emphasized the word anything ''—I can say or do that would persuade you not to take me back to Orlantha?''

Matt crossed his arms over his chest, leaned back in his

chair and stared at her. "You wouldn't be propositioning me, would you, princess?"

She should reprimand him for his impertinence, but wisdom bade her to remain calm. Reminding herself that this man held her fate in his hands—in his big, strong hands— she glanced at his taut biceps where his arms crisscrossed his chest, and she continued smiling at him.

"I'm willing to do almost anything." She caressed her neck, then slid her hand slowly downward, spreading her robe apart and laying her open palm in the center of her chest, her pinky finger slipping between her breasts.

What would she do if he took her up on her offer? Was she really willing to have sex with this man in order to gain her freedom? The thought sobered her instantly. Just as she started to speak, Matt reached across the table and grasped her chin.

"You're pretty desperate, aren't you, to even contemplate such a thing?"

Damn, she felt like crying, could actually feel the tears welling up in her eyes. She glanced away, not wanting him to see her weak and uncertain. After releasing her chin, he continued staring at her for a few minutes, long enough to embarrass her. A heated flush colored her cheeks.

"Let me make things easy for you," Matt told her. "There's nothing you can say or do that will keep me from returning you to your father. Unless…"

"Unless?" Adele's heartbeat boom-boomed in her ears.

"Unless I believe that taking you home would put your life at risk. But I hardly think you'll be in any danger from your own father."

Adele shook her head. "No, not from Father. But both he and I are in danger from Dedrick." When she saw the doubting expression on Matt's face, she said, "You don't believe me, do you?"

"l don't know," Matt admitted.

"Why would I lie to you?"

"I don't know that, either. Not for sure. But let's just say that before I'd believe you—or anyone I don't know—I'd need to see some sort of proof."

Adele sighed. "I don't have any proof. And that's the problem. If I had proof, I could take it to my father and he would call off my wedding to Dedrick and throw Dedrick in prison for treason."

"I'm sorry. I wish I could help you, but—"

Adele reached across the table, grabbed one of Matt's hands and squeezed it pleadingly. "You can help me. Call my father and tell him that you couldn't find me, that I wasn't with Yves. I need more time. Pippin and his people need more time."

"Look, honey, why don't you just tell your father that you are not going to marry the duke? He can't force you to marry him, can he? After all, it's a free country and…" Realization dawned. "Sorry, princess. Orlantha isn't a free country, is it? Your father could force you to marry old mule face, couldn't he?"

Now she was getting through to him. Finally. She squeezed his hand again and gave him a pathetic little look of total helplessness. "Please, help me, Mr. O'Brien. Matt…"

He jerked his hand free, squinted as he glowered at her and then grinned, a rather cocky, smug grin that gave Adele a sick, sinking feeling in the pit of her stomach.

"You're good, honey. You're very good. You almost had me, there. I was this close—" he indicated how close with his thumb and forefinger "—to buying your act."

Adele clenched her teeth. Trying to fight Matt O'Brien didn't work. But neither did trying to charm him. And getting any help from the innkeeper or the maid apparently wasn't possible. So, that left her with only one option—

she had to escape. But how? He watched her every minute. The man had even made her leave the bathroom door half-way open when she'd undressed. The bathroom! The bathroom window. It was small and would be a tight squeeze, but she thought she might be able to slip through it and out onto the inn's roof. After that she'd find a way to get down to the ground. If only she could steal the car keys first, she would have transportation and wouldn't have to telephone Yves to meet her and then strike out on foot in the middle of the night. But if necessary, that's exactly what she'd do. She'd slip out the window, get down to the ground, go back inside the inn and call Yves.

She would have to bide her time. Her bodyguard would have to sleep eventually. All she had to do was wait.

After Matt had seen through her little ruse, the princess had foregone any more pleasantries. They had eaten in relative silence, then she had gone to bed. Although he was nearly a foot taller and twice her size, he was forced to take the sofa, which was too short for his length and probably damn lumpy to boot. He gathered up his still-damp clothes from the floor and hung them over a couple of chairs he positioned in front of the fireplace. Her Highness went to sleep almost immediately after Matt turned off the lights. He stoked the fire before bedding down for the night.

Unable to find a comfortable position on the sofa, he tossed and turned for what seemed like hours. Finally he closed his eyes and relaxed. He'd been trained to go days without sleep if necessary, and his gut instincts told him that tonight would be one of those you'd-better-stay-awake nights. The princess had gone to sleep too quickly, had given up her persuasive tactics too easily. She was defi-nitely up to something, probably no good. If he knew women—and he did know women—this stubborn, contrary lady would attempt an escape before daybreak.

Hours later—he wasn't quite sure of the time, but figured it was well over into the morning—Princess Adele slipped out of bed, tiptoed into the bathroom and closed the door. Matt didn't move. He'd give her a few minutes. Maybe she had to use the facilities. Matt listened. Sometime in the past few hours, it had quit raining. The minutes ticked by, then he heard the creaky groans of a window opening. He shot straight up. She was going to try to escape through the bathroom window. She was probably just small enough to fit through the narrow opening. He figured she'd changed into her damp clothes that she'd laid out on the bathtub. Why, God, why had he gotten stuck with this assignment?

Matt grabbed his own still-damp clothes and dressed hurriedly. When he thought he'd given her just enough time to make it through the window, Matt opened the bathroom door. The room was empty; the window was open. He sighed, shrugged and then turned around and headed toward the door leading into the dimly lit hallway. Only the faint moans of an old building intruded on the predawn quiet. He took his time going down the stairs, through the small lobby and out the front door. The best thing to do was station himself in the corner and wait for her to descend from the roof. He hoped she didn't break her fool neck in the process.

Suddenly in his peripheral vision Matt caught a glimpse of movement about twenty feet away. He leaned back against the stone wall and held his breath. Had Adele gotten down that quickly? He stared out into the darkness, lit only by hazy moonlight barely visible after the storm. That's when Matt saw them. Two men, average size by the looks of their dark forms. They were speaking quietly. Too quietly for Matt to hear what they were saying. Then one of them pointed up, toward the roof. Both men moved forward. Matt eased slowly, carefully along the front porch until he reached the side of the inn, then he dashed off the porch and straight toward the nearest tree. He slid behind the huge tree, then looked up where he saw another dark form, small and curvy, as it climbed down a trellis attached to the side of the inn. Princess Adele. The two men waited, one on either side of the trellis.

Damn, they were waiting for Adele. But who the hell were they? And how had they known where Adele was? Unless they had followed her, followed them, to the inn. He hadn't paid much attention to the traffic once he'd felt certain that Yves Jurgen hadn't followed them. It had never crossed his mind that someone might be stalking the princess.

Matt watched while Adele descended—right into the arms of her waiting captors. Hell, he'd have to go get her, and that probably meant roughing up a couple of tough guys. He just hoped there wouldn't be any gunplay involved. He hated like the devil to deal with the foreign police.

Adele let out a piercing scream. Matt checked his 9 mm gun, sucked in a deep breath, then marched forward, like the calvary to the rescue.

# Chapter 4

Adele didn't recognize her attackers, but it was dark and she was scared to death. Although it was possible that these men were muggers, her instincts warned her that they were somehow connected to the Royalists and thus connected to Dedrick. There was no way anyone could have known where she was unless she'd been followed—or unless Matt O'Brien really wasn't working for her father.

She didn't have much time to think about what was happening to her. A sweaty hand clamped over her mouth seconds after she screamed. If Matt was on the up-and-up, maybe he'd heard her cry for help. Adele tried to fight off the assault, but she didn't have the strength to struggle against two men intent on subduing her.

Suddenly, out of nowhere, another man appeared. Taller and bigger than the two holding her. With the swift, deadly ability of a trained soldier, the man attacked, ripping her from captivity and shoving her to freedom. Then when the two culprits surged toward him, he used his entire body as a weapon. His hands. His feet. His head. He landed blow after blow, outmaneuvering and outsmarting his opponents. Adele stood to the side of the action scene and watched in silent amazement. She'd never seen anything like it outside a big-budget adventure movie. Even without being able to see him clearly in the semidarkness, she knew her rescuer was Matt O'Brien. She recognized his hard, lean physique.

When her two attackers lay on the ground, one apparently unconscious and the other moaning in agony, Matt grabbed Adele's arm and dragged her away from the inn and toward the rental car they had abandoned hours ago during the rainstorm.

"Where are we—" she tried to question him, but he pulled her with him to the car, then opened the door and shoved her inside. She didn't protest. Not this time.

She thought he'd get in the car immediately, but instead, he walked back to where he'd left the two men. She rolled down the car's passenger window and watched while Matt bent over the man who was conscious and spoke to him. She was too far away to make out what was being said, but she had a feeling Matt was getting the answers he wanted.

Just as Matt headed back to the car, the porch lights came on and Herr Gerwalt rushed outside.

"Call the police, and tell them that these men attacked two of your guests."

"But where are you going, Herr O'Brien?" Franz Gerwalt asked.

"Somewhere a little safer for Mrs. O'Brien," Matt replied, then opened the door to the car and got behind the wheel. He turned to Adele, reached out and caressed her cheek. "Are you okay, honey?"

She nodded. "I'm all right."

"I owe you an apology."

"You do?"

"Those two men followed us from Vienna. They were given orders to keep tabs on me and if I found you, to tail us. And if you escaped from me, they were ordered to drug you and take you back to Orlantha themselves." Matt shook his head. "Damn, I should have spotted them, but it never entered my head that—"

"Did they tell you who hired them?"

"One guy is still out cold," Matt said. "And the other guy wasn't saying more. But the bastard has brass balls. He actually told me that if I knew what was good for me, I'd make sure you got home to your father as soon as possible. Otherwise I'd be sorry and you could wind up dead."

"Dedrick hired them! I know he did."

"Yeah, maybe he did."

Matt started the engine, shifted into Reverse and turned the car around, then headed toward the highway. Several minutes later, when they were well out of sight of the inn, Matt glanced at her, taking his eyes off the road for a split second.

"Tell me again why I shouldn't take you straight to Orlantha," Matt said.

Adele sighed with relief. Maybe he was actually going to give her the chance she so desperately needed. Saying a silent prayer for the right words to persuade Matt, she turned sideways in the seat and looked at him. Be honest and straightforward. Don't try to play him, she told herself.

"I've already told you," she explained. "And everything I said was the truth. Not only am I in danger, but my country is in danger. From Dedrick and from the Royalists."

"And why is it that you suspected the truth about this Duke Dedrick and your father didn't?"

"Dedrick Vardan, Duke of Roswald," she corrected,

"has fooled my father and his advisors. He even fooled me for years. But Pippin is the one who brought the ugly truth to my attention."

"And you're sure you trust this Pippin guy?"

"Yes, I trust Pippin Ritter. He loves Orlantha as much as I do. As much as my father does."

"And him being the vice chancellor, an elected office, doesn't make him an enemy of the king? Looks to me like Vice Chancellor Ritter would want to see the downfall of the monarchy."

"You don't know Pippin. You don't know the people of Orlantha. They're quite happy with the way the country is jointly governed by the king and the elected council members. It's not unlike your president and congress, only—"

"The king isn't an elected official."

"Please, Mr. O'Brien, give me some time. Two weeks. Give me two weeks. I'll contact Pippin to tell him that he must do whatever is necessary to unearth evidence against Dedrick in two weeks time."

Matt pulled the car to a standstill at the intersection. "I'll give you one week. That's it. Take it or leave it."

Adele gasped. "Do you mean it? You'll actually let me go? You trust me to—"

"I'm beginning to trust you," he told her. "Those two guys back at the inn were playing pretty rough. My gut instincts tell me that you're in danger, and I'm sure your father would want me to protect you, at all costs."

"And you did protect me. You rescued me and I'm very grateful. And if you'll let me go, I promise I'll pay you more than my father offered you."

Matt shook his head. "I don't want your money. As far as I'm concerned, I'm still working for your father, and a week from today, I'm taking you home to dear old dad."

"But I don't understand."

"Do you have someplace you can go where you'll be safe?"

What was he saying? she wondered. He was still working for her father, yet he was willing to give her a week's reprieve before he forced her to return to the palace in Erembourg.

"I had planned to go to Golnar. I have an old school friend who lives there."

"Then won't that be the first place your father would expect you to go?"

"Yes, but they can't deport me once I'm there. The laws are different in Golnar, and my friend's husband is very influential."

"Hmm. All right. Then I'll need you to give me your word," Matt said. "I'm going to trust you—if you make me a promise."

"You're confusing me," she told him.

"I'll take you back to Vienna and we'll get the next flight to Golnar."

"I'm afraid you're confusing me even more. Once I'm in Golnar, you realize that you can't force me to leave with you, don't you?"

He nodded. "Why do you think I'm not going to let you go without your giving me your word you'll return with me to Erembourg in one week."

"And you'll really take me at my word?"

"Call me a fool, but yeah."

"Oh, Matt...er...Mr. O'Brien, thank you. But how will you ever explain to my father about letting me go?"

"I'm not going to let you go," he said. "I'm going to Golnar with you."

"But if my father thinks you've betrayed him, he'll send someone else after me. The only way this will work is if you allow me to escape, then follow me to Golnar."

"Not a good plan," Matt told her. "I'm supposed to

keep you safe. Anything could happen to you if I'm not there to protect you.''

Adele smiled. ''Just listen to my plan, okay? You put me on the first flight to Golnar. I'll call Dia before I leave Vienna and have her chauffeur there to meet me the minute I arrive. Peneus acts as Dia's bodyguard wherever she goes on Golnar. I'll be perfectly safe until you arrive.''

She could tell by the expression on his face that he was wary, both of her and of her plan. Of course, she couldn't blame him, not after the way she'd been acting.

''If you fly with me to Golnar and my father finds out, he won't believe that I escaped. He'll know you allowed me to go to Dia.''

Matt sighed. ''I don't like it, but—''

''Please, please. I swear I'll be safe until you arrive and I promise…I swear—'' she laid her hand over her heart ''—that I'll return to Orlantha with you in one week.''

Matt looked directly at Adele. ''Okay, I know I'll probably live to regret this, but we have a deal.'' He held out his hand.

What choice did she have? She either accepted Matt O'Brien's offer or, if she didn't, she felt certain he'd take her straight back to Erembourg this morning. ''We have a deal.'' She shook his big, strong hand. A flicker of some strange sensation tingled in her hand, up her arm and through her body. She stared at him and noticed he was studying her as intently as she was studying him.

''I…uh…we really should get started for Vienna, shouldn't we?'' She eased her hand from his.

Matt cleared his throat. ''Yeah.'' He turned the car west, straight back the way they'd come last night.

''Why have you summoned me at this ungodly hour?'' Dedrick Vardan demanded as he stood in the private office of his coconspirator. The man held too much power over

Dedrick at the present time, but that would change once the Royalists took over Orlantha and he became sole monarch. Dedrick simply had to bide his time and take orders from the man King Eduard had appointed the leader of the Royalists in Orlantha. If only his dear, distant cousin Eduard hadn't thought it necessary to assign this power-hungry bastard as Dedrick's watchdog.

"We have a problem. A major problem."

"And that would be?"

"The princess tried to escape from the American private detective the king hired to bring her home."

Dedrick shrugged. "So? Weren't our men able to prevent her escape?"

"It seems they botched the job and were taken to the local jail. And now the princess is back in the American's custody. But I find it odd that he has not called to report the incident to the king."

"Are our men still in jail?"

"No, I was able to persuade the constable that they were working for King Leopold and that the man who fought them off had kidnapped the princess."

"Good God, man, if the king hears about this, he'll know damn well that—"

"The king will hear nothing. I swore the constable to secrecy and assured him that the princess is now safe and her kidnapper apprehended."

"Then I'm to assume this private detective is en route with Adele, bringing her back to her grieving fiancé as we speak." Dedrick decided then and there that he would find many delightful ways to make dear, sweet Adele pay for scorning him. Once they were married, she would be at his mercy.

"We should assume nothing! Until this hired bodyguard either telephones the king or shows up with the princess, we can't be sure that Her Highness hasn't told this man what she suspects.''

''Why should he listen to her? Her own father doesn't believe her wild accusations about my being a Royalist.''

''Do you forget how beautiful and charming the princess is? I dare say it wouldn't be too difficult for her to wrap this American around her little finger.''

''Damn!'' Dedrick balled his hands into tight fists. ''If he has been intimate with my fiancée, I shall have to—''

''Shut up, you fool. I've found out quite a bit about this man, Matthew O'Brien. He is not just some ordinary private detective, nor is Dundee just a routine detective agency. You would do well to know your opponent. Mr. O'Brien could annihilate you in two seconds, with very little effort, so I suggest you forget about challenging him when he—*if* he brings Adele home.''

''You're intimidated by this Mr. O'Brien, aren't you?'' Dedrick laughed. ''My God, I never thought to see the day that anyone would—''

Dedrick's laughter died instantly when the man's hand lashed across his face, giving Dedrick a resounding slap. He tensed and glowered at the man he reluctantly called comrade. If he didn't need this maniacal bully, he'd kill him here and now. He'd shoot the bastard in the heart. But perhaps a bullet couldn't kill such evil. Only a silver bullet perhaps? Or a stake through the heart?

Dedrick wiped the blood from his cracked lip and grinned. ''If you can't get Adele back to Erembourg in time for our wedding, then taking over Orlantha by peaceful means may be out of the question.''

''I will see to it that the princess returns for her wedding.''

''And if you can't make that happen?''

''You already know the answer to that question. Either the princess marries you or she must die.''

* * *

Matt waved goodbye as Princess Adele boarded the first morning flight from Vienna to Golnar. He knew he was taking a big chance trusting a woman he didn't know, a woman who had tried every possible way to get away from him. He was going with his gut instincts, and in the past his instincts had seldom proven to be wrong. But just so she knew where they stood, he'd pulled her aside a few minutes ago and leveled with her.

"Look, honey, you should know, up-front, that if when the time comes, you renege on your word, I'll find a way to get you off Golnar and back to Erembourg."

She had smiled at him. "I know. I have no doubt that you're perfectly capable of forcing me to capitulate to your wishes."

With Adele off to Golnar and his ticket for the next flight in five hours in his jacket pocket, he had a couple of phone calls to make in the meantime. First call—King Leopold. Second call—Ellen Denby. He dreaded his boss lady's wrath far more than the king's.

He found a pay phone, used his phone card and punched in the private number King Leopold had given him. The phone rang twice and was promptly answered—but not by the king.

"I'd like to speak to King Leopold," Matt said.

"And whom may I say is telephoning?" Lord Burhardt asked.

"Matt O'Brien."

"Yes, Mr. O'Brien. We've been expecting to hear from you. I hope you have good news about the princess."

"I have good news and bad news," Matt said. "So how about putting the king on the phone so I can explain things to him."

"That won't be necessary, I assure you. I am the king's trusted advisor and can relay any messages to him."

"Yeah, I'm sure you can, but I want to speak directly with His Majesty. What I've got to say isn't something that should go through a third party...even a *trusted* advisor."

Matt heard the slight gasp as if Lord Burhardt were shocked that a hired hand would dare to speak to him in such a manner. Too bad. The king might trust his chief advisor but Matt didn't. There was something not quite right about Burhardt.

"I shall inform His Majesty that you wish to speak to him," Lord Burhardt said.

While he waited, Matt thought about what he was going to say. A dry run. A dress rehearsal for the act he was going to put on. Within minutes the king came on the line.

"What's this about, Mr. O'Brien?" King Leopold asked. "Do you have my daughter? Are you en route to Orlantha?"

"I found the princess in Vienna and we began our trip back to Erembourg when we got caught in a bad rainstorm, so we stopped at an inn about an hour's drive from the border."

"Then you're calling to inform me that you are bringing the princess home this morning."

"Not exactly," Matt said. "You see, during the night, the princess escaped."

"What? How is that possible? I thought you were a highly trained professional. You must be an imbecile to have allowed her to get away from you."

"I apologize, Your Majesty. Princess Adele slipped out the bathroom window and I didn't catch up with her until it was too late."

"What do you mean it was too late?"

"Your daughter caught a flight from Vienna to Golnar. I missed her by only a few minutes. But I can assure you that I'll find her. I've booked the next flight to Golnar."

"She's gone to Dia Constantine," the king said. "When

you arrive in Golnar, rent a car and go directly to the Constantine villa. That's where you'll find her. And I'm afraid your bungling the job last night will make it more difficult for you. You see, Orlantha has no diplomatic ties with Golnar, so you'll have to kidnap Adele and find a way to get her off the island. Do you think you're capable of doing this job? I find myself wondering if I should call your agency and request another agent.''

"There's no need to do that." Talk fast, Matt, he told himself. Convince the king that you're the only man for the job. "I promise you that once I find the princess again, I won't let her out of my sight for a single minute until I bring her home to you."

"Very well. Go to Golnar and contact me the minute you have Adele in your custody. If you fail again, I'll see to it that you—"

"I won't fail. I promise you I'll bring the princess home."

Half an hour later, after drinking a couple of cups of coffee and downing a Danish, Matt made his second phone call. He contacted the Dundee Agency in Atlanta and was put through to Ellen immediately.

"Matt?"

"Yeah, it's me."

"I didn't expect to hear from you so soon. Have you already completed your assignment for King Leopold?"

"Not exactly."

"Uh-oh. I don't like what I hear in your voice. What's gone wrong?"

"This assignment is turning out to be a little more complicated than I expected." Matt gave Ellen a blow-by-blow account of his brief odyssey with the princess. "I really think she's telling the truth. That's why I took matters into my own hands and decided to give her a week's reprieve."

Ellen groaned. "You do realize that you've involved

yourself in the politics of Orlantha—something that is none of your business and that goes against the policies of our agency.''

''Yeah, I know I'm not going strictly by the book on this one. But my gut instincts—''

''Is she pretty?''

''What?''

Ellen repeated, ''Is Princess Adele as pretty as her pictures?''

''Prettier,'' Matt said. ''But that has nothing to do with why I'm playing along with her for a week. One week. That's all. If her cohorts back in Orlantha can't come up with some evidence against the duke in the next seven days, I'll take Her Highness back to her father.''

''You didn't tell me where she went, where this old school friend of hers lives.''

''Some little island nation between Cyprus and Greece—''

''Golnar?''

''Yeah. How'd you know? I'd never heard of the place before.''

He sensed a slight hesitation in Ellen's response and heard an odd tone in her voice. ''I visited Golnar once, years ago. It's a lovely place. Sandy beaches, ocean views, mountain villas. And several very quaint little towns. And if you stay the week, you'll probably witness one of their many festivals. I've heard that some are quite spectacular, similar to New Orleans's Mardi Gras.''

''You certainly know a lot about this place. How long did you stay in Golnar?''

''Two weeks.''

The quick change in Ellen's tone of voice alerted Matt to her mood. Back to business! He knew better than to ask her more questions. She wasn't the type to share confidences about her personal life with her employees, not even the ones she considered to be friends.

"I'll give you a daily update," Matt said.

"Be sure you give King Leopold frequent updates, also. He's not going to like it when you keep putting off bringing his daughter home."

"I think I'll persuade the princess to speak on my behalf to her father. Maybe she can convince him that he shouldn't have me drawn and quartered."

Ellen chuckled. "Who's going to convince me that I shouldn't?"

"Jeez, boss lady, give me a break, will you? My actions could save an entire nation."

"Yeah, right. And the next thing you'll tell me is that you're going to marry Princess Adele to save her from having to go through with the wedding to the duke."

A peculiar feeling hit Matt square in the gut. Marry the princess? No way! "Hey, just because I suggested she marry somebody else doesn't mean I volunteered for the job."

"Why not? I think you'd look adorable in one of those fancy uniforms loaded down with medals. And just think, you could be prince for a day."

"I'm hanging up now, Ms. Denby."

"Be careful, Matt. If what the princess suspects is true, then her life could be in danger, and so could yours."

"I'll do my job."

"I never doubted it for a minute."


Adele sipped on the bottled water she had requested from the flight attendant and tried to block out the chattering going on all around her. She'd never flown economy class before and she found it rather cramped and noisy.

When Yves had met them at the airport with her passport, he'd lamented that he didn't have the funds to pay for a first-class ticket. She'd kissed him on the cheek and assured him that she would survive, just this once, in economy class.

Ever since she'd boarded the plane in Vienna, she'd been unable to get Matt O'Brien off her mind. He was so typically American. Uncultured, brash, opinionated…and fair-minded. If not for his willingness to trust her, she'd be standing before her father at the palace right now, listening to a stern lecture. But Matt had given her seven days—only one short week—to prove her accusations against Dedrick. As soon as she arrived in Golnar, she would call Pippin and tell him the situation.

But what if Pippin couldn't come up with the evidence by the end of the week? Adele's mind kept returning to one thought—a suggestion made by her American protector. *Marry someone else.* If she married another man, albeit in name only, there was no way her father could force her to go through with the wedding to Dedrick. Yes, that's what she'd do if she had no other choice. She'd marry someone else. But who? Surely Theo and Dia could find her a suitable temporary husband.

## Chapter 5

The Constantines' chauffeur met Adele at the airport. Before departing the airplane, she'd donned the sunglasses and scarf she had purchased at the Vienna airport. If she didn't hide her identity, some tabloid reporter might spot her, and she simply couldn't deal with the paparazzi right now. She had enough problems without those sleazy news people chasing after her, asking questions, snapping photographs. If they knew she was at the Constantine villa, Theo would have to hire a small army to keep them from his door. And that certainly wouldn't make Theo happy. She suspected Dia hadn't told her husband why she was coming for a visit, although if he'd been reading more than the business section of the newspapers lately, he might suspect she was on the run.

The ride from the airport to the villa took thirty minutes, leading directly through the downtown area of Dareh, the capital city of Golnar. A mixture of modern and ancient, Dareh possessed the allure of an old-world town and the exotic charm of a Mediterranean seacoast city. Miles of sandy beaches as well as miles of rock cliffs spanned the coast that half circled the capitol. Donkeys vied with small economy cars on the narrow back streets, and antiquated buses from the fifties chugged alongside taxis and motorists on the main thoroughfares. Catering to tourists and locals alike, modern banks and hotels stood alongside quaint restaurants and cafés as well as unique shops that sold everything from Persian rugs to Parisian-designed bikinis. In the northern edge of Dareh, which the limousine passed in its trek out of the inner city, was an open-air market, unchanged for hundreds of years. The voices of bargaining buyers and sellers rang out like a singular hum carried on the wind. When Adele rolled down the window to see the market more clearly, the mingled scents of game birds roasting over open fires, fresh garlic, rich spices and broad-bean stew assailed her senses.

Most of the residents of Golnar spoke Greek, but with so many European, Russian and American tourists flocking more and more to the picturesque island, English was spoken fluently by many residents, as was Russian. The people of this small nation were mainly of Greek descent, with some Turkish blood flowing in their veins from generations of intermarriage between the two peoples. But unlike Cyprus, the blend of cultures here had formed a single people not divided by religious or political differences. Greek Orthodox was the state religion and Greek the national language, but many local customs had deep roots in both cultures. And if there was one thing the Golnarians loved, it was celebrations of any type, especially festivals.

Outside the small town of Coeus, the Constantine villa perched at the top of the green hills that broke off abruptly to the rear and exposed the high, jagged banks of the cliffs, as if nature had sliced the hills in two with a giant blade and one half had dissolved into the Mediterranean below.

The house itself overlooked the sea, with tiered balconies clinging to the hillside.

The villa, once a monastery, had been purchased in the early part of the twentieth century by Theo's grandfather, and each generation had modernized the sprawling compound. Two stories of whitewashed stucco and native rock topped by a red tile roof, the ancient structure seemed to have risen fully formed for the earth. A long, narrow driveway led along the edge of the cliff toward the main house that faced inland. By the time the chauffeur stopped the limousine and opened the back door, Dia came rushing through the enormous, two-story-high front doors, across the porch and through the arched entryway. On her heels were her daughter, the child's nanny and two galloping cocker spaniels.

"You're here at last!" Dia threw open her arms and encompassed Adele in a best-friends hug. "I have your room ready and have told Theo that you'll be staying with us for a week."

Adele hugged Dia, who stood several inches taller than she, then released her and grasped her hands. "And what did you tell Theo about my visit?"

"The truth," Dia replied, then broke into a wide grin. "Well, as much of the truth as he needs to know. You understand how my Theo is. An old-fashioned man but a dear one."

"Old-fashioned? Don't you mean he's a male chauvinist?"

Both women laughed.

"What's a chauvinist?" Phila Constantine asked as she came forward and stared quizzically at Adele.

"Phila, sweetheart." Adele turned from mother to daughter, bent down and kissed Phila's rosy cheeks. "You've grown a foot since I last saw you." Adele patted the child's head, then glanced past her to the nanny. "Miss

Sheridan, you're going to have to put some heavy books on Phila's head to slow down her growth, or the next time I visit, she'll be as tall as I am.''

The Constantines' nanny, Faith Sheridan, smiled timidly and nodded. ''Yes, ma'am, Your Highness.''

''Aunt Adele, you didn't tell me what a chauvinist is. That's what you called my papa, isn't it?'' Phila's big brown eyes, identical to her father's, stared at Adele.

''Talk yourself out of that one,'' Dia said.

Adele took Phila's hand into hers as the group walked toward the villa's entrance. She stopped abruptly when she heard Dia issue orders to the chauffeur to bring in her luggage.

''Oh, I'm afraid I didn't bring anything with me. I left in a bit of a hurry.''

Dia's cheeks flushed. She cleared her throat. ''Oh, no problem. We'll go shopping directly after lunch and buy whatever you need. If we were the same size, I'd be happy to lend you anything of mine, but you're pounds lighter and inches shorter.'' Dia turned to the chauffeur. ''That will be all, Peneus. But Her Highness and I will be going back to Dareh in about two hours.''

''Yes, madam.''

When the foursome, along with the playful spaniels, entered the massive entrance hall with its white marble floor, Phila tugged on Adele's hand.

''What is a chauvinist?'' Phila demanded.

Dia moaned. ''You must answer her, Adele. Otherwise, she'll nag you until you do. She's just like Theo that way. Insistent to the point of aggravation.''

''Well, a male chauvinist is a man who...who is rather old-fashioned in his ideas about women,'' Adele said, and thought that she'd given a rather diplomatic response.

''My papa likes women.'' Phila beamed with delight. ''He tells me all the time that he adores me and Mama.

And he's very nice to Faith and Mrs. Panopoulos and Aunt Dora and—''

"Yes, yes, my pet." Dia placed her hand on her daughter's shoulder. "Papa is a wonderful, old-fashioned man and we love him dearly, don't we."

"Yes, Mama." Phila turned to Adele again. "I'm to be allowed to have dinner with you and Mama and Papa tonight. And so is Faith. Aren't you pleased?"

"Yes, I'm very pleased. Your parents must think you're quite grown up to allow you to join the adults for dinner."

"Only tonight, because it's a special occasion."

"I see."

"Phila, please go with Faith." Dia tapped the face of her wristwatch. "It's time for your music lessons. Mr. Mylonas is waiting."

"Yes, Mama. Bye Aunt Adele." Phila went with her nanny, but before she got five feet down the corridor leading to the music room, she turned back and called, "I'm so glad you've come for a visit."

The companion spaniels kept pace with Phila and Miss Sheridan as they disappeared down the hallway. Dia led Adele to the sunroom, a twenty-foot by thirty-foot pavilion that had once been part of the enormous central courtyard. Potted trees and large plants, some flowering, gave the area a garden atmosphere. The glass and metal table was set for two with exquisite china, crystal and silver.

"Sit, sit," Dia instructed. "We'll have something light here at the house because I want to take you to this marvelous café in Dareh for a midafternoon snack. They have fabulous coffee and tea and scrumptious desserts."

The moment the two women sat, a servant appeared carrying fruit salads, and another brought a bottle of chilled white wine and filled their glasses. Then the two silently disappeared, leaving the old friends alone.

"So, how long will it be before your father telephones Theo and demands your return to Golnar?" Dia asked.

"I'm not sure. It depends on how persuasive Matt—Mr. O'Brien—was when he spoke to Father. If he believes Mr. O'Brien can deliver me to the palace, then he might not bother Theo. However, my guess is that when Father realizes I won't be returning immediately, he'll speak to Theo." Adele studied Dia's frowning face. "Is my being here a problem for you?"

"No, of course not. It's just that if your father is more persuasive than you are, Theo might be inclined to agree with King Leopold. You do realize that even though he likes you a great deal, Theo has always thought you were a bad influence on me. It amazes him that an Orlanthian princess has such a modern, twenty-first-century attitude toward men and women, democracy and...well—" Dia waved her hand in a circular motion "—about everything."

"As I recall, when we attended boarding school together, you were considered a modern thinker yourself."

Dia smiled. "Yes, and I'm afraid sometimes I annoy my husband."

"Then it's a good thing the man worships you." Adele lifted her glass of wine to her lips and took a sip. "Besides, I believe that by the time Phila is a teenager, she'll have brought her papa's attitudes into the twenty-first century."

Deftly changing the subject, Dia said, "Tell me about this Mr. O'Brien. How ever did you talk him into allowing you to come to Golnar without him?"

"I didn't. Not exactly. He'll be arriving later today."

"And will he expect to stay here?"

Adele nodded. "Yes, I'm afraid so. And in a room next to mine, if that's possible. You see, even though my father has hired him to return me to Golnar, Matt...er...Mr. O'Brien seems to consider himself my bodyguard."

"You keep referring to him as Matt. Just how well did you become acquainted with this man during your brief encounter?"

"Not well at all, I can assure you. He's totally American. Rather crude and rude, without any regard to my position. He kept calling me *honey,* as if I were some peasant girl."

Dia's lips twitched. "He called her Highness, Princess Adele Johanna Milisande Reynard, *honey?* My dear, he sounds perfectly delightful. And what every woman secretly wants—a man she cannot intimidate. Let's be honest, most members of the male population of Europe are intimidated by your title."

"I do not want Mr. Matt O'Brien!" Adele protested quite vehemently. "The man is uncouth and disrespectful. And when I saw him last, he badly needed a shave and a haircut."

"You have me dying of curiosity," Dia said. "I simply cannot wait to meet your protector."

Matt arrived in Golnar midafternoon. His flight had been delayed due to some sort of mechanical problems that had to be taken care of before takeoff. He'd grabbed a quick bite at the Vienna airport, but his growling stomach reminded him that it was past time to eat. With only a duffel bag to carry through customs, he whisked through the Dareh airport in record time, rented a car—an older model Fiat—with no air-conditioning, no radio and reeking of cigarette smoke. The dealership had apologized about the car, but told Matt it was best they had left from a small fleet of rentals. It seemed autumn was the peak tourist season on Golnar. Using the directions that Adele had written down for him before she'd left Vienna, he headed out of the city and along the narrow winding highway leading to Coeus. As a Pave Low pilot during his years in the Air

Force, he and the five other crewmen that had been required to fly the twenty-one-ton behemoth had set their MH-53J down in many foreign countries. Some lands had seemed truly alien to him. Ugly barren deserts or miles and miles of little more than humid swamps. But Golnar was a Mediterranean paradise, a Greek isle with a Middle Eastern flair. As he passed the open markets the smell of food lured him to stop, but he resisted the urge and continued his journey. Thirty minutes later he pulled up in front of a set of massive stone pillars connected by a scroll-design iron gate that, thankfully, was open. He drove directly up to the villa. The damn thing was as big as a small hotel. But why shouldn't Theodosios Constantine reside in a sprawling estate. From the rushed report he'd been given over the phone from the Dundee Agency's own Lucie Evans, a former FBI agent, Constantine was a billionaire many times over and practically owned the entire island of Golnar. Over a third of the population owed their livelihoods to the Constantine family, whose shipping empire, begun by Theo's grandfather, had broadened to numerous enterprises over the decades.

When Matt knocked at the twenty-five-foot-tall front doors, a male servant responded and asked Matt something in Greek, a language in which he knew only half a dozen words.

"Do you speak English?" Matt asked.

"Yes, sir, I speak English," the small, slender, dark-haired man replied with a heavy accent.

"I'm Matt O'Brien. Princess Adele is expecting me."

"The princess not here. Gone. She and Mrs. Constantine."

"Gone? Gone where?"

"To Dareh. To shop."

"Damn!" What was she thinking? Didn't she realize that just as her father had figured out she would run straight to Golnar, so would whoever the hell was after her—be that person Dedrick or someone else connected to the Royalists.

"Do you know exactly where in Dareh they went?" Matt asked.

"No, not know. Shopping. Many stores."

"It's important that I find Princess Adele. Is there anyone here at the villa who might know exactly where they went?"

The servant shook his head.

"I might be able to answer that question," a deep male voice said in slightly accented English.

Matt glanced past the servant to the dark-eyed, black-haired man entering the grand foyer from the right. He was about six feet tall, lean and quite fit. Matt surmised, from the description of Theo Constantine Lucie had given him over the phone, that this man must be the lord and master of the villa.

"Mr. Constantine?"

"Yes, I'm Theo Constantine. Who, may I ask, are you and what is your business with Princess Adele?"

Figuring the wisest course of action was to wait for the man to come to him, Matt did just that. Theo moved forward with languid movements, totally unhurried and with an air of utmost confidence.

"I'm Matt O'Brien." Matt held out his hand. "King Leopold hired me as the princess's bodyguard. I'm to protect her until she returns to Orlantha."

Theo shook hands with Matt. "You're an American." Theo's black eyes narrowed speculatively as he released Matt's hand and stared at him.

"Yeah. Yes, sir. I'm with the Dundee Agency out of Atlanta, Georgia, in the good old U.S.A." Matt whipped out his I.D. for Constantine's inspection.

"Why would King Leopold hire an American security

officer to protect the princess when he has his own royal guards?'' Constantine asked as he studied Matt's I.D., then returned it to him.

Just as Matt had figured. Either Adele had left out some pertinent information when she'd telephoned her friend or Dia Constantine had chosen to leave her husband in the dark about Adele's predicament. Hell, he hated being caught in the middle this way. But past experience had taught him that in most cases honesty was the best policy. He had enough trouble as it was with the princess—he certainly didn't need to make an enemy out of a man as powerful as Constantine.

''May I speak frankly—man-to-man?'' Matt asked.

Theo dismissed the servant with a wave of his hand, then motioned for Matt to come with him. ''Join me in the library for a drink, won't you, Mr. O'Brien?''

''Thanks.''

Matt followed Theo down the hall and into a two-story library with a carved metal spiral staircase leading from the main level to the second. The walls of the upper room were lined with bookshelves, which were filled with thousands of books. The downstairs contained a man's private den-cum-home office, with a large fireplace, heavy wooden furniture and modern office equipment, everything from a computer with a twenty-inch monitor to a bank of telephones.

''You look like a whiskey man to me,'' Theo said. ''Scotch all right?''

Matt nodded as he continued visually exploring the library. ''Quite a room. Do you manage your holdings from here, Mr. Constantine?''

Theo punched a button on the wall, and a painting disappeared behind a slender, antique commode to reveal a well-stocked glass and chrome bar. As he lifted a bottle of scotch and undid the lid, Theo replied, ''Yes, I can handle everything from here. But I do have an office in Dareh. However, I must admit that I work from home as much as I do from the city. I prefer the tranquility here at the villa, and I enjoy the extra time it gives me with my wife and daughter.''

''An ideal situation,'' Matt said. ''One of the privileges of being a very rich man.''

Theo poured the whiskey and handed one glass to Matt and kept the other. ''Yes, one of the privileges.'' Theo lifted the liquor to his lips and sipped. ''Now, Mr. O'Brien, what would you like to say to me, man-to-man?''

Matt took a hefty swig of the fine, aged scotch and let the whiskey burn a sweet trail down to his belly. He didn't think he'd ever tasted anything finer. ''Princess Adele ran away from the palace when her father refused to cancel her wedding to the Duke of Roswald.''

Theo cocked his eyebrows as he focused his attention directly at Matt. ''So that is why it was reported she was seen in Paris with that ne'er-do-well Yves Jurgen.'' Theo sipped his whiskey, then motioned for Matt to sit. ''I can't say that I blame Adele for not wanting to marry Dedrick. The man's a pretentious idiot, but King Leopold has been determined to fulfill the obligations of Adele's engagement to the duke, even though the practice of betrothing children is outrageously archaic.''

Matt sat, sipped on the best damn scotch he'd ever drunk and said, ''The king hired my agency to track down the princess and return her to Erembourg.''

''And you tracked Adele here, to my country?''

Matt shook his head, then hurried through a shortened version of his brief association with the princess. He ended his tale with ''So, I've agreed to give her one week's grace period. After that, I'll have no choice but to take her home.''

Theo grinned. ''Interesting. Very interesting.'' Theo

laughed. "I am not laughing at you, Mr. O'Brien. I am amused that Her Highness and my wife thought it necessary to keep me in the dark about Adele's true reason for coming to Golnar."

"And why would they do that? Why would your wife think it necessary to be less than totally honest with you?"

Theo chuckled. "Because I am an egotistical tyrant at worst and an overprotective, rather old-fashioned husband and father at best."

"And if the princess's life was truly in danger, you wouldn't want your wife and child exposed to that danger."

"Mmm. Yes, I suppose that is why Dia thought it best not to inform me that Adele was running not only from her father, but from someone's rather inept henchmen."

"I can assure you that if Dedrick, or whoever sent the first two goons, sends someone else after the princess, he will send someone more capable."

"Then you truly believe that Adele is in danger?"

"I'm not 100 percent sure," Matt said. "But I'm willing to give her the benefit of the doubt. For a week, anyway."

"Very well." Theo set his empty glass on a marble-topped antique mahogany table to his left. "If you will accept total responsibility for Adele while you are in Golnar, I have no objection to your staying here at the villa as her bodyguard."

"Thank you." Matt finished off his whiskey and placed his glass beside Theo's. "Now, Mr. Constantine, where might I find the princess?"

Theo smiled warmly, but his dark eyes surveyed Matt with astute perception. "I believe you are who you say you are, Matt, but you will forgive me if I make several quick phone calls to verify what you've told me."

"Certainly," Matt replied. "Would you like for me to wait outside?"

"That won't be necessary."

Theo Constantine made three phone calls and although Matt tried to feign indifference, he couldn't help hearing the man's end of each conversation. After the third call— to Ellen Denby—ended, Theo turned to Matt. "Everything seems to be in order. I apologize if my—"

"No apologies necessary," Matt assured him. "I'd have done the same thing in your place."

"Dia was eager to take Adele to a new café in Dareh after their shopping spree. I believe you can find them on the east side of the city, at the Odyssea Café on Lidinis Street. It's a rather quaint old building painted a light shade of tan, and there is a red-and-white awning over the entrance and the restaurant extends outside into a sidewalk café."

Matt nodded, then stood. "You do understand, don't you, Mr. Constantine, that regardless of whether the princess is willing, at the end of one week, I will be taking her to Orlantha and turning her over to her father?"

Theo gazed at Matt, a serious expression on his face. "I believe your giving her an entire week was more than generous of you, Matt…may I call you Matt?" Matt nodded. "And you must call me Theo. I have a feeling that by week's end you and I are going to be friends."

Matt breathed a sigh of relief. Thank God Theo turned out be an all-right kind of guy. He understood that Matt had a job to do and he'd pretty much assured Matt he wouldn't get in his way.

"I think for the duration of our stay here in Golnar, it might be wise for me to keep the princess here at the villa," Matt said. "Just in case."

"You must do as you think best, but I warn you that Adele and Dia together are quite a formidable force," Theo said. "That is one reason I dread those two spending too much time together. Only God above knows what mischief they will get into.''

''I consider myself warned.''

Matt shook hands with Theo again, then Theo walked him outside to his rented Fiat. As he drove out of the driveway, he glanced in his rearview mirror and caught a glimpse of a servant handing Theo a cellular phone.

Finding the Odyssea Café had been relatively easy, although it blended into the scenery, being only one of many restaurants on Lidinis Street. The building next door, another modernized old structure, boasted intricate iron banisters surrounding small, second-story balconies.

Matt parallel parked the Fiat, locked the car and headed toward the café. If he was lucky, he'd find Adele and her friend enjoying a late-afternoon snack. As he approached the sidewalk café with red-and-white-striped umbrellas over the tables matching the canopy over the restaurant's entrance, he caught sight of the princess sitting with a strikingly attractive black-haired woman at a table about fifteen feet away. The two were laughing and talking the way old friends usually do. Stacked in three other chairs at their table were boxes and sacks, no doubt filled with feminine treasures from their shopping spree. Matt took his time, assuring himself that Adele wouldn't run when she saw him. After all, she was expecting him. They'd made arrangements for him to follow her, hadn't they?

When he was within ten feet of their table, the princess turned her head ever so slightly, almost as if she had sensed his presence. Her gaze searched through the customers, then moved across the sidewalk café to where he stood. When she saw him, she threw up her hand and waved, a warm smile on her face. A tight knot of something odd, something alien, formed in his stomach. He couldn't remember when he'd ever been so damn glad to see a woman, unless she was lying naked in his bed, waiting for him with outstretched arms.

Adele returned her attention to her friend as Matt made his way between tables. Suddenly, in his peripheral vision, Matt noticed a dark car nearby, and at first he thought the driver was trying to parallel park the black sedan. But the hood of the vehicle faced the sidewalk. A warning signal went off inside his brain, the result of years as a soldier and more recently as a security agent. When he turned his gaze fully toward the car, he realized immediately that the driver had either lost control or was deliberately heading straight toward the sidewalk café filled with afternoon patrons. Adele! She and Dia Constantine sat at a table nearest the street and would therefore be the first two people hit if the car didn't stop.

Following gut instinct, Matt shot across the sidewalk in front of the black car, missing the hood by mere inches. "Get out of the way!" he yelled to Adele, who looked in his direction, gasped and then screamed. He dove toward her, jerked her out of her chair, reached over and grabbed Dia Constantine's arm and pulled both women out of harm's way just as the late-model black Mercedes crashed into the table where they'd been sitting.

Matt kept the women moving farther and farther back and then into the café, fearing the out-of-control vehicle would continue its perilous route. But suddenly, as if the driver realized he had missed his target, the car backed up and sped off down the street.

Dia Constantine leaned against the door frame, her huge gray eyes staring sightlessly into space. Adele clung to Matt, her ragged breathing pressing her breasts against his chest. Unconsciously he lifted one arm, wrapped it around her and threaded the fingers of his other hand through her hair. She tilted her face and looked up at him. Her soft, pink lips parted on an indrawn breath.

"Are you all right?" he asked, his gaze caressing her face.

She nodded. "What...what happened?"

"I'm not sure, but—" He felt her shivering. "It's all right. You're not hurt and neither is your friend."

"Yes, thanks to you. You saved our lives."

"Adele..." He probably shouldn't have used her given name, seeing that she was a princess, but it was rather difficult to remember proper protocol when you had your arms wrapped around a woman and she was looking at you as if you were the most wonderful man on earth. "You realize this might not have been an accident, don't you? I'd say the driver of that car was either trying to kill you or frighten you to death...or possibly get close enough for his partner to grab you."

She trembled from head to toe as she comprehended his meaning. "The Royalists will stop at nothing to force my return to Orlantha. And if I don't marry Dedrick, they are willing to kill me to accomplish their goals. Oh, God, Matt, what am I going to do?"

"You're going to let me take care of you," he told her. "I promise I won't let anyone hurt you."

## Chapter 6

After dealing judiciously with the local police, assisted in great part by the that fact that Mrs. Theo Constantine was involved, Matt secured the ladies in the limousine and followed closely behind in his rental car. He'd learned from Dia that her chauffeur also acted as her bodyguard whenever she left the villa. Apparently her personal security hadn't acted as quickly or successfully as Matt had. The chauffeur, a man she called Peneus, seemed rattled by the attack, probably not only afraid for Dia, but fearful for his job once Theo found out what had happened.

On the drive from Dareh to the villa, Matt kept a close watch to make sure no one followed them. He couldn't be absolutely sure the target of the "accident" had been Princess Adele, but what reason would anyone have to want to harm Dia? Due to Theo's great wealth, Matt suspected that the greatest threat to the Constantines might be kidnapping.

The minute the chauffeur opened the limousine's back

door, Dia jumped out of the car and ran toward the house, calling her husband's name. Adele exited more slowly, apparently still slightly shaken and a bit dazed. Matt parked the Fiat, pocketed the keys and got out as quickly as possible.

Standing on the porch beneath the villa's twenty-five-foot entrance arch, Adele turned and looked at Matt. When their gazes met, he understood that she was waiting for him. A totally masculine sense of pride surged up within him. This beautiful, wealthy, aristocratic woman needed him—and she knew she needed him. He could see the understanding in her eyes, the knowledge that he—Matt O'Brien—had saved her life and she could depend on him to keep her safe. Odd how suddenly nothing else seemed to matter except protecting Adele. His assignment to find her and return her to her father would have to take a back seat to a more important issue—making sure she was safe.

When he approached her, she lifted her face and looked up at him. In her loafers she stood nearly a foot shorter than he, the top of her head reaching just above his shoulder. It took every ounce of his willpower not to reach out and pull her into his arms. She looked so small and lost, so sad and vulnerable.

"Dia is very upset," Adele said.

"As she should be," Matt replied. "You two came very close to being run down, perhaps killed."

"Dia thinks the driver and his partner might have been trying to harm her. She's gone to tell Theo what happened and ask him if he has some enemy who might want to kill her."

"You don't think Dia was the target, do you?"

"Do you?" Adele's gaze locked with Matt's.

"Explain to me why Dedrick would want to kill you? I thought the guy wanted to marry you so he could be the prince and start changing your government from within."

"Pippin says that since Balanchine's military power doesn't match that of Orlantha's, then the Royalists would much prefer taking control of my country through peaceful means. Dedrick marrying me is the ideal situation. But if I won't marry Dedrick, then their next course of action will probably be to kill me and make it look like an accident. Then, in a few years, after Dedrick persuades my father to name him his successor, they will kill my father."

"Pippin seems to know an awful lot about the Royalists, doesn't he?"

"If you're implying—"

"I'm not implying anything. Just making an observation," Matt said. "By the way, if something happened to you, why would your father name old mule face to be his successor if the two of you weren't married?"

"Dedrick is one of three people directly in line to succeed to the throne if I die without an heir. His mother was my father's cousin as are Count Elend and Bernadette Billaud, the Duchess of Ghislaine. Count Elend is seventy-seven and the duchess is seventy and in poor health, and both are childless. So it would stand to reason that Dedrick, a young, healthy man of thirty-four, would be the logical choice."

"I see." Matt considered the situation for several minutes, then said, "Do you trust Pippin Ritter with your life?"

"Yes, I do. Why?"

"Call him and tell him what happened in Dareh today, then tell him that the Dundee Agency is going to send him some help."

"What do you mean—"

Matt gently grasped Adele's shoulders. "We need to find proof against Dedrick, and the sooner the better. The Dundee Agency provides detective services. It's our business to find people, to find evidence, to find proof of guilt.

You tell Pippin that I'm going to contact my boss and request that a couple of our agents go to Orlantha and work with Pippin, speed up the process by putting the Dundee Agency on the job.''

"Oh, Matt, would you do that? I...oh, dear, I'm afraid I might not be able to get my hands on that much money. Most of my assets are frozen now. I had to depend on Dia to buy my new clothes today.''

"Don't worry. We'll figure out something. If necessary, we can bill King Leopold after we get the evidence we need against the duke.''

Adele threw her arms around Matt's neck and hugged him. From behind them, someone cleared his throat. Adele and Matt broke apart instantly and turned to face Theo and Dia Constantine where they stood in the open doorway of the villa's front entrance.

"Dia has told me what happened today, Mr. O'Brien...Matt,'' Theo said. "It seems I am in your debt. You saved my wife and the princess. I should like very much to reward you.''

"That's not necessary,'' Matt replied.

"But I insist. I will write you out a check for—what amount do you think, my dear?'' Theo turned to his wife. "Is a hundred thousand American dollars satisfactory?''

"I think you should give him more,'' Dia said.

"Look, I appreciate the offer, but I can't— Hey, here's an idea. Princess Adele's assets are temporarily frozen while she's at war with her father, and she's in need of some money right now to pay the fees of a couple of Dundee agents.''

"Oh, Matt, that's a great idea.'' Adele looked to Theo. "Please, Theo, say yes. Matt plans to contact his agency and request two agents be sent to—''

Dia cleared her throat loudly and shook her head. Adele groaned, then bit down on her bottom lip as an I'm-sorry-

I-almost-let-the-cat-out-of-the-bag expression crossed her face.

Theo slipped his arm around his wife's waist. "It's all right, my dear, Matt filled me in on the situation earlier today, when he first arrived at the villa."

Dia smiled. "Then you aren't upset?"

Theo kissed Dia's forehead. "I am upset only because you were nearly killed this afternoon...and perhaps because you felt it necessary to be less that completely honest with me about the purpose of Adele's visit."

"What did you tell Theo?" Adele asked Matt.

"Pretty much everything," Matt admitted.

Adele turned immediately to Theo. "I'm very sorry that by simply being with me this afternoon, Dia was almost killed. I truly didn't believe that—"

"We will not send Adele away!" Dia said forcefully. "She's my friend, she's in trouble, and I intend to help her."

Theo grinned. "Yes, of course, my dear. If you wish Adele and Matt to stay on here at the villa, if you wish for me to pay for these Dundee agents to go to Orlantha, I will." Theo looked to Matt. "Exactly what will these Dundee agents be doing in Orlantha?"

Before Matt could respond, Adele said, "They're going to help Pippin prove that Dedrick is a Royalist and therefore a danger to Orlantha." She took a deep breath, then continued, "The Dundee Agency not only specializes in personal protection, but in investigative work, too."

"Tell me, Matt, are you now convinced that the princess is telling you the truth about the Duke of Roswald?"

"Unless you know of a reason why someone would have wanted to kill your wife today or to issue you a warning by frightening her, then I'd say Princess Adele was the target of either an assassination attempt or a kidnapping attempt. So, the answer to your question is yes."

Theo turned and gave a quick bow to Adele. "Then I am at the princess's service. My money, my power. Adele is very dear to Dia and therefore to me. She is, after all, our precious Phila's godmother."

"Are you interested in a little professional advice?" Matt asked.

"And that would be?" Theo looked at Matt point-blank.

"Beef up security around the villa. Hire your wife and daughter their own personal bodyguards and don't rely on the chauffeur, no matter how competent, to do double duty."

"But here on Golnar we Constantines have always been safe," Theo said. "This is my country, my island, no one would dare—"

"That's definitely old-fashioned thinking," Matt said. "I know you told me you were an old-fashioned man, but you can't honestly think that because your family has controlled Golnar for three generations that you're safe from the same threats that other wealthy men face every day."

Dia gasped. Adele looked at Matt in awe—and with respect.

"We have servants who are loyal to a fault, and they are all the protection we have ever needed here at the villa," Theo said. "And whenever we travel away from home, I have security with us at all times."

"It's your life and the lives of your family members," Matt said, "so it's your decision about how to ensure your safety and theirs. However, if you're serious about helping the princess, you might want to engage some private security for the villa during her stay."

"Then you expect another attempt to be made? To what? Kidnap her? Or perhaps kill her?" Theo's classic Greek features tightened, changing his face from handsome to menacing.

"Yeah, it's a possibility that I'd be a fool to rule out.

And if something happens, I would do everything in my power to protect you and your family, but make no doubt about it, Princess Adele is my first priority.''

Adele wished she could control the erratic beating of her heart, the increased tempo of her pulse, but she was powerless to stop her purely feminine reaction to Matt O'Brien's protective, possessive statement. In all the years she had known Theo Constantine, she had never seen anyone brave enough to stand up to the man and to contradict him. But Matt had been totally unafraid. She thought it utterly amazing that a middle-class working American man, a mere commoner, with no wealth, power or title, possessed so much self-confidence.

''If you think my staying here will put Dia and Theo and little Phila at risk, then perhaps we should make arrangements to stay in Dareh,'' Adele said.

''No!'' Dia cried. ''You are safer here.'' She turned to her husband. ''You will hire guards for the villa, at least for the time being, as Mr. O'Brien suggested, won't you Theo?''

Theo hugged his wife to his side, kissed her temple and replied, ''Yes, I will arrange for professional security here at the villa.'' He held out his hand to Adele, which she accepted. ''You will stay here with us.''

''Thank you.''

Theo looked squarely at Matt. ''I will take care of my woman and my child. You take care of your…of the princess.''

''Now that that's settled, let's go inside,'' Dia said. ''It's almost dark and I'd like to go to Phila and spend some time with her before her bedtime. She's quite upset that we aren't having dinner together tonight as planned.'' Dia held out her hand to her husband. ''Come, Theo, Phila will want you to finish that story you began last night.''

Once Theo and Dia disappeared inside the villa, Adele spoke. "Perhaps you should telephone your boss first, before I call Pippin. That way I can tell him the name of the Dundee agents coming to Orlantha and when to expect them."

"Do you think Theo will mind if we use the phones in his library to make our calls?" Matt asked.

Adele giggled.

"What's so funny?"

"You are. Only a moment ago you were issuing orders to one of the wealthiest men in Europe, and now suddenly you're concerned about using his telephones?"

"I suppose my basic bossy, take-charge nature is constantly at war with the good manners Aunt Velma tried to drill into me." Matt grabbed her arm. "Come on. Let's make those calls and get the ball rolling."

While Adele telephoned Pippin Ritter to bring him up-to-date, Matt sat across the room from her using another of Theo's telephone lines. He dialed Ellen's private home number, since with the time differences, it was early morning in the U.S. He hoped she didn't chew him out for calling at the crack of dawn, but the sooner she sent a couple of agents to Orlantha, the sooner they'd be able to help the vice chancellor collect evidence against the duke. As he listened to the ringing phone and waited for Ellen to answer, he heard the hum of Adele's voice, but since she spoke softly and not in English, he really couldn't make out what she was saying.

"You've reached 555-8017. I'm unavailable to take your call at present. At the sound of the tone, please leave your name, number and a brief message."

Damn! Ellen's answering machine had picked up.

As soon as he heard the beep, he said, "Hi, there, boss lady. It's Matt O'Brien. If you're there, how about picking up the phone. I've got a job for a couple of our guys, and it's urgent.''

''At such an ungodly hour, this had better be important, O'Brien,'' Ellen said.

''Not a morning person, are you?''

''Cut the crap. Why do you need two agents? Can't you handle the princess without assistance?''

''There's been another attempt made to either abduct or perhaps kill Adele—Princess Adele.'' He elaborated, explaining the incident at the Odyssea Café. ''What we need is a couple of agents to go into Orlantha, undercover, meet with Pippin Ritter and see if they can't get the goods on Dedrick Vardan.''

''And who's going to pay for this little venture?''

''Theo Constantine.''

''*The* Theo Constantine?''

Matt thought Ellen's voice sounded peculiar. ''Is something wrong? You sound kind of funny.''

''No, I'm all right. Just surprised. Mind telling me how Theo Constantine is involved?''

''He's married to Adele's best friend, Dia, and since the guy is loaded, he's happy to pick up the tab.''

''Theo is married?'' Ellen asked.

''Do you know him?''

''Yes…I met him. I was a guest at a party in his home years ago. At the time Theo was quite a playboy. Somehow I can't picture him married.''

''Not only married, but a father.''

''He has children?''

''One. A daughter. Adele is the child's godmother.''

''He's very fortunate.'' Ellen cleared her throat. ''So, tell me, when did you get on a first-name basis with the princess?''

''What?''

''You've been referring to Her Highness as Adele.

That's sort of chummy, isn't it, for a princess's body-guard?''

"Sorry, I guess with all that's happened, I've sort of lost track of my manners."

"I don't mind, if the princess doesn't," Ellen said. "Now, when do you want these agents sent to Orlantha? And do you have a preference about which agents should go?"

"I want them there yesterday," Matt replied. "And if they're free, I'd like you to send Lucie Evans and Jed Tyree."

"Lucie's available. But Jed's tied up until next week. Domingo Shea just got back from Vegas yesterday."

"Dom's free? Hell, yes, send him."

"Lucie and Dom will be on the next flight out of Atlanta. And the code phrase will be 'warm for this time of year' and the response should be 'I prefer the warmth. I don't like cold weather.' So, is there anything else I can do for you?"

"Yeah, how about calling King Leopold and feeding him some cock-and-bull story about why the princess and I won't be back in Orlantha right away."

"I think perhaps the princess isn't able to travel for at least forty-eight hours, maybe longer, because she's come down with a stomach virus. How does that sound?"

"Perfect."

"Matt?"

"Yeah?"

"Are you becoming personally involved with the princess?"

"What makes you...I've known the woman twenty-four hours. And most of that time she has been an A-number-one royal pain. I'm doing my job. I'll protect her until I feel that it's safe to turn her over to her father."

"Be careful, Matt. Personally and professionally.

There's something about Golnar that tends to affect people in odd ways. People can become personally involved very quickly there, in that island paradise.''

"Speaking from personal experience?'' The minute the question came out of his mouth, Matt regretted having asked. "Don't answer. None of my business.''

"You're right. It is none of your business.''

"I'll keep in touch. Let me know how the king takes the news that there's been an unavoidable delay in returning the princess to the palace.''

Just as Matt said goodbye and hung up the receiver, Adele waved at him. He looked up from where he was perched on the edge of Theo's desk and smiled across the room at the princess.

She held her hand over the phone's mouthpiece. "Is everything set?'' she asked.

"Two of our best agents, Lucie Evans and Domingo Shea, both experts at investigation, will be on the next flight to Orlantha. Tell Pippin to send one of his people to pick them up at the airport and use the code phrase, 'warm for this time of year,' with 'I prefer the warmth. I don't like cold weather.' as the response.''

Adele relaid the message, assured her friend that she was safe and in good hands, then said goodbye and turned to Matt with a smile.

"How can I ever thank you for your help?''

She was looking at him with those soulful brown eyes, her lips slightly parted and her body leaning toward his. Didn't she realize what her expression and body language were saying to him? Maybe she had no idea she was sending him some pretty powerful signals.

"I'm just doing my job,'' he told her.

When she shook her head, her dark curls bounced. "Your job was to return me to my father.''

"Yeah, I know. And that's what I intend to do—return

you to your father safe and sound, with the proof of the duke's treachery in your hand.''

His instincts told him that the princess was about to propel herself directly at him, into another hug of gratitude. Damn, if she wrapped herself around him, he couldn't be held responsible for what he'd do. In an effort to protect himself from embarrassment, he grabbed her arm and practically dragged her out of the library.

''Where are we going?'' she asked, scurrying to keep pace with Matt's long-legged stride.

''I thought you'd want to freshen up before dinner, and I certainly could use a breath of fresh air. I'll probably wander around the grounds and see just what sort of security Theo needs.''

''I'll go with you.''

''No! I mean, you don't have a wrap, and the sun has already set. It's probably chilly outside.''

''I'll grab a wrap from the entry closet,'' Adele told him. ''Dia keeps all sorts of sweaters, coats and jackets there.''

''Are you sure you—''

Before he could finish his sentence, Adele rushed ahead of him into the grand entrance hall and went straight to one of several doors that opened up to storage spaces. By the time he caught up with her, she had put on a cashmere cardigan.

When he approached, she slipped her arm through his and said, ''I want to show you the view from the balconies. The sea is magnificent. I often wish Orlantha bordered the Mediterranean.''

As they walked together out of the villa and down the path to the tiered balconies, Matt felt a bit like the condemned man being led to his own hanging. The princess was being too damn sweet to suit him. His suspicious nature warned him that she was up to something—something that would probably mean big trouble for Velma O'Brien's nephew Matt.

Ellen stepped into the shower, turned the water on full blast and let the warm spray drench her from head to toe. The two brief phone conversations with Matt O'Brien late last night and early this morning had shaken her badly. And it took a great deal to unnerve Ellen Denby. She prided herself on being tough, shrewd, perceptive and un-emotional. But she'd come damn near close to exposing her innermost feelings to an employee. Those who knew her thought of Ellen as a woman without weaknesses. And for the most part they were right. Purposefully she kept others at arm's length, never forming lasting attachments beyond the normal comradery with the men and women at Dundee's.

But just the mention of Golnar flooded her mind with memories she had buried deep within her long ago. She didn't want to remember. Remembering was far too pain-ful. Even now. After nearly fifteen years. But once the dam burst and the memories engulfed her, she couldn't turn back the flood.

She'd been twenty-one, fresh out of college, traveling with a group of girlfriends through Europe for the summer. They'd gone to Golnar to participate in one of the many festivals for which the small island country was known. In the midst of the Mardi Gras-type atmosphere that perme-ated the celebrations, she'd gotten separated from her friends. That's when she met him. Nikos. Odd that she never knew his last name. Not until nearly a year later. And even then, she hadn't been sure it was his real name.

*No! Don't think about it. Don't do this to yourself. It happened a long time ago. You've built a good life for yourself. You're strong and in control, and the nightmares seldom bother you anymore. If you can't stop thinking*

*about him, about those two brief weeks you spent with him,
and about the ungodly price you eventually paid for four-
teen days of ecstasy, you will be pulled back into that deep,
dark abyss from which you barely escaped. Life as you
had known it ceased to exist after that.*

Ellen scrubbed her body as if the thorough cleansing
could wash away the memories—and the unbearable pain.

She could feel him in her arms, the warmth of his body
against hers. Could smell his sweet scent. Could hear his
cries.

Oh, God, the cries. The sheer terror. And then the silence. After all these years she could still hear his final cry
only seconds before he died. And the agony ripped through
her as if it had happened only moments ago.

As she fell to her knees on the tile floor, Ellen wept
uncontrollably, and the shower's warm spray combined
with her salty tears.

## Chapter 7

"I don't like all these guards at the villa." Dia Constantine looked out the window and sighed. "Theo says it's only a precaution, just in case. And it's only temporary. But their presence here makes me edgy."

"It's not as if Theo hired a small army. There are only two guards posted outside and one inside the villa."

Dia shrugged. "Yes, I know, but even Phila has noticed them. I dismissed her concerns by telling her that those men are here to guard you because you're a princess."

"Quick thinking. After all, I've told her that I grew up with guards surrounding me," Adele said. "I pay them little attention and so should you. Just pretend they aren't there."

"Mmm. I'll try." Dia moved away from the window and turned to Adele, who was busy putting the clothes she'd purchased in Dareh onto hangers and placing them in the large, ornately carved wooden armoire. "Tell me truthfully, Adele, can you ignore Mr. O'Brien the way you do other guards?"

Adele placed another garment in the armoire, then turned to face her friend. Dia always had been a bit too perceptive about Adele's actions and reactions, but she supposed that was because Dia had known her for such a long time and they had shared so many confidences over the years.

"Matt O'Brien is not the type of man who can be easily ignored," Adele admitted.

"He's very good-looking, isn't he? I mean, honestly, who could help but notice those incredible blue eyes and that—"

"You're a married woman!"

"I may be married, but I'm hardly blind, am I?"

Adele laughed. "What would Theo say if he heard you drooling over Matt?"

"I'm not the one doing the drooling. I'm merely stating facts. You, my dear Princess, are the one who was drooling when you and Matt came in from your walk last night. Do tell me what happened between the two of you out there on the balcony?"

"Nothing happened." And that's the truth, Adele thought. Nothing worth mentioning. She had been on her best behavior around Matt, showing him how cordial and accommodating she could be. After all, they'd certainly gotten off on the wrong foot, hadn't they? In order to persuade Matt to do her an enormous favor, she needed him to at least like her.

"Dia, I'm going to tell you something, but I must swear you to secrecy first."

Dia rushed to Adele, grabbed her hands and looked her in the eyes. "I swear that whatever it is, I'll not tell a soul."

"Not even Theo."

Dia nodded. "Not even Theo."

"I'm going to get married."

Dia stared at Adele, puzzlement etched on her features. "The whole world knows you're engaged to Dedrick."

"I'm not going to marry Dedrick. I plan to marry someone else before I return to Orlantha."

"What?" Dia shrieked the question.

"It was Matt's idea. He said that if I married someone else my father couldn't force me to marry Dedrick."

"Who are you going to marry?"

Before Adele could respond, a knock on the door interrupted them, and one of the maids opened the door and walked in, then said, "Mrs. Constantine, there's a telephone call for the princess."

"If it's my father again—"

"I've given instructions to relay the same message to King Leopold whenever he telephones." Dia looked pointedly at the maid. "Didn't you tell the king that Her Highness isn't well enough to speak to him?"

"Yes, madam, I've told the king exactly that the four times he has called," the maid replied. "But this call is not from the king. It's from the vice chancellor."

"Pippin?" Adele rushed to the bedside table, reached out and grasped the extension phone.

"You may go now." Dia dismissed the maid with fluttering hand movements.

Adele lifted the receiver, "Pippin?"

"Your Highness, how are you?"

"I'm fine. But tell me, what's going on there? Have you been able to find any proof against Dedrick?"

Pippin sighed. "No, Your Highness. And I have some bad news to relay."

Adele's heartbeat accelerated. "Tell me."

"Word has reached me that the Royalists have hired a trained mercenary and given him orders to either return you to Orlantha within the week or—" Pippin cleared his throat "—or to eliminate you and make your death appear to be accidental. We feel certain that yesterday's mishap at the Odyssea Café was an attempt to either frighten you into returning home or abduct you…or kill you.''

''This doesn't come as a huge surprise to us, does it?''

''I'm deeply concerned,'' Pippin said. ''Even in Golnar, you aren't safe. Perhaps you should come home and pretend you're going to follow through with the wedding plans. It might be safer for you here in Erembourg. I feel relatively certain that we can trust your father's palace guards.''

''You're right. I'm not safe even here in Golnar. I'll come home soon. And, Pippin?''

''Yes?''

''I plan to bring a surprise with me.''

''What sort of surprise?''

''A husband.''

''Your Highness, we must have a bad connection. I thought you said your surprise was a husband.''

''That's exactly what I said. I'm going to get married…in name only, of course. There is no way my father can force me to marry Dedrick if I'm already married.''

''God help us. I'm not sure how the Royalists will react to such news. And what if King Leopold refuses to recognize the marriage? What if he disinherits you? That would be playing right into Dedrick's hands.''

''I know my father,'' Adele said. ''He will not disown me, he will only threaten to. I'll tell him that I fell madly in love and couldn't help myself. He won't be pleased, but he'll eventually understand. His marriage to my mother was a love match, you know. But in the meantime Father will rant and rave and swear he will disinherit me. And Dedrick will think perhaps the throne can be his without marrying me. It's an almost foolproof plan.''

''Who is he? Who is this man willing to be your temporary husband? Is it Yves Jurgen? Your Highness, the man is highly unsuitable. And no one would believe that it's a love match."

"It's not Yves. And I'd rather not say who it is. Not yet. You see, I haven't proposed to him, and there's a possibility that he'll refuse and I'll be forced to find another candidate."

"Who would dare refuse you?"

"Oh, I know one man who might."

"Please, Princess, be careful. Remember that you cannot trust everyone."

"I'm well aware of that fact." Adele glanced at Dia, who sat on the edge of the bed and listened attentively to Adele's conversation. "By the way, have the Dundee agents arrived?"

"I'm expecting them this afternoon," Pippin replied. "Let's hope they can help us. Time is running out. The Royalists are becoming more bold in their actions, and once Dedrick finds out that you're planning to marry someone else, there is no way to predict what they will do next."

"Don't worry about me. I have a twenty-four-hour-a-day guardian."

The moment Adele hung up the phone, Dia said, "I know who you're going to marry."

Adele smiled. "Do you really? So, tell me, do you approve of my plan?"

"If he marries you, a man like that will expect a wedding night."

A shiver of apprehension shot up Adele's spine. The thought flashed through her mind of lying naked in his arms. "There will be no wedding night. If he agrees to marry me, it will be with the understanding that the marriage is in name only and a temporary arrangement. Just until we get the evidence we need against Dedrick."

"What if he turns you down?"

"Then you and Theo will have to find someone for me. But my feminine instincts tell me that my first choice is the right choice."

"When do you plan to ask him?"

"This evening. And if he says yes, we'll get married as soon as possible."

Matt paced the floor in Theo Constantine's home office. With the latest report from Pippin Ritter confirming that Adele was the target of yesterday's mishap at the Odyssea Café, he realized that the princess wouldn't be safe anywhere. And since it was his job to return her safely to Orlantha, his number-one priority had become simply to keep her alive. But as long as Dedrick Vardan and the Royalists posed a threat, Her Highness would still be in danger once he returned her to her father.

"You are wearing a hole in the floor," Theo said. "There are ways to solve every problem. It's all a matter of finding the right solution."

Matt halted and glared at Theo. "If Pippin Ritter's information is correct, the Royalists have hired a mercenary, which means we're now dealing with a professional." Matt raked his fingers through his hair. "Damn! I've sent two of Dundee's best agents to assist in digging up the dirt on old mule face, but it would help a great deal if I knew someone who had a pipeline directly into the Royalists' territory. Somebody who knows all the inner workings of the group."

"I know such a man," Theo said.

Matt stared at Theo. "You know someone with ties to the Royalists?"

Theo shook his head. "I know a man who has ties to every militant group in existence worldwide."

"You're kidding?"

"I would not joke about something this important. About Adele's life."

"Who is this guy?"

"A mystery man," Theo said. "He prefers to remain in the shadows. It is much safer for him that way. After all, he has ties to and knowledge of every dissident faction in Europe, Asia and the Middle East."

"How can we contact this man?"

"This gentleman will be attending the private party that Dia and I are hosting this coming Saturday night. My wife and I agreed that we will not cancel our plans out of fear. I will arrange for more private security, of course. So, if you wish, I will set up a private meeting between you and my *friend*."

"Saturday night," Matt said. "Two days from now." Matt nodded. "Set up the meeting."

"Before I make these arrangements, I must caution you—you must never tell anyone other than the people directly involved in this case of yours of your meeting with him or reveal anything about your conversation with him. If you do, your life will be in danger."

"Who the hell is this man?"

"It is safer for him and for you if I tell you no more."

Matt nodded, but decided then and there to contact some old friends in the military later that day to see if they could find out anything about some mysterious man who had ties to all the militant organizations in the world. When he'd been in the air force, he'd heard a name whispered within the inner circles, but even the top brass didn't seem to know the man's true identity. Matt wondered if Theo's acquaintance and the man he'd heard about might be the same man. El-Hawah. Arabic for *the wind*. A man as elusive, unpredictable and unstoppable as the wind itself. El-Hawah was a legend. Some believed he didn't exist, that he was a fictitious character created by the overzealous imaginations of undercover agents worldwide. The famous El-Hawah had made numerous enemies over the years but had somehow managed to escape death or capture time and again. And no two descriptions of the man seemed to match.

The rest of the day passed uneventfully. Matt put in a call to an old air force buddy and asked him to call in some favors and do some checking on this mysterious El-Hawah and see if there might be any connection between the man and Theo Constantine. And after King Leopold's sixth call to Adele, Matt decided if the princess wouldn't talk to her father, maybe he should. He assured the king that Adele was recovering from her stomach flu, but she wouldn't feel like traveling for a few more days. Thankfully, His Majesty bought the lie and seemed genuinely concerned about his daughter's health.

Although the three local bodyguards that Theo had hired conducted themselves professionally and appeared to be well trained, Matt kept a close eye on Princess Adele. She seemed to be totally oblivious to his presence, a habit she no doubt had perfected from years of being watched by the palace guards. Her Highness had spent the entire day with Dia Constantine, who was constantly aware of his intrusive presence. He'd caught Theo's wife eyeing him skeptically from time to time, as if she weren't quite certain about him. Did the woman distrust him? Or was there some other reason for her close scrutiny?

The two women had joined Phila and her nanny outside on the top balcony where they all took turns reading aloud from the latest Harry Potter book. Playacting the parts of the characters, the foursome entertained themselves for over an hour. During that time, Matt studied each one in turn. He could see why Theo had chosen Dia to be his wife. Her exotic beauty and gentle nature would be enough to attract any man. Young Phila was her mother's daughter—a rare beauty in the making. Someday she would undoubtedly have suitors lined up outside the villa. Faith Sheridan puzzled Matt. He suspected that beneath the loose-fitting white blouse and tan skirt lay a rather nice figure. And behind a pair of dark-framed glasses were a pair of large, expressive blue-gray eyes. He rather liked Faith, the shy, soft-spoken nanny who seemed quite content with her life as a servant in the Constantine household. And that's what puzzled him. Why would someone that young, with the potential to be quite attractive, choose to be a nanny? Of course, the woman's personal life was none of his business.

But Adele Reynard's personal life was his business. First her father and then she had put him in a position where he had no choice but to become embroiled in every aspect of the princess's life. The sane and sensible part of his nature reminded him that this was an assignment, not unlike others he had taken on over the past few years. Guard a client. Protect her from any and all harm. Simple enough. Yeah, except when he let his emotions get involved. He'd already broken the cardinal rule of maintaining an impersonal and professional attitude toward the client at all times. When he looked at the lady, he didn't see Her Highness, he saw a desirable woman.

So, get over it, he told himself. No way would she ever think of him as anything other than her bodyguard. He was nothing more to her than a useful tool in her quest to safeguard her throne and her country from the royalists. And even if she were interested in him—which she wasn't—having an affair with a princess might prove to be more trouble than it was worth.

When Phila's nanny reminded her it was time for her art class, Dia went inside with them, leaving Adele and Matt alone on the balcony. Adele rose from her chair, turned and gazed out at the sea below the tiered balconies. Matt walked over to stand beside her.

"Have you ever been married?" Adele asked.

"Huh?" Her question surprised him. "Married? Me? No."

"And you aren't engaged or in a committed relationship?"

Matt shook his head. "Why the personal questions?"

"Just curious."

"My life's pretty much an open book," Matt said. "No secrets. No hidden agenda. No conspiracies. Dull stuff compared to your life."

"I suspect you're making fun of me."

"Sorry. I didn't mean to offend you."

"I'm not offended. You're right to feel as you do. After all, what would a commoner, an American commoner, know about life at the Erembourg court? My way of life may seem superficial and superfluous to you. You probably think of a monarchy as an outdated way to govern a country. But I was raised from birth to put the needs of Orlantha before my own needs, to consider the people's rights before my own, to dedicate my life to serving my country and her people."

"In theory it sounds noble," Matt admitted. "So, are you telling me that if old mule face wasn't a suspected member of the Royalist, you'd marry him?"

Without hesitation Adele replied, "If marrying Dedrick was what was best for Orlantha, yes, I would marry him tomorrow."

"What about love?"

"What about it?"

"You'd marry Dedrick and spend the rest of your life with him even though you don't love him?"

"If he were a good man, I would probably learn to love him, in time."

Shaking his head, Matt chuckled. "You royal folks sure do things differently from us regular guys. I'd hate to marry somebody I didn't love and who didn't love me. Marriage is difficult enough as it is without going into it lacking the most important ingredient."

"Since you've never been married, what makes you such an expert on the subject?"

"I didn't say I was an expert. I just said I wouldn't want to marry somebody unless the lady and I were in love."

"Tell me exactly, what is love?"

Thinking she had to be kidding him, Matt was surprised to find, when he looked directly at her, that Adele appeared to be completely serious.

"I'm not sure *exactly*," he admitted.

"Haven't you ever been in love?"

"Sure I have, but…well, it was a long time ago. I was just a green kid. And she was just a kid, too."

"So, what happened? What was it like being in love? And if you loved this woman, why didn't you marry her?"

He could see now that he'd opened a can of worms when he'd brought up the subject of marrying for love. He hadn't ever told anyone about Valerie Ralston. Only Aunt Velma had suspected the truth. And to be honest he hadn't thought much about his "true love" in years. Maybe the old adage about time healing all wounds was right. He could think about Valerie now without that painful ache in his gut. But the sense of rejection remained a part of him as much today as then.

"You want the truth?" Matt asked.

Adele nodded.

"My aunt Velma was a domestic servant…you know, a housekeeper, a maid. We lived in Louisville, Kentucky, and she worked for several different families over the years. She was working for the Ralston family when I was seventeen. The Ralstons had a daughter. Valerie."

Adele focused her attention on Matt, watching him intently. "Let me guess—the two of you fell in love, but her father forbade her to marry beneath her. But, goodness, Matt, if you were only seventeen—"

"Her parents wouldn't even let her date me, so we sneaked around for over a year, until she was eighteen. That's when I asked her to marry me."

"And she said no?"

"Not only did she say no, she told me that she couldn't believe that I'd thought she would even consider marrying me. Didn't I know that when she married, she'd marry someone in her social circle, someone at least as rich as her daddy."

"But she had misled you, hadn't she? She'd told you that she loved you and you thought—"

"What are you, a mind reader?"

"Do I...do I remind you of Valerie?"

"What?"

"Do I—"

"No!"

"But I thought perhaps because you and I aren't social equals that I might—"

"Valerie was a tall, thin, blue-eyed blonde. So in appearance the two of you are nothing alike. But, yeah, maybe that snobby attitude of yours does remind me a bit of Valerie...and a dozen other rich, society gals I've known over the years."

"Were you in love with any of these other women?"

"No. Never. I learn pretty quick. I had to get burned only once to make me shy away from fire."

"I see. I...Matt?"

"Hmm?"

"May I ask you another question?"

Matt eyed her suspiciously. "I'm not playing true confessions with you again. My private life is just that—private.''

"I apologize if I seemed nosy, but you are the one who brought up the subject of marriage.''

"Correction," Matt said. "You brought up the subject of marriage. All I said was that I thought people should marry for love.''

"There are other reasons for people to get married.''

"Yeah, I know. There are all kinds of reasons. Political reasons. Financial reasons. Selfish reasons that have nothing to do with love. But you'd know all about that, wouldn't you, since the upper class in Orlantha believe in arranged marriages.''

"Most arranged marriages work out quite satisfactorily. My father's marriage to Muriel was arranged, and they're quite content with each other.''

"Then the queen isn't your mother?''

"No, my mother died when I was three," Adele said. "She was the love of my father's life. He was betrothed to his cousin, Dedrick's aunt, but he fell in love with my mother and refused to marry anyone but her.''

"If your father married for love the first time, why is he so insistent that you marry old mule face? He's got to know that you don't love the man.''

"But I'm not in love with anyone else," Adele explained. "If I were in love with another man...if I were to marry someone else, then... Don't you see, Matt, you suggested it yourself—I should marry someone else, and that way I can't be forced to marry Dedrick. Married to someone else, I could return to Orlantha.''

"Even if you marry some other guy, what would that accomplish in the long run? Your father might decide that you weren't fit to inherit the throne and he might turn it over to Dedrick.''

"That's what I'd like Dedrick to believe. Knowing my

father the way I do, I'm sure he'll fuss and fume and make all kinds of threats. He'll even threaten to denounce me, but he won't. He will eventually accept my marriage, but in the meantime we'll have found the proof we need against Dedrick. Once Dedrick and the Royalists are no longer a threat, then I can have my marriage annulled and—''

''Okay, I admit that screwy as your plan sounds, it just might work. If you're sure about your father—that he'll be outraged enough to be convincing, so that Dedrick will believe the king is considering denouncing you in favor of him.''

''Oh, I'm sure of father's reaction. Believe me, this will buy us the time we need. We can get married here on Golnar. Theo can twist some arms to wave the two-week waiting period so we can get married in a few days, and then I'll call my father and—''

Matt grabbed Adele by the shoulders. She gasped. Their gazes clashed as they stared at each other.

''What do you mean *we* can get married?''

''Oh. Sorry. I never did ask you, did I?'' She smiled faintly. ''Matt O'Brien, will you marry me?''

## Chapter 8

"Marry you?" the words croaked from Matt's tight throat.

"Yes, will you marry me?" Adele repeated. "A temporary marriage in name only. You're the ideal choice—while you're posing as my husband, you can also protect me. And it's not too great a stretch of imagination for people to believe that we've fallen madly in love, if we say that it was love at first sight."

"You expect me to marry you?" Matt shook his head as if puzzled by her request.

"Why do you seem so surprised? After all, it was your idea."

"My idea? I don't think so."

"Yes, you told me, while we were in the car on the way from Austria to Orlantha, that I should marry someone else so I wouldn't be forced to marry Dedrick. Don't you remember?"

"Yeah, I remember, but I wasn't talking about me. No

way, honey. You're going to have to find yourself another groom.''

"Please, Matt." Adele hadn't counted on him refusing her. Didn't he realize he was turning down an offer of marriage to the heir to the throne of Orlantha? "I need you. The people of Orlantha need you. Don't you understand that I'm honoring you by giving you the privilege of—''

Matt laughed, a mirthless sound filled with sarcasm. "You forget you're talking to an American commoner. Being 'prince for a day' doesn't impress me.''

"I see." Appealing to his noble side hadn't worked, so perhaps she should offer him a different inducement. "What if I agree to pay you a sizable amount of money to marry me and remain my husband until we can prove to my father that Dedrick is a Royalist?''

"How much is a sizable amount?''

Adele huffed. *Mercenary American lout!* How was it possible that a man so physically appealing could be such an emotional oaf? "Half a million U.S. dollars. Once our marriage is annulled. I'm sure my father will consider it a small price to pay for your assistance in saving his country and his daughter.''

"Hmm." Matt clicked his tongue as he considered her offer. "Being married to you would require hazardous-duty pay, which would up the asking price considerably.''

"One million dollars." Adele smiled sweetly, determined not to allow this greedy, uncouth, aggravating, irritating, rude man to get the best of her. If she didn't believe that he was the absolutely perfect choice to pose as her bridegroom, she wouldn't consider demeaning herself this way.

Matt let out a long, low whistle. "You know, for that amount of money, I'm tempted.''

"Then you'll marry me?''

Matt shook his head. "I said I was tempted. I didn't say I'd lost my mind."

Adele stomped her foot on the tiled balcony floor. Tension tightened her muscles as she tried to control her anger. "Very well. If you can't be persuaded to do something noble and selfless, even for a million dollars, then I'll have to find someone who will."

Matt grinned. "I didn't say I couldn't be persuaded."

There was something rather lascivious about Matt's smile. The bottom dropped out of Adele's stomach, and the erratic rat-a-tat of her heartbeat drummed inside her head.

"But you said...you implied that—"

Matt reached out, lifted a flyaway strand of hair from her cheek and looped it behind her ear. Her breath caught in her throat as her gaze locked with his.

"Maybe you didn't offer me what I want," he said.

"A million dollars is a lot of money. Are you saying that there's something you'd rather have?" Even to her own ears, her voice sounded nervous and breathy. Was he implying what she thought he was? And if so, would she be willing to meet his price? Would she sacrifice herself for Orlantha?

Matt caressed her cheek. Adele took a step backward, common sense warning her to put some distance between the two of them. As much as she needed this man, she was intelligent enough to be wary of him. Despite the fact that he'd saved her from harm more than once, he was, in fact, little more than a stranger.

"You want a temporary, marriage-in-name-only deal, right?" Matt kept his gaze fixed on her face.

She nodded.

"I don't have a problem with the temporary part," he told her. "But the in-name-only part gives you all the advantages and leaves me with none. After all, I'd be doing you a favor, so the least you could do would be to make the deal worth my while. On a personal level.''

How dare he! There was no longer any doubt in her mind. The man was asking her for sex. Sex as payment for him marrying her. If courtesy and good manners had not been drilled into her since childhood, she would slap his silly, grinning face. To whom did he think he was speaking? She was Princess Adele Reynard of Orlantha, heir to the throne. And he was a commoner. A foreigner. He was nothing!

''Mr. O'Brien, consider the proposal withdrawn!'' Rage boiled inside Adele. She turned and ran from the terrace, opened the nearest set of French doors, went into the villa and slammed the doors behind her.

Outside on the balcony, Matt O'Brien barely restrained his laughter until he was certain Her Highness was out of earshot. Damn, she was an easy mark. He supposed he should feel guilty for messing with her that way, but who the hell did she think she was, acting as if his marrying her on a temporary basis would be some great honor for him? And the woman actually thought she could buy him. A million dollars. A hell of a lot of money. More than he'd ever had; probably more than he ever would have. But no amount of money was worth selling his self-respect. He had learned long ago that the world wasn't always fair, didn't allot the same gifts to everyone and didn't necessarily reward hard work. Others could put you down, take away your livelihood, your material possessions and even your life. But self-respect was one thing that no one could ever take away from a person.

In his peripheral vision, Matt noticed Dia Constantine open the French doors through which the princess had gone so hastily several minutes ago.

''Mr. O'Brien?'' Dia approached him.

He turned to face her. ''Yes, ma'am?''

"Adele told me what happened and she's furious with you. Do you think it's wise to antagonize her? Adele is unaccustomed to being told no. She usually gets what she wants."

"Then maybe her not getting what she wants this time will be good for her."

"Ah, is that why you turned down her proposal—you wanted to teach her a lesson?"

"So you already knew what she had in mind." Matt studied Dia's expression. "I'm sure you and Theo can find her a more suitable gentleman to play the part of her husband."

"I'm sure we can, but..." Dia hesitated. Matt didn't like the peculiar look in her silvery-gray eyes.

"But what?" he asked.

"Oh, nothing. Nothing at all. I just thought of a rather interesting gentleman who would be simply perfect for Adele."

An odd tightening in his gut warned Matt that trouble was brewing. Just who did Dia have in mind? And was this guy really suitable? "Whoever he is, I'll need to run a check on him. We can't allow her to marry just anybody."

"You're quite right, Mr. O'Brien." Dia laced her arm through his. "Walk me to Theo's library, will you? I'll have to get their phone numbers from him."

"*Their* phone numbers?"

A suspicious Cheshire Cat grin lit Dia's face. "While we were talking, I thought of another gentleman. And since Adele needs a husband immediately, I think it best to act quickly, don't you? I'll invite both Stavros and Antonio to dinner tonight. That way Adele can get to know them in a social setting, and by tomorrow night's party here at the villa, she can announce her engagement to the one she chooses."

"Hey, don't you think that's moving awfully fast?" Something about Dia's little plan didn't sit quite right with Matt. He was not jealous! he told himself. No way. It was a simple matter of making sure the princess didn't make a huge mistake by choosing some jerk to play the part of her husband. After all, it was his job to protect her—even from herself, if necessary.

"Time is of the essence, is it not?" Dia led Matt into the house and along the corridor toward Theo's library. "King Leopold will not wait much longer for you to return Adele to Orlantha."

"It's hardly fair to expect the princess to ask some guy to marry her after meeting him only once."

"She has known you only a few days," Dia said. "And she asked you, didn't she?"

"That's different. I'm her bodyguard. She knows who I am, who I work for and what I'm all about. Adele... Princess Adele knows that her safety is my top priority."

"Yes, of course." Dia knocked on the closed library door, and when Theo responded, she opened the door and walked in with Matt on her arm. "Theo, darling, I need a couple of telephone numbers. I want to invite two special guests for dinner tonight."

"With our party tomorrow night, why would you want guests tonight?" Theo asked.

"Adele is husband hunting," Dia replied.

Theo's mouth dropped open.

"I was thinking of Stavros and Antonio as candidates. You do have their numbers, don't you?"

"You don't mean Stavros Christofides and Antonio Fabrizio?"

"Yes, dear, that's exactly who I mean."

"Dia, you've totally confused me. Why is Adele husband hunting? I thought her problem was trying to rid herself of the fiancé she already has. Why would she need— Aha. Marry one man to avoid marrying another. Who's idea was this?''

''It was Mr. O'Brien's,'' Dia said as she turned to smile at Matt.

''Is this true?'' Theo asked.

Matt shook his head, then nodded. Damn! ''Yes and no. The first night I met the princess, I did suggest maybe she should marry someone else, but—''

''Mr. O'Brien was the logical choice, of course,'' Dia explained. ''But I'm afraid he rejected Adele's proposal, so I'm going to provide two candidates for Adele's approval, and then Mr. O'Brien can check them out and—''

Theo lifted his hand to gesture stop. ''Enough! You're giving me a headache with this confusing nonsense.'' Theo turned to Matt. ''Did Adele ask you to marry her?''

''Yeah, she did.'' Matt couldn't bring himself to make eye contact with Theo.

Dia eased across the room, cuddled up against her husband and said softly, ''And when Mr. O'Brien turned down her offer of a million dollars as a bonus and instead asked for s-e-x during their make-believe marriage, Adele withdrew the offer.''

A look of total bafflement crossed Theo Constantine's face. He glanced from his wife to Matt and then back to his wife.

''I can explain about that.'' Heat rose up Matt's neck and warmed his face.

''No need to explain,'' Theo replied. ''I believe I understand what happened.'' He slipped his arm around his wife's waist. ''I'd like to speak to you alone, darling.''

''Yeah, well, I should go check on Adele,'' Matt said. ''Princess Adele.'' Let Theo talk some sense into his wife. God knew somebody needed to.

The minute Matt closed the library door, Theo grasped Dia's chin and forced her to look him in the eye.

"What is the real reason you want to invite Stavros and Antonio here tonight?"

Dia caressed Theo's hand that clutched her chin. "I want to help Adele, of course. She needs a husband right away."

Theo released his wife. "Ah, you're playing a game, aren't you? Stavros is a conceited idiot. And Antonio is a money-hungry womanizer. Adele would never consider marrying either man, not even on a temporary basis."

"Probably not," Dia agreed. "But if Mr. O'Brien thinks she might marry one of them, then—"

"You're setting a trap for Matt, aren't you?" Theo sighed. "Be careful, my dear, that your plan doesn't backfire on you."

"Since you are a man and thus a better judge of other men than I am, don't you think that once Mr. O'Brien sees Adele heading toward danger, he will come to her rescue? Wouldn't you have done so for me?"

"Yes, of course I would have, but then I am in love with— My God! You're playing matchmaker, aren't you? You think there is something romantic between Adele and Matt?"

"Don't you think there is?"

Theo shrugged. "There is tension between them, yes. But something romantic? I'm not sure."

"But I am sure." Dia patted her husband's arm. "Adele is very attracted to Mr. O'Brien, and unless I'm very much mistaken, he feels the same."

"Heaven help us if you're wrong." Theo laughed. "And heaven help Matt if you're right."

Adele sat between Theo and Dia's two guests at the dinner table that night and wondered why on earth her friends had thought that either of these men could be husband material. For the delicate job of pretending to be her husband, she needed an intelligent man, with the ability to at least pretend to be in love with her. And he had to be someone that everyone would believe she could love.

Intelligence ruled out both of these "candidates," as Dia referred to them. Candidates indeed! Candidates for "loser of the century." Her own dismay seemed to be equaled only by Matt's seething, just-below-the-surface animosity toward Stavros and Antonio. He had been studying the two since the moment they arrived at the villa, and it was apparent that his appraisal of them was similar to her own.

Tall, slender and beautiful in an effeminate way, Stavros Christofides was unable to pass a mirror without inspecting himself. Smiling at his own reflection, he would shake his head just to see the light dance off his black curls. And his favorite topic of conversation was—what else?— Stavros. But Adele had to admit that he had impeccable manners, if you could overlook his egotistical self-centeredness.

A stocky, swarthy Italian, who claimed his uncle was a count, Antonio Fabrizio had kissed Adele's hand six times in the past two hours. The sixth time she'd jerked her hand away just as his lips began moving up her arm. It was obvious that he considered himself a true Casanova and probably believed that she found him irresistible. His favorite topic of conversation was love. He loved love. He loved the ladies. And the ladies loved him. And he loved Adele's dress, her hair, her eyes, her smile.

Adele realized that Theo was as uneasy as she and Matt, although he hid his discomfort well. The consummate host, Theo did his best to remain charming throughout the evening. Only Dia seemed thoroughly entertained by Stavros and Antonio. She smiled, laughed and even giggled a few times. Apparently she saw something special in her guests that no one else could see.

When they adjourned to the terrace, they were served brandy, and Theo offered the gentlemen cigars. Matt and Stavros declined, but Antonio accepted, and soon he and Theo were enjoying their after-dinner pleasures.

"Isn't it a glorious evening," Dia said. "So warm and pleasant. And just look at that sky."

Stavros reacted immediately and rushed to Adele's side before Antonio could flick his cigar ash into his empty brandy snifter.

"Princess, would you care to take a walk with me to one of the lower balconies?" Stavros bowed from the waist quite gallantly.

"Uh, er—" How could she refuse him without an excuse? She could hardly say, *I find you quite annoying*.

Before Adele could respond, Dia lifted Adele's arm and slipped it through Stavros's. "She'd love to, wouldn't you, Adele?" Dia gave Adele a little push. "Now, you two go on and enjoy the moonlight. The lower terraces are quite romantic in the moonlight."

Adele glared at Dia, who seemed totally unaware of Adele's displeasure. Out of the corner of her eye, Adele noticed Matt move toward her, then stop abruptly. A fierce scowl marred his handsome face. Some irrational, completely feminine part of her wanted to scream, "Save me, Matt. Please save me." But as Stavros led her from the balcony and down the steps to the next level, Matt neither said nor did anything. Some protector he was turning out to be.

With a man other than Stavros, she might have found this night truly romantic. A three-quarter moon, twinkling stars in a black sky, the sound of the surf below, a secluded balcony overlooking the sea, the scent of flowers in the air. But Stavros knew nothing about romancing a woman.

The only thing Stavros knew anything about was Stavros. His favorite color, his favorite cologne, his favorite song, etc., etc. Just when Adele thought she would scream at any moment, she heard someone coming down the rock steps from the upper balcony. For a split second her heart caught in her throat. Matt?

"I will not allow you to monopolize the princess," Antonio said. "You are probably boring her senseless with your prattle."

Adele's heart sank.

"Go away you pesky Italian," Stavros said. "Your presence is an unwanted intrusion." Stavros looked soulfully into Adele's eyes. "Your Highness, tell this insignificant person to go away, that you wish to be with only me."

Before Adele's brain could barely register the comment, Antonio stormed forward and jerked her away from Stavros. Antonio pulled her into his arms, pressing his body intimately against hers, then peered into her eyes and said, "You want a real man, do you not, *mia amora*. Not this strutting peacock."

"I, uh—" She shoved against Antonio's chest. "Please, let go of me."

He tightened his hold and brought his lips within a hair's breadth of hers. The thought of his lips actually touching hers nauseated her. If he kissed her, she would throw up.

"Unhand Princess Adele this instant." Stavros marched forward, his arms raised, his hands balled into fists.

If Adele hadn't been so aggravated, she would have laughed. This was just what she needed—two blithering idiots fighting over her. What in this world had Dia been thinking inviting these two imbeciles to dinner tonight?

Antonio shoved Adele behind him and faced his opponent. "You dare to challenge me? You skinny boy, you.

You are no match for me. I am an excellent fighter. I have fought for and won many a lovely lady.''

"Please, don't do this," Adele said, but her plea fell on deaf ears.

Stavros landed the first blow. His fist clipped Antonio's shoulder. Then Antonio lunged at Stavros, who side-stepped and laughed when Antonio nearly ran into the hedge row across the back wall. Adele closed her eyes momentarily and blew out an exasperated, disgusted huff.

Suddenly, as if from out of nowhere, a big arm slid around her waist and pulled her away from the humorous battle scene. While her two would-be suitors were duking it out, her rescuer whisked her down the winding rock steps to the terrace below, then, before she could catch her breath, he hurried her along, down the next set of steps. When they reached the narrow beach, far below the villa, Adele turned and stared up at the man whose features she could make out plainly in the moonlight. She eased away from him. He grabbed both of her hands, but didn't try to force her to come closer. They stood and stared at each other, the waves lapping near their feet, the sea breeze caressing them.

"You're not going to ask either of those bumbling idiots to marry you," Matt O'Brien said.

"I'm not?" she asked, her tone teasing.

"Does Dia think you're desperate enough to actually consider either of them?"

"To be honest, I don't know what Dia was thinking."

"If you're determined to find a husband..."

Adele moved toward Matt. Slowly. Never breaking eye contact. "I am determined to do whatever is necessary to protect Orlantha from Dedrick and the Royalists."

"I don't think it will be necessary for you to marry Stavros or Antonio." Matt glanced up toward the terraces overhead.

Adele heard the sound of voices, faded echoes in the wind. "Do you think they've realized I'm gone?"

"Probably not," Matt said. "They seemed far more interested in themselves than in you."

Adele laughed. "They did, didn't they?"

Matt's smile vanished. Adele's heart skipped a beat. He tugged on her hands until she willingly moved directly in front of him, only a few inches separating their bodies.

"I owe you an apology," he said.

"I think you owe me more than one apology, so would you mind being specific—for which infraction of etiquette and simple good manners are you apologizing?"

Matt cursed softly under his breath, then reached out, grabbed the back of her neck and drew her to him. Adele's breath caught in her throat. Hypnotized by his intense stare, she was momentarily rendered speechless.

"I'm apologizing for letting you think that I'd marry you if you'd agree to have sex with me."

"Oh...that."

Adele licked her lips. Matt was big and tall and muscular. He exuded an aura of strength and virility that lured her as powerfully as any aphrodisiac. She could feel his heat. Sense the tension inside him. And instinctively understood that he felt what she felt, needed what she needed, wanted what she wanted.

"Matt?"

"You're not going to marry anyone else," he told her, his voice gruff and husky.

"No, I'm not going to marry anyone—"

He tightened his hold around the back of her neck, lowered his head and whispered against her parted lips. "Damn it, woman, what am I going to do with you?"

Apparently a response was irrelevant. Within seconds he was doing to her exactly what she wanted him to do. His mouth covered hers with an urgency born of continuous restraint. Soft lips pressing hard. Moist tongue thrusting. Two bodies straining for closer contact. And when she clung to him, the heat within them combined like gunpowder and a lit match, and the detonation rocked Adele to her very core.

Matt murmured her name against her face as he kissed her cheeks, her forehead, her chin and then returned to ravage her mouth once again. She held on for dear life, giving kiss for kiss, losing herself completely in the moment, savoring every passionate exchange.

And just when she thought she would die from sheer pleasure, Matt lifted her off her feet and swept her into his arms.

# Chapter 9

Adele preened in front of the cheval mirror. She seldom bought off the rack, but she'd had little choice when she arrived in Golnar without anything except the clothes on her back. She had phoned Yves and instructed him to simply ship the clothes she'd purchased during their Paris shopping spree to the palace in Erembourg. After all, she would be returning home in a few days. As she studied her reflection, Adele had to admit that few people would ever guess this dark-plum silk dress hadn't come straight from one of the Paris couture houses. The addition of minute silver beading that crisscrossed the gown from shoulders to hem in dipping waves added that extra touch of elegance. She stuck out her foot that peeped from beneath the edge of the slim skirt. The high-heeled sandals were a plum leather, an almost perfect match to the dress.

When someone knocked on the door, she held her breath for a split second, thinking it might be Matt. But when Dia asked if she could come in, Adele sighed. She hadn't been alone with Matt since early morning, and with so many servants buzzing around throughout the house, they'd had little chance to talk privately. After what had happened between them last night, she thought surely he would need to discuss their plans. He hadn't out-and-out said that he would marry her, but after the way he'd kissed her—and the way she'd responded—Adele believed his agreement was a foregone conclusion. But she couldn't be completely sure, could she? Not with a man like Matt O'Brien.

"Here are the earrings you wanted to borrow." Dia came into the room and handed Adele a pair of plum-colored Austrian crystal and diamond earrings that dangled two inches long on sterling silver wires.

"Thanks." Adele slipped the silver wires through the holes in her ears, then turned her head this way and that so that the stones caught the light. "These are perfect."

She turned around and smiled at her best friend. Dia looked like an exotic model in her gray satin gown, which clung to every curve of her statuesque body. "You look fabulous, as always."

Dia curtsied playfully and laughed. "Your lady-in-waiting, Princess."

Adele rolled her eyes toward the ceiling, then grinned and asked, "What time are you expecting the first guests to arrive?"

"Officially the party begins at eight, but there will be a few eager guests show up at seven-thirty." Dia checked her diamond-studded wristwatch. "We have almost an hour. It's barely six-thirty."

"Have you seen Matt?" Adele asked.

Dia smiled. "I believe he's still in his room. Theo had a tuxedo delivered for him this afternoon. We can't have your future husband wearing jeans to his first public outing, can we?"

"He's not my future husband. Not yet. He hasn't agreed to marry me."

"But he will," Dia said. "I had no doubt that once he thought you might get stuck with Stavros or Antonio, he would do the gallant thing and rescue you. After all, that is his job, isn't it—rescuing fair damsels in distress?"

Adele laughed. "You could have at least warned me what you were up to last night. For a while, there, I thought you'd lost your mind. Stavros and Antonio have to be two of the worst husband candidates in the world."

"Yes, they are, aren't they? And wasn't it breathtakingly romantic—" Dia laid her hand over her heart "—the way Matt swept you away from both of them and took you to the beach to be alone?"

"It wasn't exactly romantic. It was overwhelming. You know, Dia, if you and Theo hadn't shown up when you did, I'm not sure what might have happened."

"Well, catching you and Matt in such a passionate embrace certainly let the wind out of your two new admirers' sails. Stavros and Antonio couldn't leave fast enough." Dia placed her hand on Adele's shoulder. "Are you falling in love with your bodyguard?"

Adele gasped. "What a silly question. Most certainly not. No. Matt O'Brien has a certain earthy, animal magnetism that…interests me. As it would any woman. And I think he finds me attractive."

Dia blew out a long whistle. "I'll say he finds you attractive. The way you two were going at it last night on the beach, in another five minutes he'd have had you on the ground with your dress hiked up to your waist."

"Dia! How vulgar! I was about to put a stop to things just as you and Theo showed up."

"Sure you were."

"I was!"

"If he agrees to marry you, he's going to expect sex."

"Then, I'll have to make him understand it's out of the question. We can hardly have the marriage annulled if we—"

"No one would know if you did. Just you and Matt."

"Dia!"

"Are you going to ask him tonight?"

"Ask him to marry me? Yes, I hope to find a few moments alone with him."

"Perhaps you should suggest he take you for another walk on the beach."

"Absolutely not. I don't want to give him the wrong impression."

"Too late. You gave him quite an impression last night, and right or wrong it's the one that he'll remember."

"I'll simply have to correct any mistaken assumptions." Adele lifted the sheer silk shawl off the hanger and put it on, draping the edges over her arms on either side so that they flowed loosely atop the skirt of her gown. "Maybe I can speak to Matt and we can clear things up before the party. If he agrees to marry me, we can announce our engagement at the party. Do you think Theo would make the announcement for me?"

"I'll persuade Theo." Dia grasped Adele's arm. "But now isn't a good time to speak to Matt."

"I thought you said he was still in his room dressing."

"He is, but…" Dia pulled Adele closer and whispered, "Theo has invited a special guest tonight, a man who is an old acquaintance. This man, Mr. Khalid, is internationally infamous."

"Theo always invites interesting people to his parties. But what does this Mr. Khalid have to do with my not talking to Matt before the party?"

"Theo has arranged for Matt to speak to Mr. Khalid about the Royalists, and Dedrick in particular. Theo agreed that I could tell you about Matt's meeting with Mr. Khalid."

"I must confess that I'm confused. How does—?"

"Mr. Khalid knows people. All sorts of people. Theo believes that he can find out the information you need about Dedrick."

"Is this man some sort of spy? Or is he a criminal?"

"Both, I suspect. And I'm certain Khalid is an alias. I have no idea how Theo knows the man, but he seems to trust him. He has told me very little and warned me not to mention Mr. Khalid to anyone. He made an exception for you, of course."

"And Matt is going to meet with him tonight?"

"Before the party. In private. Mr. Khalid is already here. In the library. Waiting."

Matt followed Theo into the room, then stood aside while Theo closed and bolted the door to his private domain within the villa. A lone man sat in a darkened corner of the library, his face half in shadows. Matt held back and waited while Theo crossed the tile floor and spoke quietly to his guest.

"It is good of you to come tonight," Theo said. "And I appreciate your arriving early to speak to my new friend, Matthew O'Brien. As I've told you, Matt works for the Dundee Agency and is presently employed as Princess Adele's bodyguard. I explained the circumstances."

The man rose from the chair, his movements quick and precise, like a large, black panther responding to the scent of nearby prey. Theo motioned for Matt, and when Matt came up beside the other two men, he realized how tall this mystery man was. A good four inches taller than Theo and probably two or three inches taller than Matt. So that would make him at least six-four. A large man. Muscular and lean in his black tuxedo. His thick black hair hung past his shoulders, and a neatly trimmed black mustache and goatee added to his ruthless appearance despite his formal attire. A white scar, the width of a pencil, marred the perfection of one bronze cheek.

Matt held out his hand. "Thank you for meeting with me."

The man took Matt's hand and they exchanged a firm, solid shake. "You may call me Khalid."

The guy's accent sounded upper-class British, but Matt caught another underlying accent. English probably wasn't his native language, but he had mastered it to perfection. Almost. What was Khalid's nationality? Matt wondered. It was hard to tell by just looking at him. His physical appearance hinted of a Middle Eastern heredity, perhaps Greek and Turk. And a hint of something else. British, maybe? Or at least Anglo-Saxon.

"Mr. Khalid, I need information about a group who call themselves the Royalists," Matt said. "I need to know who in Orlantha are members of this organization, and—" Matt glanced at Theo, double checking to make sure Theo trusted this man completely and Theo nodded "—if Dedrick Vardan, Duke of Roswald, is a member of this group, I need some sort of proof that he is."

"Proof that will hold up in court?"

Khalid's black eyes studied Matt, as if he were a specimen under a microscope. Hell, this guy was giving him the heebie-jeebies. And it took a lot to unnerve Matt O'Brien. An aura of danger and indescribable power emanated from Theo Constantine's mysterious guest. Matt had run into a lot of different kinds of people over the years, in the air force and since joining Dundee, so he'd learned how to judge others and divide the good from the bad. But he was getting some mighty confusing vibes from this guy. Matt's instincts warned him that this was a man who was both good and bad, and more than capable of destroying any enemy in his path. And doing it with a certain amount of satisfaction.

Matt cleared his throat. "If you can get that sort of proof, it would be good."

"That type of proof might be impossible to find," Khalid said.

"I understand. What I have to have is enough proof to convince King Leopold of the duke's treachery."

"As you know, the duke is betrothed to Princess Adele," Theo said, "and the wedding is set for a few weeks from now."

"You are doing this with Princess Adele's knowledge and approval," Khalid said to Matt.

"Yes," Matt replied. "And if it's a matter of money—" When Matt heard Theo's indrawn breath, he realized he'd made a really stupid mistake. "Sorry. I assumed you'd need a reason to do such an enormous favor. I realize it won't be easy coming up with this kind of information. I already have a couple of Dundee agents working with Orlantha's vice chancellor."

"No offense taken, Mr. O'Brien." Khalid clamped his large hand down on Theo's shoulder. "I will do this as a favor for an old and trusted friend."

"Thank you," Matt said. "I'll be in your debt."

"Yes, thank you," Theo said. "The princess is very dear to my wife."

The corners of Khalid's lips lifted ever so slightly, but he did not smile. Matt wondered if this guy had ever smiled. He looked as if he might be made out of stone. Or at least some hard, unbendable material. Steel? Or something even more sturdy? Some new high-tech material that was indestructible? Matt wasn't sure. But he sensed he could trust this stranger to get the proof he needed.

Dedrick and his comrade shared a private talk after their secret meeting with the handful of other royalists who resided in Erembourg. Sitting across from each other in a local tavern, Dedrick flirted with the waitress while his friend scowled at him.

"Bring our drinks, girl," the man ordered, and the waitress scurried away to fetch their ale. He turned his heated glare on Dedrick. "Your scandalous womanizing will be the ruin of you."

"At least I do not have ice water flowing through my veins as you do."

"Humph! I do not want to have to jerk you out of some woman's bed in the morning when Princess Adele is returned to the palace. You are to go straight home from here and get a good night's sleep, so that when your bride is returned to you and King Leopold summons you, you will arrive at the palace fresh and with your wits about you."

"How can you be certain that this man—this mercenary—you hired will be able to bring Adele home?"

"He is a professional. He will use whatever means necessary."

"He'll probably have to kill the agent the king hired," Dedrick said. "His Majesty informed me only today that he trusts this man to protect Adele and bring her safely home."

"We cannot take any chances. We need the princess home now. I do not trust this Mr. O'Brien. Nor do I trust the princess. The marriage must take place, and she must be persuaded that you are not a Royalist. Once she is back in Erembourg, I think you should suggest moving up the date of the wedding. The sooner she is your blushing bride, the better."

"I agree." Dedrick smiled wickedly. "I rather like the fact that she will be an unwilling bride. She will learn quickly that I am not a man who will abide her hysterics."

"You will do nothing to anger the king." He reached across the table and grabbed Dedrick by the throat. "Marrying the princess is only the first step in our plan, you fool!"

Dedrick gasped for air. His comrade released him.

"One day I shall make you pay for every insult." Dedrick rubbed his throat.

"But until that day, you will follow my instructions. Once you and Princess Adele are husband and wife, you will give her no reason to go crying to her father. Is that understood?"

"You take all the fun out of it."

His comrade growled.

Dedrick huffed. "I understand. I will handle Adele with kid gloves. Until I rule Orlantha and Balanchine."

Adele didn't even see Matt until after the party had already started. Dia had joined Theo downstairs to greet their guests, and Adele stood on the landing with Phila and Faith Sheridan as they watched the early arrivals. Adele could remember when she'd been allowed to spy on her father's guests when she was Phila's age. She'd taken great delight in being a voyeur, and dreamed of the day when she would be old enough to attend the grand affairs at the royal palace.

"All the ladies look so beautiful," Phila said.

"Yes, they're lovely," Faith agreed, a wistful look in her eyes.

Adele wondered if the plain, shy Miss Sheridan had ever attended an elegant gala. Probably not. Such a shame. Everyone, even quiet, shy little nannies should get a chance once in their lives to be Cinderella at the ball.

"There's Mr. O'Brien," Phila said. "He is very handsome. Almost as handsome as my papa."

When Adele saw Matt, her heart skipped a beat. He *was*

very handsome. Tall, broad-shouldered, classically good-looking in a very Black-Irish sort of way.

"Who is that talking to Mr. O'Brien?" Phila asked.

Adele hadn't noticed anyone except Matt. Devastatingly attractive in his black tuxedo, he had gained and held her complete attention. Her gaze traveled from Matt to the man beside him. Adele gasped. Taller than Matt. Dark skin. Long black hair. Mustache and goatee. And a vicious white scar on his right cheek. Just looking at this man from a distance made Adele's blood run cold. Was this the mysterious Mr. Khalid? Of course it was. Who else could it be? The infamous Mr. Khalid who might be a spy or a criminal. And what else was he? Adele decided that she was probably better off not knowing.

"I have no idea who he is," Adele lied. "He's probably a business associate of your papa's." No, Mr. Khalid was no ordinary businessman, Adele thought.

"Phila, we can stay only a few more minutes," Faith told the child. "Your mama said fifteen minutes of observing and that was all."

Phila groaned. "Yes, I know."

Adele patted Phila's cheek. "Don't be sad, sweetheart. Before you know it, you'll be old enough to wear a beautiful gown and join your parents at their parties."

Phila shook her head. "That will be ages and ages from now. I'm only seven, and Mama says I must be sixteen before I can attend one of their parties, and then I can stay only until midnight."

"Well, I must join the festivities now," Adele said. "I'll see you in the morning."

"Good night, Aunt Adele."

Adele kissed her godchild, then smiled at Faith Sheridan who returned the smile.

When she began her descent from the landing, she looked down to see Matt waiting alone at the bottom of the staircase. He was gazing up at her, watching her closely. A scene from an old American movie flashed through her mind. Rhett Butler at the bottom of the stairs, smiling devilishly at Scarlett O'Hara.

When she reached the foot of the stairs, Matt took her arm and draped it over his. "Good evening, Your Highness."

"Good evening, Matt."

"You look beautiful," he told her quietly.

"So do you," she said.

He grinned.

As he led her through the throng of guests, she leaned over and whispered, "Did Mr. Khalid agree to help us?"

Matt stopped dead still and glared at her. "How did you know?"

"Dia told me."

"Theo shared that information with her?"

"Of course. She's his wife."

"You are aware of the fact that Khalid probably isn't his real name and that even meeting him could prove to be dangerous if you—"

"Is he a spy?"

"Is that what Dia thinks?" Matt asked.

"Either that or some sort of international criminal."

Matt groaned.

"What's wrong? Why that reaction?"

"You don't need to know who or what he is," Matt told her. "Theo made it perfectly clear that the man's true identity is none of my business."

"How does Theo know him?"

"Did anyone ever tell you that curiosity killed the cat?"

Adele made a face at Matt, who promptly led her out onto the dance floor. Theo had flown in a small orchestra from Athens and they played modern renditions of classical and semiclassical music, tunes suitable for dancing.

Matt swept her along with the rhythm, his strong arms holding her, his talented feet quite adept, never once making a misstep.

"You're a very good dancer," she said.

"So I've been told."

"I'll bet. And from more than one woman, no doubt." Matt shrugged.

"Lots of women?"

Matt grinned. "What did I tell you about curiosity?"

"Sometimes you can be rather aggravating." Tilting her chin, Adele turned up her nose in a haughty manner.

Matt chuckled. "If that's not the pot calling the kettle black, I don't know what is."

"The pot calling the kettle…?" Adele looked at him, puzzled by his comment. What an odd thing to say. It must be some sort of Americanism, she thought. "Is that your way of telling me that I, too, can, on occasion, be aggravating?"

"Princess, since the moment I met you, you've been nothing but aggravating."

"Is that so? Well, I seem to recall that last night you didn't find my company all that unpleasant. On the contrary—"

Adele gasped when Matt hurriedly danced her across the room, through a set of open French doors and out onto the upper terrace. Several people strolled on the terrace, a few were sitting and one couple was huddled in a dark corner. Matt pulled her to a halt near the edge of the balcony.

"Why did you do that?" she demanded. "What will people think?"

"They'll think I wanted to be alone with you." He glanced around at the other people on the terrace. "Looks like we might have to find another place for privacy."

"Why do we need privacy?" Her heartbeat thumped loudly, sending a pulsating cadence through her body.

"To talk," he replied.

"Oh." Why did she feel disappointed by his answer? she wondered. What had she hoped he would say?

"Hey, honey, if you want a repeat of last night, then we should head down to the beach."

She knew he was joking with her. It was easy enough to see that he could barely keep from laughing. "You're right. We need to talk. About last night, for one thing."

"What's to talk about?" he asked. "What happened seems self-explanatory to me."

"I can assure you that I'm not in the habit of—"

"Yeah, that was pretty obvious."

Adele huffed loudly. "How dare you!"

"How dare I what?"

"How dare you imply that my kissing technique was amateurish. I'll have you know that I've kissed dozens...hundreds of men. And no one has ever complained."

"I wasn't complaining," he told her. "Just making an observation."

"That my kisses are less than adequate?"

"I wouldn't put it that way. I enjoyed our kissing, even if I could tell you haven't had a great deal of practice."

"I told you that—"

"Yeah, I know. You've kissed hundreds of men." Matt shook his head, feigning sadness. "Undoubtedly these men didn't teach you very much."

Adele spluttered. She saw red. Literally. A red rage that colored everything around her. Okay, so she had exaggerated the number of men she'd kissed. Not hundreds. A couple of dozen. And at least half of those had been relatives and close friends whom she had kissed on the cheek. Dedrick had kissed her once, and she'd been so disgusted by his actions that she'd refused to allow him near her again.

"There's a lot I could teach you," Matt said.

"I do not want you to teach me anything. All I want is for you to agree to—"

"There you are, Princess." An elderly gentleman walked toward them, and she immediately recognized him as Theo's uncle, Milo Spaneas. "I hope your young man can spare you for a dance."

"Of course, Mr. Spaneas. I'd love to dance with you."

"Uncle Milo," he corrected her. "You are like a sister to our dear Dia, therefore I am Uncle Milo to you. Always."

Adele lowered her voice, smiled sweetly at Matt and said, "We'll finish this discussion later."

Matt bowed. "I'm at your command, Your Highness."

Adele took Uncle Milo's arm and went inside with him. Matt stayed on the terrace for a few minutes, his mind fighting a battle with his libido. He'd known what Adele was going to ask him—she wanted him to marry her. But even after the passion they'd shared last night, she still wanted only a marriage of convenience.

A voluptuous redhead in a gold gown that hugged every inch of her ripe figure sauntered toward Matt. Oh, boy! Now there was trouble. If his guess was right, Mrs. Big Silicone Boobs was a rich, middle-aged divorcee on the lookout for her next conquest.

"Hello," she said. "I'm Claudina Gallo. And you are?"

"Matt O'Brien."

"An American?"

Matt nodded.

"I adore American men."

He needed to get inside and find Adele. Even with the extra security Theo had added tonight, both outside and inside the villa, Matt should stay fairly close to Adele throughout the party.

"Would you care to dance, Ms. Gallo."

"I would adore to dance," she replied.

He led the clinging Italian lady inside and luckily found Adele dancing with Uncle Milo. The orchestra completed one piece of music just as Matt took Ms. Gallo into his arms. When he started to release her, she whimpered.

"I adore these moments between the dances," she said.

Matt groaned inwardly. Apparently the senora adored everything. The music began again, and Matt caught a glimpse of Uncle Milo dancing with Dia, and Theo with Adele. He breathed a sigh of relief, then smiled at his dance partner.

Nothing was wrong, Matt told himself. Everything seemed perfectly normal. So why was it that all of a sudden the hairs on the back of his neck were standing at attention? Gut instinct warned him that something was off-kilter. But what? As he led Ms. Gallo around the dance floor, Matt's gaze scanned the room. In his peripheral vision he caught a glimpse of Mr. Khalid in the adjoining dining room. The same uncertainty Matt felt showed on Khalid's face. Matt slowed enough to look directly at Theo's mysterious friend. Khalid urgently shoved his way through a throng of guests and headed straight toward the dance floor. Oh, God! Matt thought. Something's happening. What? What the hell had he missed?

Two tuxedo-clad men pulled semiautomatic handguns from inside their jackets and brandished their weapons. One man held the guests at bay while the other zeroed in on Adele. How the hell had these men gained entry to a private, by-invitation-only party?

Matt released Ms. Gallo so quickly that she almost lost her balance. He barged past the couples standing transfixed on the dance floor while Mr. Khalid, a 9 mm gun in his hand, came around from the other side—both he and Matt with the same destination. One of the intruders reached out for Adele. Theo shoved her aside and blocked the man's path. Matt pulled his SIG Saur P229 from his hidden shoulder holster.

Then, over the thunder of his own heartbeat, he heard the deafening sound of gunfire.

# Chapter 10

From the moment the man's hand touched her, the world began to move in slow motion around Adele. She heard Dia scream. Saw Theo collapse in front of her. Felt herself being jerked forward and then dragged alongside the husky man with a brown beard and keen, menacing brown eyes. Trying to assimilate all the information her brain had absorbed in the past few minutes, she realized that Theo had been shot and that she was being kidnapped. Adrenaline pumped through her body at an alarming rate. Fear ate away at her insides like an insidious acid.

The orchestra stopped playing. People stood rigid as statues. Whimpers, cries and murmurs blended together, creating a frenzied melody to replace the music.

Rapid shots in quick succession. More screams. Loud gasps. In her peripheral vision Adele caught a glimpse of the second intruder as he grasped his chest and dropped to his knees. His hand opened. His weapon hit the floor with a loud clang, then he fell forward, flat on his face. While

Mr. Khalid walked over to inspect his kill, the man gripping Adele's arm so fiercely paused in his hurried escape. The six extra guards Theo had hired for tonight's party swarmed into the villa from their vantage points outside on the grounds. Caught between the guards on one side and Matt and Mr. Khalid on the other, Adele's kidnapper pulled her directly in front of him. Holding his pistol to her head, he backed up against the wall. Sweat moistened her face, coated her palms and trickled down between her breasts. She closed her eyes and said a prayer, pleading with God for her life.

A gunshot echoed inside her head. A wet stickiness splattered across her neck, shoulder and the side of her face. Had she been shot? Was she dying? No, that wasn't possible. She felt very much alive.

Matt had attacked so quickly that Adele didn't realize what had happened until she saw him directly in front of her, grasping her shoulder and jerking her away from the man who slumped into a heap on the floor. That's when she saw the gun in Matt's hand. Adele gasped.

"Are you all right?" Matt asked.

She nodded.

Mr. Khalid entered the foyer and, using his foot, turned the dead man over on his back. Adele knew she shouldn't look, but she did. Her mouth opened on a silent scream. Blood had gushed from a single shot in the center of his forehead and had oozed down the corner of his mouth. Matt had killed this man, taken him out with an expertise that was both amazing and frightening.

Still holding the gun in one hand, Matt wrapped his other arm around Adele's shoulders and hugged her to his side. Then he and Mr. Khalid issued orders to Theo's hired guards. The first order was to telephone the police and send an ambulance immediately.

"Theo was shot trying to protect me," Adele said.

With his free hand—the other still held his gun—Matt whipped out a handkerchief from his pocket and tenderly wiped the specks of blood from her face, neck and shoulder. Adele trembled. He pressed a kiss against her temple, then led her from the foyer and into the room where Dia sat on the dance floor with Theo cradled in her arms. The guards guided the stunned guests from the room.

Mr. Khalid knelt beside Dia. Matt and Adele came over and stood behind him as he flipped open Theo's tuxedo jacket and then ripped apart his bloodstained white shirt. He eased Theo onto his side to expose the exit wound. Tears streamed down Dia's face, but she didn't speak or move; she simply stared at the bloody, gaping wound in her husband's side. No one questioned Mr. Khalid's actions because he seemed to know exactly what he was doing. Was he, among other things, a doctor or a trained medic? Adele's traumatized brain wondered.

"Theo, can you hear me?" Khalid asked.

Theo's eyelids fluttered, but he did not open his eyes. Not at first, but when Dia whispered his name softly, his eyelids opened. Dia bit down on her bottom lip and fresh tears filled her eyes.

"Yes," Theo replied weakly.

"They're both dead," Khalid said. "But everyone else is safe."

"Adele?" Theo asked.

She knelt down beside Mr. Khalid and lifted Theo's hand. "I'm fine. Thanks to you and..." Her voice broke with emotion.

"We've sent for an ambulance," Khalid said. "Just lie here in your wife's arms and wait. It's a nasty wound, but you'll live."

"You promise?" Theo tried to smile.

"You have my word," Khalid replied.

"You must go," Theo said to his friend. "Before the police arrive."

Khalid nodded. "I will leave you in good hands. Your friend, Mr. O'Brien, is quite capable." Khalid stood, shook hands with Matt and said, "I will send word when I have the information you need."

When Mr. Khalid left, Adele had the oddest notion that he had somehow disappeared into the night. Like a ghost. Or like the wind.

Matt lifted her to her feet. "We have no proof, but it's a sure bet that one of those guys was the mercenary the Royalists hired. Undoubtedly Dedrick and his friends are tired of waiting for me to bring you home to Orlantha. I'd say he's more than eager to marry you. He's desperate."

"He wants to become my husband before I can prove to my father that he's a traitor. And he knows it's only a matter of time until I have the proof." Adele stared at the gun Matt still held. "Can't you put that away now?"

Matt obliged her by slipping the SIG Saur P229 into his shoulder holster. "I'm sending two of the guards to the hospital with Theo and leaving the rest here with Phila and Ms. Sheridan."

"Do you think they're in danger?"

Matt shook his head. "No. I believe you were the only target. My guess is their orders were to bring you back to Orlantha immediately and do whatever it took, to kill anyone who got in their way."

"Meaning kill my bodyguard if necessary." The thought of Matt dying to protect her sent shock waves through Adele's system. She shivered.

Matt draped his arm around her shoulders. "You're trembling, honey. Maybe we should have the doctor check you out."

"I'm fine," she told him. "Or at least I will be once I know for sure that Theo is going to be all right."

"I agree with Mr. Khalid. Theo should be okay," Matt assured her. "We'll follow behind the ambulance. Is the nearest hospital in Dareh?"

"Yes, but there's a clinic in Coeus. I believe they'll dispatch an ambulance from Coeus, the nearest town. And the local doctor will probably be with them, since the patient is Theo Constantine."

"Good. The sooner Theo sees a doctor, the better."

"I thought you said—"

Matt hugged her to him. "Theo is going to be okay. Mr. Khalid willed it, didn't he? And my guess is that not even Death would double-cross that guy."

"Why do you suppose he left in such a hurry?" Adele asked. "Do you think he's wanted by the police?"

"Possibly. Interpol. Scotland Yard. The FBI. Khalid is no small-time hood. He's big-time. International."

"How is it that Theo knows this man? Dia said he was an old acquaintance."

"I think we're both better off not asking too many questions about Mr. Khalid. All I want from him is proof you can take to your father about Dedrick's treachery."

"Will you be indebted to him? Will I?"

"To Khalid?" Matt shook his head. "He said he was doing it as a favor to Theo."

"Then I'll owe Theo an enormous debt of gratitude."

Off in the distance the distinct sound of emergency sirens wailed through the night. The local authorities and hopefully the doctor were only minutes from the villa.

Adele leaned heavily on Matt, grateful for his strength and for his care and concern. When he had come into her life, only a few short days ago, she had thought of him as her enemy. Strange how quickly things can change. At this very moment she knew exactly what Matt O'Brien was— he was her hero.

* * *

Daybreak over the Mediterranean surpassed mere beauty. Sublime might be a better adjective to describe the pastel glory of the sun's first light as it banished the darkness. Matt brought the rental Fiat to a quick stop in front of the villa. With armed guards situated at various points on the grounds, the place had the look and feel of an armed camp.

Adele, who had been dozing the last ten minutes of the drive from the Dareh hospital, woke abruptly. She stretched and yawned, then glanced at Matt. "I hated to leave Dia."

"She insisted we come back to the villa, clean up and get some sleep. Besides, Dia expects you to explain to Phila in simple terms what happened last night, and to reassure her that her father is going to be fine and will come home in a day or two."

"I'm sure Ms. Sheridan had a terrible time with Phila last night. Thank God she managed to keep her in her room." Adele reached over and ran the back of her hand along Matt's rough cheek. "Thank you for remembering Phila last night, and sending one of the guards upstairs to tell Ms. Sheridan what happened and to let her know the villa would be guarded."

"Sure thing." Matt felt awkward having so much praise lavished on him. Adele, Dia, Theo—who'd insisted on seeing Matt the moment he awoke after surgery—had all acted as if he were some sort of superhero. He reminded them that he hadn't acted alone.

"Yes, Khalid is a man you can count on," Theo had said. "Just as you are, Matt." Theo had reached for Matt's hand, and when Matt leaned down to grasp Theo's hand, Theo had said, "Contact Doran Sanders and tell him what has happened, if he doesn't already know. His number is programmed into my phone. He can take over Constantine,

Inc. for the time being. And you, Matt—you must take care of things at the villa for a few days." An understanding had passed between the two men. Caring for things at the villa meant looking after Theo's family, too.

"I'll handle things," Matt had assured Theo.

Adele's voice returned Matt to the here and now. "Are you all right?" she asked. "You have the oddest expression on your face."

"Yeah, I'm fine," Matt opened the car door. "Come on, honey. You need a bath and some sleep." He rounded the Fiat's hood, swung open the passenger door and offered Adele his hand.

She placed her hand in his. "Will you stay with me? I mean…will you stay in my room for a while? I really don't think I could bear to be alone."

Matt tugged on her hand and assisted her out of the car, then, without releasing her, headed her toward the villa's entrance. A guard stepped aside to let them pass and another guard inside the house opened the double doors.

"Any problems?" Matt asked.

"No, sir, no problems," the interior guard replied in heavily accented English.

"I'll be in Mr. Constantine's office for a few minutes," Matt said. "After that I'll be upstairs with the princess, if I'm needed for anything."

"Yes, sir."

Matt escorted Adele to the foot of the stairs, then released her hand. "Go on up and take a bath. I'll be up after I make that call to Doran Sanders."

Adele nodded. "Do you suppose you could ask Cook to prepare us some tea? Perhaps a nice, soothing herbal tea?"

Matt grinned. "I'll see what I can do."

Adele smiled weakly, and Matt knew she was putting up a brave front. Protected, spoiled, indulged, pampered.

He had no doubt that that described Adele's former life—her life before Dedrick Vardan and the Royalists had made plans to use her in their ruthless schemes. Before unscrupulous men had become the architects of her future, determined to force her into an unholy marriage, and even sending their henchmen after her, Princess Adele had been living a fairy-tale life. Now she was living a nightmare. And he was right in the middle of her ongoing bad dream.

Matt watched her climb the stairs, noted the weariness in her and longed to lift her into his arms, hold her and comfort her. Every masculine instinct within him wanted to promise her that he'd find a way to give her back her old life. But he couldn't make such a promise. No one could turn back time to those carefree days. But something told him that once he'd seen her through this trial of fire, Adele Reynard would be a better person. And perhaps so would he. After all, it wasn't every day that a guy got the chance not only to save a princess, but to help her save a country.

Adele slipped into a pair of pale coral silk lounging pajamas. She sat on the edge of the bed and towel dried her hair. Several sharp, soft knocks at the door gained her attention.

"Princess?"

"Come in, Matt."

The moment he entered the room, Adele stood to meet him. She tossed the towel into a nearby chair and met Matt in the center of the luxurious Persian carpet. He held a silver tray with both hands.

"Tea for Her Highness," he said.

She smiled. "How thoughtful of you."

"It was thoughtful of Cook," Matt replied. "But she didn't seem to mind. She was already in the kitchen and had made coffee for the guards."

Adele smiled. "Yes, very thoughtful of her."

Matt chuckled. "You're used to servants waiting on you hand and foot. I'm not. And I have to admit that I've always had a certain, er, disdain for people who can't take care of themselves." When Adele opened her mouth to speak, he added, "My aunt Velma slaved all her life for people like that, and I doubt any of them ever thanked her."

"All of us are not useless and ungrateful," Adele told him.

"Yeah, I know." He shrugged. "It's just a hangup from my childhood."

"I understand." She was, as Matt was, a product of her childhood, of her own particular upbringing. While he had been raised as the ward of a household servant, she had been reared as a princess.

Noting Matt's damp hair and the jeans and cotton sweatshirt he wore, Adele realized he'd also showered. "Please, set the tray on the table." She nodded to the Chippendale mahogany and walnut tea table nestled between two white Donghia silk-covered, tufted chairs.

Matt complied to her request. "I brought two cups. Thought I'd join you. Although I admit I'm not much of a tea drinker."

"Strong, black coffee?" she asked.

He grinned. "Got me figured out, haven't you, Princess?"

Adele sat in the chair on the left, poured the tea from a silver pot into the two china cups, then held up one of the cups and saucers to Matt. He sat across from her and accepted the offering.

"Did you get in touch with Mr. Sanders?" Adele sipped her tea, which was delicious, mild, with just a hint of mint.

"Yeah. He'd already heard about what happened here ast night and is holding a press conference in a couple of hours."

"What does he intend to say? Surely he won't accuse the Royalists. We don't have any proof yet and—"

"Calm down, honey." Matt placed his cup and saucer on the tea table. "Sanders is going to say that two unknown gunmen crashed the party, one of them shot Theo, and the incident is under investigation. You won't be mentioned, other than to say that you were one of the guests at the party."

Adele took a deep, calming breath. "I suppose I should telephone my father to let him know I'm all right."

"He'll want to know when you're coming home."

"Yes, I'm sure he will. And he'll probably want to speak to you, too."

"Should I tell him that you were the target, not Theo? That the gunmen's goal was to abduct you?"

Would her father believe Matt? she wondered. Why shouldn't he? Why should it be so difficult for him to believe the truth? After all, what reason would Matt have to lie?

"I'll tell him and you can confirm it." Adele finished off her tea, set down the cup and saucer and rushed over to the bedside table. After lifting the telephone receiver, she dialed her father's private number. Lord Burhardt answered. "This is Princess Adele. I wish to speak to my father. Immediately."

"Princess, how are you? We've been concerned since we heard about the incident at the Constantine villa last night."

"I'm perfectly all right. Now, will you please put my father on the line?"

"Yes, of course, Your Highness."

Matt walked over and stood beside her, his gaze connecting with hers. She offered him a weak smile, then sat on the edge of the bed.

"Adele, my dear daughter," King Leopold said. "How

are you? How is Theo? What the devil happened? Was it the result of some rival business interests trying to kill Theo? A vendetta against his family? What is this world coming to?"

"I'm fine. Theo was shot and is in hospital but will be all right." Adele paused, garnered her courage and continued, "Father, Theo was not the target. The two intruders who crashed the party came there to abduct me."

"What?" King Leopold yelled. "Who would dare—?"

"The Royalists," Adele replied.

"Damn! It's time I rid Orlantha of these lunatics. I need proof that those men were hired by—"

"By Dedrick and his fellow Royalists."

"I refuse to believe that Dedrick is a Royalist. You're using that lie to try to get out of marrying him, to get out of doing your duty."

"My duty is to Orlantha. To protect my people from terrorism, from being taken over by another nation that will set Orlantha back a hundred years."

"Is Mr. O'Brien there with you?" the king asked.

"Yes. Why?"

"I wish to speak to him."

Adele held the telephone out to Matt, who took it and said, "O'Brien here."

Listening to Matt's end of the conversation, Adele soon realized several things: her father believed Matt's assessment, that the intruders had intended to kidnap her; despite Matt's opinion that Dedrick might well be a Royalist, her father refused to believe it; and he expected Matt to bring her to Erembourg immediately.

"Your Majesty, the princess has asked to be allowed to remain in Golnar with Dia Constantine until her husband is released from the hospital," Matt said.

Adele smiled as she rose to her feet and hugged Matt.

Brilliant idea. Absolutely brilliant. Surely her father wouldn't refuse.

"Thank you, sir. And yes, the minute Mr. Constantine is released from the hospital, I will bring the princess home."

When Matt hung up the receiver, Adele danced around the room. "You just bought us some more time."

"A couple of days at most."

Adele yawned. "Excuse me."

Matt clutched her shoulder and marched her to the bed, then pulled back the covers. "You're exhausted. Lie down and get some rest. Sleep, if you can."

Adele didn't protest when he assisted her into bed, then lifted the covers to her shoulders. She reached out and grabbed his hand.

"Don't leave me."

"I won't." He glanced across the room. "I'll sit over there and drink some tea."

She tugged on his hand. "Sit down here for just a few minutes, will you?"

"That might not be such a good idea," Matt told her.

"I trust you. After all, you're my protector, aren't you?"

"I'm your bodyguard," he replied. "I'm trained to protect, and if necessary, in the line of duty, to kill for you or die for you."

She squeezed his hand. "You know what I want...what I need."

Matt sat on the bed, leaned over and kissed her forehead. "It's hard enough as it is for me to keep my hands off you. If I agree to what you want, what do you think will happen?"

Adele reached up and put her arms around his neck, then pulled him down to her. With their lips only inches apart, she whispered, "Marry me and find out."

# Chapter 11

If a man had ever been tempted, Matt O'Brien was. He wasn't sure whether she was kidding around or if she meant what she'd said. But right at the moment it didn't matter, because she was looking at him as if he was everything she'd ever wanted. Common sense tried to warn him, but his male libido overruled caution. He lowered his head and brushed his lips across hers. Tentatively. Giving her a chance to pull away, to change her mind. But her lips softened under his and opened on a passionate sigh. Her compliance erased even the slightest doubt about what he was doing or the knowledge that he would probably regret it later.

While he took her mouth hungrily, she clung to him, her breasts pressing against his chest and her lips parting in welcome. For several intense moments, Matt ceased to think and simply enjoyed the reckless abandon. He lifted one hand; then his splayed fingers worked through her damp hair and cupped the back of her head. His other hand moved down her back and gently nudged her closer and closer. And all the while the kiss continued, growing hotter and wilder with each passing moment.

Matt eased her down onto the bed, following her descent and placing his body over hers. Bracing himself above her, he spread kisses from her forehead to her neck, then nuzzled the exposed cleft between her breasts.

Adele sighed. "Matt…"

He caressed her hips, then slipped his hands beneath her and cupped her buttocks. He brought her lower body up and against his arousal, his mouth covering her breast through the thin barrier of silk. He suckled her greedily. Adele whimpered and writhed beneath him. Every masculine instinct within him urged him on. But when he eased up her pajama top and licked a trail from one tight nipple to the other, Adele lifted her hand and grasped his shoulder.

"Please, Matt, stop."

"What?" Hell, had she just asked him to stop? She had to be kidding. He was hot and hard and about as ready as a man could get.

"I'm sorry. I…I shouldn't have let things go this far."

Matt's mouth sucked on one nipple, then laved it lovingly with his tongue.

Adele moaned. "Oh, please, please stop."

With his body still intimately covering hers, Matt lifted his head and glowered at her. She stared at him, all the longing he felt reflected in her big brown eyes.

"You don't want to stop any more than I do. You want it bad, honey. You want me." He rubbed himself against her, his sex hard against her soft mound.

"I…I want you to marry me," she said.

Matt lifted himself up and off her, then stood by the side of the bed and glared down at her. "Is that what this is all about? You don't want to give away any free milk because you're afraid I won't buy the cow?''

"What?" Adele jerked her pajama top down to cover herself, then sat up in bed and tilted her head. Looking directly at him, she asked, "Is that another Americanism? I don't see what free milk and buying a cow has to do with our situation."

Matt harrumphed. "It means you aren't going to put out unless I marry you."

"What a vulgar thing to say." Adele huffed, but she kept her gaze fixed on Matt. "Sex has nothing to do with our getting married. You know precisely why I want you to marry me."

"Yeah, I know. But you're crazy if you think sex has nothing to do with you and me." Narrowing his gaze, Matt's eyelids half closed as he scanned Adele from head to toe, lingering over her breasts. "Our marriage would be temporary. I understand that. I'd be doing you a favor, wouldn't I?"

"Yes, you would. Does this mean that—"

"It means that a real marriage between two people as different as you and me would be impossible, but a red-hot affair wouldn't be."

Heat suffused her body, warming every inch of her inside and out. She had never had an affair, not even a luke-warm one. It wasn't that she was completely innocent, but her sexual experience was limited to two brief encounters when she'd been at Cambridge. Constantly afraid that she would follow the path of so many European princes and princesses and allow her love life to become fodder for the paparazzi, her father had kept a close watch on her—even when she'd lived out of the country.

"I'm not sure now would be the appropriate time for me to have a red-hot affair," Adele told him. "I can't let my personal feelings get in the way of my duties. I mustn't think of myself or what I might want. Not until I've rid Orlantha of Dedrick and his fellow Royalists.''

"One is not exclusive of the other," Matt said, then shrugged. "But if you can handle a platonic relationship, so can I." He walked across the room and sat in one of the tufted chairs on either side of the tea table. "Lie down and close your eyes, Princess. I'll stick around until you go to sleep."

Was it that easy for him to change modes? To go from passionate, demanding lover to professional bodyguard? Damn! What had she expected—that he'd ravish her, refuse to take no for an answer? Hadn't she been the one who'd called a halt to things and transformed from a passionate woman into a single-minded princess with only one goal?

"Matt?"

"Huh?"

"*Will* you marry me?"

He crossed his arms over his chest and relaxed into the chair so his head rested against the back. Then he closed his eyes. "I'll probably regret it, but...yeah, I'll marry you."

Adele's heart skipped a beat. A temporary marriage in name only, she reminded herself. Matt O'Brien was little more than a stranger to her and totally unsuited to the job of being her prince consort. But he was the perfect choice to be her temporary husband.

"Thank you," she said, her voice a mere whisper. "I'll be in your debt forever."

"Yeah, yeah." Matt opened his eyelids just a fraction and peered at Adele. "Six months after our annulment, you'll barely remember my name."

"That's not true. I'll always—" She stopped herself abruptly. She'd said enough. If she told him that she would always remember him, that years from now when she was wed to a man more suited to being a prince, she would think of him with fondness. With more than fondness.

"Maybe we'll get lucky," Matt said. "Maybe your friend Pippin or Theo's friend Khalid will come up with some evidence against Dedrick before we have to follow through with a phony marriage."

"Yes, maybe…but if not… We should marry as soon as possible."

"Sure. Whenever you say."

Adele sighed, then closed her eyes and allowed herself to relax. She was doing the right thing, wasn't she? Of course she was. With Matt as her temporary husband, she had all the cards stacked in her favor. Someone to guard her twenty-four seven and time to continue the search for evidence against Dedrick. Of course there was one slight problem—the sexual attraction between Matt and her.

Across the room Matt kept watch over Adele. He did his best not to be obvious about it, but he simply couldn't take his eyes off her. And the more he tried to push aside thoughts about her, the more vivid those thoughts became. He could taste her lips, feel her body, hear her soft whimpers. His sex grew hard again. She had played him like a fiddle. Oh, yeah, she'd lured him in with all her sweet charms and then—snap—hooked him so fast he hadn't known what happened until it was too late.

She kept telling him no, over and over again, but the look in her eyes said something else. That look said *maybe*. It said *I want you, even though I know we're all wrong for each other.*

But hadn't she said aloud, *Marry me and see what happens?*

Oh, he had every intention of marrying her, and he already knew what would happen. But he didn't think the princess knew.

* * *

Adele spent most of the day with Phila and Ms. Sheridan. Matt admired the way she'd handled explaining to Phila what had happened to her father. She'd covered the vital details, but had given them to the little girl in terms a seven-year-old could understand, if anyone of any age could ever truly understand violence.

Late in the day, after Dia had telephoned and spoken with Phila and Adele, Ms. Sheridan escorted the child to the kitchen for her evening meal. During her conversation with Dia, Adele had informed her that she and Matt wished to marry as soon as possible, and Dia had promised that she would arrange everything. While staying at the hospital with Theo, she could make telephone calls to expedite matters.

Alone for the first time since early morning, Adele and Matt smiled awkwardly at each other.

"I should call Pippin and tell him our plans," Adele said.

"I can't believe that Dia can put together a wedding, even a quickie wedding, by day after tomorrow."

"Mrs. Theo Constantine can accomplish anything she chooses to, especially in Golnar."

"Yeah, so it would seem. She might not have the title, but in her own way, Dia is queen of Golnar, isn't she?"

"I suppose you could look at it that way."

"How do you think your Pippin will take our big news?" Matt asked.

"He's not my Pippin. He's my friend. Nothing more. And he'll understand my motives and agree that I'm doing the right thing."

Ten minutes later Matt stood in Theo's library cum office and smiled to himself when he heard Adele defending her decision to marry her bodyguard.

"But Pippin...please calm down. Don't raise your voice

to me.'' Adele glanced at Matt, a frown creating lines in her forehead. ''It's a marriage in name only. A temporary affair. No, I don't mean affair. I mean situation. We'll have the marriage annulled as soon as we've dealt with Dedrick and the Royalists and then put the whole affair—the entire situation behind us.''

''Ask him if either Lucie or Dom is there with him,'' Matt said.

''Pippin, Matt, er, Mr. O'Brien wants to know if either of the Dundee agents is there with you.'' Pause. ''Hmm.'' She looked at Matt. ''No, neither of them are there. They're both out following up leads. Did you want them to telephone you?''

Matt shook his head. ''They'll call if they find something important.'' Walking over, he held out his hand. ''Let me speak to Pippin.''

Adele glared at him quizzically.

Matt motioned for her to give him the phone.

''Pippin, Mr. O'Brien would like to speak to you.'' She handed over the receiver.''

''Matt O'Brien here. I just wanted to assure you that Adele…Princess Adele is in good hands. I'm keeping watch over her day and night.''

Adele gasped. Matt grinned. She frowned at him.

''You should know that I do not approve of the princess taking such drastic steps,'' Pippin Ritter said. ''She's taking a terrible risk by marrying you and assuming that King Leopold will not disown her.''

''It's her choice to make,'' Matt replied. ''She's willing to go to any lengths to protect her country from the Royalists. She told me that you love Orlantha as much as she does. Was she wrong?''

''Are you questioning my devotion to Orlantha?''

''Nope. Just wondering.''

''Then wonder no longer, Mr. O'Brien. My only concern in this matter is Princess Adele's welfare. I warn you that if you are anything less than a gentleman with her, I shall…'' Pippin cleared his throat. ''She has placed her trust in you. Do not disappoint her.''

''Believe me, I aim to please.''

''Damn you, man, if you—''

''I promise that I will be everything the princess needs in a husband. She can count on me to fulfill my duties to her.''

''I'm warning you, Mr. O'Brien…''

''Well, thank you, Pippin, I'll convey your congratulations to my bride.'' Matt hung up the phone and turned to Adele, who stood a few feet away, tapping her foot nervously.

''Why do I get the distinct feeling that you were doing a lot of double talk?'' Adele marched over to Matt. ''Pippin didn't actually congratulate us, did he?''

''What do you think?''

She eyed Matt suspiciously.

''The guy's got a thing for you,'' Matt said.

''He does not.''

''Oh, honey, he does. My guess is that your Pippin would love to be in my shoes right about now.''

''That's utter nonsense. There has never been anything the least bit romantic between Pippin and me. We are friends. Dear friends.''

''A dear friend might act protective, but not proprietorial. All his huffing and puffing is because he's afraid I'll get in your pants.''

Adele cringed. ''Must you always be so crude!''

''Excuse me, Your Highness. Let me rephrase. Mr. Ritter's greatest concern is that you and I will consummate our marriage.'' Matt grinned. ''Was that better?''

''Pippin actually said something about us…about you and me… He told you not to—''

"He warned me to be a gentleman at all times. I think he was getting around to telling me that if I didn't, he'd have me castrated."

Adele closed her eyes momentarily and sighed loudly. "Oh, God."

"Did you ever think that Pippin might be lying to you about Dedrick? That Pippin doesn't want you to marry old mule face because he wants you for himself?"

Adele's eyelids sprang open instantly, and her gaze shot daggers at Matt. "Pippin would never lie to me about Dedrick."

She spoke with such certainty, without even a hint of doubt, that Matt believed her. And despite the vice chancellor's macho blustering, Matt's gut instincts told him that Pippin Ritter was as trustworthy as Adele thought he was. But his instincts also told him that the guy was most definitely in love with Adele.

"Okay," Matt said. "I believe you."

"Thank you."

"So, moving on to the next topic—our marriage. Do I need to buy a new suit? Get a haircut? Pick out a ring?"

"Pick out a ring?" Adele asked.

"Yeah, you know—a wedding ring."

"Oh, that. Well, yes, I suppose we will need rings. I'll phone Dia's jeweler in Dareh and have him bring some rings to the villa, and we can choose what we like. Also, an engagement ring would add a romantic touch, don't you think? Something sweet and not too large since you aren't a wealthy man. Perhaps only two or three carats."

"You want a two- or three-carat diamond engagement ring?"

Adele looked directly at him. "Too big? Too small?"

"Too much," Matt said. "I thought this was supposed to be a temporary marriage. Why go to all the trouble of choosing an engagement ring? And as for the wedding rings, just tell the jeweler our sizes and tell him to send a couple of plain gold bands.''

Adele tensed instantly. She sucked in her cheeks and glared at Matt. ''Temporary marriage or not, I am a princess. It will be expected for me to have an engagement ring. If you were as madly in love with me as we want people to believe, you would be willing to spend every penny you have to buy me a proper ring.''

''Yeah, honey, the operative word there is *if.*''

''If the cost is bothering you, don't concern yourself. I shall pay for the rings.''

''With what? I thought you were short on cash.''

''I'll simply ask Dia to extend my loan.''

''Sure, why not? What's a few more thousand to a woman married to a billionaire?''

''You really do have a thing about wealthy people, don't you?''

Damn! Why hadn't he just kept his mouth shut? ''Yeah, I told you I did.''

''Don't you think it's time you moved past those childhood insecurities and prejudices?''

''I'll make you a deal, honey. I'll think about giving rich, powerful, snobbish people the benefit of the doubt, if you'll come down off your high horse for a while and start acting like a woman instead of a princess.''

Adele stared at him, her expression one of surprise...even shock. As if he had slapped her. Hell, what had he said? Why was she acting so odd?

''I believe my actions this morning proved to you that I can be a woman. A woman with needs and desires.'' When Matt came toward her, she held up a restraining hand. ''But my duties as a princess must, at this time in my life, come first. I do not have the luxury of...of not acting like a princess.''

Holy Moses! He'd made of mess of it now. Why

couldn't he get it through his thick skull that Adele was, first and foremost, the heir to the throne of Orlantha? She might be a gorgeous, desirable woman, who had him tied in knots and made him so horny he was half out of his mind, but she was no ordinary lady. She was a princess. A real, live, honest-to-God princess. And a guy like him didn't have a prayer with a woman like her.

"I apologize," Matt said. "I guess I'd like to forget who you really are and what's at stake here."

Tears misted her eyes. "Yes…I understand. Sometimes I wish that I could forget who I am and what my obligations are."

Theo Constantine arrived home by ambulance to much fanfare. A horde of international reporters had been hounding the villa for more than twelve hours—ever since Doran Sanders's press conference alerted the world that Theo had been shot by unknown assailants in his own home, during a private party. And the fact that Princess Adele had been present only added fuel to the news people's fiery determination to get a story. The first reporters had shown up late yesterday afternoon. Local people from the Dareh newspaper and television station. By dawn this morning the villa had been surrounded. Matt had put the guards on alert and had notified the local authorities, who had sent several policemen to oversee the vast horde.

The ambulance came to a slow, even stop in front of the villa, and the attendants hopped out and hurriedly opened the back doors. After assisting Dia, they rolled Theo out and carried him inside on the stretcher. The minute they were behind closed doors, Theo ordered them to help him to his feet.

"Theo, please, darling." Dia fluttered around him. "You promised Dr. Arvanitidhis that you would go straight to bed and—"

"I told the doctor what he wanted to hear." Once they had him on his feet, Theo waved away the attendants. "I refuse to be treated like an invalid." Theo held out his hand to Matt, who moved forward and put his arm around Theo's waist to support him. "See me to my office." He turned to Dia. "I'm sure you and Adele have a great deal to discuss about the wedding tomorrow."

"But Theo—"

"Go, woman!" Theo reached out and caressed his wife's cheek. "I promise to lie down on the chaise in the library and do little more than issue orders to Matt."

"You promise?" Dia asked for his reassurance.

Theo smiled. "Of course. I promise."

Once safely ensconced in his library, with the door closed and the two men alone, Theo kept his promise and allowed Matt to lead him to the chaise. He stretched out, then glanced around the room.

"It is strange, is it not, that a man takes his life for granted," Theo said. "I have always been a lucky man. Born under a lucky star. I have great wealth. Power. The respect of my peers. And look at my wife...my daughter. Could any man ask for more?"

"You've sure got it all," Matt agreed.

Theo looked Matt square in the eyes. "My arrogance has made me foolhardy. I truly believed I and my family were safe here on Golnar, that despite my great wealth, I was immune to danger here on this island that my family has ruled for several generations."

"I see you've been doing some thinking while you were in the hospital."

"I will not take my safety or the safety of my family for granted. Not ever again." Theo shook his head sadly. "I did not want Phila to grow up surrounded by guards, but..." Theo sighed. "These local men that I hired are adequate, but they lack the sharp skills of true professionals. It was you and Ni—Khalid, who acted quickly the night I was shot. I need the men who protect my family to be better trained than these locals.''

''So hire guys from Athens or Rome or—''

''You misunderstand,'' Theo said. ''I want my own people around me. Men from Golnar. Men that I trust implicitly. But I want them properly trained. Would the Dundee Agency send several agents here to train my men?''

''Why not send them to the U.S. for training?'' Matt suggested. ''Send two at a time to Atlanta for a six-week period, and that would leave four here with you and your family.'' Matt sat on the edge of Theo's massive desk. ''Unless you know of some reason any of you are in immediate danger—''

''No, no.'' Theo shook his head. ''I know of no reason. But I have learned—the hard way, as you Americans say—that often someone else's danger can affect me and mine.''

''Adele would never have come here if she'd thought she was putting anyone's life at risk.''

Theo grinned. ''Not even the pretense any longer, huh, my friend?''

''What?''

''Adele. Not Princess. Not Her Highness.''

Matt shrugged. ''Sometimes it just slips out. I forget.''

''But of course you should refer to her as Adele. After all, tomorrow she will become your wife.''

''In name only.''

''Ah, is that what you and she are telling yourselves?''

''It's what we've agreed to and—''

''I fell in love with Dia the first moment I saw her at the palace in Erembourg. I knew immediately that I must have her.'' Theo laughed. ''Of course, it was weeks later that I understood sex would not be enough to satisfy me. I was hopelessly besotted with the lady, and she knew within a few days that I was hers forever.''

"It's not like that with Adele...with the princess and me."

Theo lifted his eyebrows skeptically.

"Yeah, okay, we're attracted to each other," Matt admitted. "But that's as far as it goes. Besides, can you see me actually being her prince consort? I'm a white-trash redneck from Kentucky whose father and grandfather and great-grandfather were all coal miners."

"My great-grandfather was a fisherman," Theo said. "Matt, Matt, my new friend, my good friend, if I were King Leopold, I would much prefer to see my daughter bring some fresh, vital blood into the family than to see her marry some insipid, inbred aristocrat." Theo patted his chest with his clenched fist. "I would say to myself, 'Think what fine, strong grandsons this American stud will father.' I would welcome you as my daughter's husband."

"God, Theo, you could sell air conditioners to Eskimos."

"I could do what?" A puzzled look crossed Theo's face.

"Never mind," Matt said. "It was a compliment. But you're forgetting a couple of things."

"What would that be?"

"Number one—you aren't King Leopold. And number two—Adele and I are not in love."

"Yes, I see your point," Theo said. "But you are getting married tomorrow. And tomorrow evening there will be a wedding night. Who is to say how you and she will feel after...once you are husband and wife?"

# Chapter 12

Adele looked at the ring on her finger. A square-cut ruby surrounded by small diamonds and set in platinum. When Matt had knocked on her door shortly before bedtime last night, she had thought he was simply checking on her before going to bed in his room adjacent to hers. With one hand braced against the door frame, he'd leaned toward her and held out his open palm, showing her the ring.

"It seems your friend Dia was one step ahead of us," Matt had said. "She knew you loved rubies and thought a ruby-and-diamond engagement ring would be something you'd like. After dinner tonight, when she asked to speak to me alone, she gave me this."

It seemed that Dia had thought of everything to make this day as perfect as any real wedding might have been, if it had been put together on the spur-of-the-moment. When Adele had mentioned this fact at dinner last evening, Theo laughed and told Adele the wedding had been a godsend for Dia and him.

"Planning your wedding gave my wife something to distract her and keep her from smothering me with too much attention while I was in the hospital," Theo had told them before he turned and gazed lovingly at Dia. "As much as I like your attention, my love, I prefer to receive it when I am able to fully appreciate it."

Everyone had understood Theo's meaning, but no one commented, not even Dia, who'd simply blushed like an innocent.

Today, as Adele inspected the chapel on the Constantine estate, she could hardly believe her eyes. Small, able to hold no more than twenty or thirty people at most, the interior of the Mediterranean-style chapel was decorated with cream-colored roses and satin ribbons. The dark wooden pews were laced with delicate cream satin ribbons that ended in large bows at the end of each pew. A white cloth floor runner led her eye up the center aisle. Afternoon sunshine shimmered through the two stained-glass windows, filling the room with rainbows of light.

Why had Dia gone to so much trouble for a marriage destined to be annulled within months, perhaps even within weeks? When this was all over, Adele didn't want to have beautiful memories haunting her. Couldn't Dia understand why she'd requested a simple wedding ceremony without any fanfare, with only a judge and not a minister or priest to officiate? The less this seemed like a real wedding, the easier it would be to forget.

Dia came up behind Adele and placed her arm around Adele's shoulders. "What do you think? Do you like it? I bought out every florist on Golnar to get enough cream roses."

"It's lovely." She turned to her friend, wrapped her arms around her and hugged her fiercely.

Dia pulled free, grasped Adele's shoulders and looked directly at her. "You're crying. Oh, please, don't cry. I'm sorry if I was a bit too extravagant. I know you said simple, but I couldn't allow you to get married without flowers...without—'' Dia snapped her fingers, and a servant girl came forward with a bouquet of cream roses in her hand. "This is your bridal bouquet. It's quite small. Nothing elaborate.''

Adele accepted the bouquet from the servant girl, who bowed and ran away quickly. "Please tell me that you didn't hire a photographer or put together a reception.''

Dia had the decency to bow her head.

"Oh, you didn't.''

Dia lifted her eyes first, smiled meekly, then lifted her head and said, "Trust me, Adele, despite what you think right now, you *will* want to remember this day.''

"A photographer?''

Dia nodded. "People won't believe the wedding is real if you don't have pictures.''

"A reception, too?''

"Only a small one. Very intimate. Just us. I did not invite outsiders.''

"Thank God for that, at least.''

"Come back to the house,'' Dia said. "You must change into your wedding outfit. Madame Vasilis finished the alternations only moments ago. It will fit you to perfection.''

"Thank you, Dia. For everything.''

"You deserve a royal wedding with all the trimmings,'' Dia told her. "King Leopold should walk you down the aisle at the Erembourg Cathedral, with the organ playing and the choir singing and—''

"I shall have that type of wedding someday. When I marry the man destined to be my mate for life,'' Adele said, and even she detected the sad note in her voice.

"Are you so very sure that Matt O'Brien is not that man?''

"You know he isn't. Matt and I come from two different worlds. Even if we were in love—which we are not—there is no way a marriage between us would work."

"Why, because you don't think Matt is good enough for you?"

"What a terrible thing to say."

"Is it true?"

"It might have been when I first met him," Adele admitted. "But not now. Oh, I know I'm a terrible snob, but… It really doesn't matter. The truth is that Matt would be miserable trying to fit into my world. Can you see him at court? He would be bored to death."

"It would seem you've given the matter a great deal of thought."

"Perhaps I have, but you shouldn't read anything into that admission. I am not in love with Matt O'Brien."

"If you say so." Dia smiled.

Two hours later Adele and Matt stood before Judge Caspar and exchanged their vows. The judge spoke English with a thick accent and kept grinning at them as he performed the ceremony. Matt wore a new black suit, a white shirt and a striped gray tie. Theo had ordered the new suit for Matt, and the tailor had come along for last-minute alterations when he'd delivered it early this morning. Shortly before they left the villa to walk the quarter mile to the chapel, Dia had pinned a boutonniere on his lapel, kissed his cheek and thanked him for marrying her dear friend. Dia had kept pace with the rapid speed of Theo's wheelchair, and Phila had sat in her father's lap for the ride, while Ms. Sheridan followed several steps behind the family.

Although Theo wasn't able to make it through the ceremony standing, he served as Matt's best man seated at his side. Dia was Adele's matron of honor and had preceded her down the aisle, right before Phila, who'd served as flower girl. The adorable child, decked out in a frilly pink dress, had strewn rose petals on the bride's path from doorway to altar. A middle-aged female harpist had played "Here Comes the Bride." It might be a make-believe marriage, Matt thought, but this wedding was all too real.

Matt stared at Adele throughout the ceremony, memorizing her every feature, from the depth and clarity of her chocolate-brown eyes to the full lusciousness of her bow-shaped pink lips. He had wondered what she would wear, had even secretly hoped she would chose a traditional wedding gown. But she hadn't, and for the life of him he didn't know why he was disappointed. She looked gorgeous in a pink silk suit. No, not exactly pink. Sort of a reddish, purply pink. What had Dia called it? Fuchsia? What the hell sort of name was that for a color?

Matt's gaze drifted upward, taking in the small diamond tiara his bride wore. A perfect match to her other diamond jewelry. Thank God this wasn't a real marriage. There was no way on earth he could afford to keep this woman in the style to which she was accustomed. He couldn't see her living in his Atlanta apartment, buying groceries at the supermarket and selecting her clothes in a department store.

When it came time to exchange rings, Dia and Theo produced matching platinum bands, and within minutes those symbols of everlasting love were on the third fingers of Matt's and Adele's left hands. He continued holding her hand as the judge pronounced them husband and wife. Well, it was legal now. Princess Adele was officially Mrs. Matthew O'Brien. Heaven help them both.

Matt could feel the slight trembling in Adele's hand. She was as unsure as he—and probably just as scared. She was looking at him, her eyes misted with tears, her lips slightly parted. Kiss her, you idiot, he told himself. Finish this thing the right way. But if he kissed her, could he make it a brief, meaningless gesture? That's what she would expect, wasn't it?

Matt pulled Adele tenderly into his arms; she went willingly. Then he lowered his head and brushed his lips against hers. She sucked in a deep breath.

What the hell, he thought. She wouldn't kill him in front of witnesses, would she? Matt took her mouth passionately, and when he finally let her come up for air, Adele was breathless for a couple of seconds and slightly unsteady on her feet.

The judge chuckled and said, "I present to you Mr. and Mrs. Matthew O'Brien."

Smiling gleefully, Dia hugged first Adele and then Matt. Phila jumped up and down in childish delight. After shaking Matt's hand, Theo slapped him on the back. And the photographer snapped picture after picture. The happy couple kept their phony smiles in place long enough to suit Dia, who gave the photographer orders to take plenty of pictures at the reception.

The others went ahead of them, leaving the newlyweds alone.

"We should return to the villa," Adele said. "Dia has arranged a small reception."

"She's a good person," Matt said, "your friend, Dia. I like her."

Adele exited the chapel at Matt's side. "She likes you, too."

An odd expression crossed Adele's face. She quickened her pace. He rushed to keep up with her along the rock pathway, then continued quietly at her side for several minutes. When they neared the villa, Matt reached out, squeezed Adele's hand and halted for a moment.

"Are you all right?" he asked.

"Yes, I'm fine. Really."

"Not the wedding day you dreamed of, huh? And certainly no Prince Charming for a groom."

"Don't…" She pulled away from him and hurried along the walkway in front of him.

"Adele!" He caught up with her before she reached the villa, grabbed her hand and whirled her around to face him. Tears trickled down her cheeks. He wiped away the tears with his fingertips. "Don't cry, honey. It'll be all right. I promise. I'll make sure everything comes out just the way you want it."

"Oh, Matt." She cried even harder then.

Women! He'd never understand any of them, least of all his blushing bride. Correction. Make that his weeping bride.

He didn't know what to do, so he did what he wanted to do. He put his arms around her and kissed her. She whimpered a few times, then flung her arms around his neck and put everything she had into returning his kiss. And she just about knocked his socks off.

A long, loud whistle broke them apart. Matt lifted his head and glanced over Adele's shoulder. Waiting outside the villa's entrance, Dia and Theo, still sitting in his wheelchair, were watching the newlyweds.

"Save that for tonight," Theo called.

Dia laughed. "Come on. You have to cut the wedding cake so the photographer can take more pictures before he leaves."

The reception had been as lovely as the wedding, with more food than a hundred people could have eaten. Champagne flowed, a small string quartet filled the house with music, and the photographer took roll after roll of pictures. Adele wasn't sure how she made it through those unbearably bittersweet hours. But she did. Perhaps her determination to save Orlantha had given her strength. Or perhaps it was knowing that Matt would be with her through the days ahead, that she could count on him in every way.

An hour after the reception officially ended and every-one had changed out of their dressy attire and into causal clothes, Matt and Adele entered Theo's office. They were moving on to the next phase of their plan.

Their marriage was a ruse to buy time for Pippin, the Dundee agents and Mr. Khalid to find proof against Dedrick. For their plan to work, King Leopold would have to threaten to disown Adele, which she felt certain he would. Of course, Dedrick might or might not believe the king would eventually name him his successor and it was Dedrick's reaction that Matt had said was pretty much a luck of the draw. Even though Adele felt certain Dedrick would cease to think of her as a threat, Matt wasn't as certain. But she pointed out the obvious to him.

"I'm already in danger from Dedrick, so what differ-ence will it make? I say we call my father now so that word will get to Dedrick immediately. I realize we have no guarantee how Dedrick will react, but I'm telling you—I know this man. He'll see my marriage to you as a god-send and—"

"Why don't we wait until our return to Golnar before telling your father that we're married?" Matt asked.

"Because there's a good chance that my father's certain reaction of disowning me will actually keep me safe from Dedrick. It's worth taking a chance, isn't it?"

"I don't know. Somehow my gut instincts sense danger either way. I just don't like taking a chance when your life is at stake."

"I know my father and I know Dedrick. Please, Matt, let's do this my way."

"Dedrick could decide that since you're married to me and of no use to him, he should eliminate you before you have a chance to return to Golnar and change your father's mind.''

Suddenly Theo Constantine swept into his office, his dark eyes filled with rage. ''I have very bad news.'' He marched across his office and turned on the television. ''It seems word of your marriage somehow leaked out and it's being broadcast on the evening news in Dareh.''

Adele's heart skipped a beat. ''Oh, God! What if Father hears about my marriage before—''

''I will find out who is responsible for this,'' Theo said. ''How dare anyone here on Golnar betray my confidence!''

Dia came rushing into her husband's office. ''Adele, you should telephone your father before someone else does. Oh, my, what an unfortunate turn of events.''

The foursome listened as a local news anchor in Dareh finished his announcement about the princess marrying an American commoner at the home of Theo Constantine this very afternoon.

''I have to call Father immediately.'' Adele looked to Matt for agreement.

''Damn!'' Matt scowled at the television. ''Yeah, go ahead and call him. We don't have much choice now.''

Matt came to Adele's side. Theo and Dia sat together on the leather sofa. Adele held her breath as she dialed her father's private number. Just this once she wished Lord Burhardt wouldn't answer. No such luck.

''This is the princess,'' she said. ''May I speak with my father.''

''How are you, Your Highness?''

''I'm fine, thank you.''

''Will you be returning home to Orlantha soon?''

''Yes, as a matter of fact, I'm setting sail on Theo Constantine's yacht tomorrow and should be home day after tomorrow.''

"How wonderful. Your father will be greatly pleased, as will the duke."

"Please, tell my father that I wish to speak to him."

"Certainly, Your Highness."

Adele's gaze locked with Matt's. He squeezed her shoulder. She offered him a fragile smile.

"Adele, my dear girl, Lord Burhardt tells me that you're coming home," King Leopold said. "I must say I'm delighted."

"I...I hope you'll be just as delighted when I tell you my wonderful news." Adele took a deep breath. Matt's grip on her shoulder tightened.

"What news?"

"Father, you might want to sit down to hear this."

"You're worrying me, Adele. But you said the news was wonderful, didn't you?"

"It is wonderful." *Please, God, help me convince him that I'm madly in love with Matt.* "I...well, you see...I've fallen in love."

"You've done what?"

"I've fallen in love with Matt O'Brien, the Dundee agent you sent to find me and bring me home. He's the most incredible, wonderful, marvelous man I've ever met. Father, it was love at first sight for both of us."

"Nonsense. You hardly know the fellow," King Leopold huffed. "Besides, the man's an American."

"That American is my husband. Did you hear me, Father? Matt and I were married today, here in Golnar."

"What!" the king shouted. "Have you lost your mind? You cannot marry someone else. You are betrothed to Dedrick."

"I'm sorry, but I don't love Dedrick. I don't even like him. And I do love Matt. He makes me very happy."

"I'll have that damn man drawn and quartered. I'll make you a widow before you—my God, Adele, don't you dare give yourself to him. Do you hear me? Dedrick will expect a virgin bride. You come home immediately and we'll have this marriage annulled.''

Adele giggled. *Dedrick would expect a virgin bride? The whoremonger of Erembourg?* ''I shall do no such thing. I love Matt madly and I plan to remain Mrs. Matthew O'Brien for the rest of my life.''

King Leopold sputtered and fumed and cursed loudly, then he said what Adele had expected him to say. ''If you are determined to defy me by staying married to that man, then I will have no choice but to denounce your marriage and to disinherit you. Tell him that. Tell your *husband* that you will not inherit the throne of Orlantha or one penny of my money. See if he wants to stay married to you then.''

Adele held her hand over the mouthpiece and whispered to Matt. ''He's threatening to disinherit me. No throne. No money.''

Matt took the telephone from her. ''King Leopold. Matt O'Brien, here. I want you to know that I love your daughter and I couldn't care less about her being a princess. And I don't want a dime of your money.'' Matt handed the phone back to Adele.

For a split second she escaped into a fantasy world where her marriage to Matt was real and he meant every word he'd said to her father, that they were in love, married and planning on staying married for the next fifty or so years. But reality intruded all too soon. Her father growled ferociously.

''Did you hear him, Father? No annulment. Not now. Not ever.''

''Then you leave me with little choice,'' King Leopold said. ''I warn you.''

''I love you, Father. Matt and I will see you in a few days. After our honeymoon.'' She hung up the phone quickly, not wanting to listen to her father rant and rave anymore.

She turned and laid her forehead on Matt's shoulder. He caressed the back of her neck, then patted her head in a comforting gesture. She lifted her head and smiled at him.

"Well, it's done," she said. "And Father reacted just as I'd thought he would."

"How long do you think he'll stay that angry?" Matt asked. "Once he's cooled off and forgiven you—forgiven us—we'll have lost our advantage."

"It should take him a few days after I return to the palace, a week at most, before he forgives me. Despite all his outrage and hysterics, my Father loves me, and he would never disown me."

"Let's hope we have a week," Matt said. "We need all the time we can get."

"I am sure that Khalid will come through for us," Theo said. "If he cannot get the information you need about a rebel group in Orlantha, then no one can."

Dia jumped up, clapped her hands together and said, "Enough of this! There will be time to deal with national crises once you are back in Erembourg, but for this evening why not put your concerns aside and celebrate your wedding day."

The others stared at Dia in puzzlement.

"My dear, surely you haven't forgotten that this wedding today was a farce," Theo said. "How can Matt and Adele celebrate something that has no meaning for them?"

Adele's breath caught in her throat. If only that were true. If only this day's events were meaningless to her. "Theo's right." Adele smiled at her best friend, her matron of honor. "Dia, I know you're a romantic and you did everything within your power to make today special, but nothing has changed for Matt and me. He's still only my bodyguard."

Dia frowned. "Yes, of course. Even so, we can still celebrate. We can toast to the success of your plan and celebrate how very cleverly you're fooling your father and Dedrick and all those nasty royalists."

Theo chuckled. "Humor her." Theo pulled Dia close and kissed her cheek. "My wife is determined to celebrate something. So, let us adjourn to the parlor and open another bottle of champagne."

Adele forced a smile. "One more drink, and then I think I'll say good evening. I'm rather tired after our big day."

"Yeah, me, too," Matt said. "I never realized how nerve-racking getting married could be."

Everyone laughed, even Adele, although she felt more like crying.


"Can you believe our good fortune?" Dedrick lifted his glass in a toast and clicked glasses with his comrade. "The foolish girl up and married some American oaf, the damn agent King Leopold sent to fetch her home. Can't help finding humor in the irony of it, can you?"

"The king is angrier than I've ever seen him. He is threatening to disown the princess, and I am doing all I can to fuel his wrath. We don't want him having any second thoughts about publicly denouncing her."

"I have every confidence in you," Dedrick said. "Keep whispering in his ear every chance you get. Whisper my name often. Once he has disinherited Adele, the people of Orlantha will expect him to name a successor." Dedrick tapped his chest. "And who else would he choose other than me, his dear cousin's only son?"

"If Adele returns to the palace, she will try her best to convince her father to accept her marriage to this American commoner. We can't allow that to happen."

Dedrick cocked one eyebrow. "Yes, I see your point. When it was possible to force her to marry me, we needed her. But now that she is married to someone else, she is expendable.''

''Exactly.''

''Then I see no reason not to dispose of her and her new husband. And, naturally, in his grief over the loss of his little princess, the king will turn to me, who will be at his side, mourning right along with him.''

''The king says that Adele is returning to Orlantha by yacht, which will no doubt dock somewhere in Italy. Once they cross the border into Orlantha, we will have a very unpleasant surprise waiting for the princess and her bridegroom.''

Dedrick poured more champagne and made another toast. ''To the future king of Orlantha and Balanchine.''

''To you, Your Majesty.''

Dedrick tossed back his head and laughed hardily, then downed the glass of champagne in one long swig.

## Chapter 13

Matt supposed there were worse ways to spend a wedding night, but right offhand, he couldn't think of any. Logic told him that since the marriage wasn't real, then neither was the wedding night. But try using logic on a guy's libido. With or without a legal piece of paper that said Adele was his lawfully wedded wife, he wanted her more than he'd ever wanted anything. And that was saying a lot, because a poor kid from Kentucky had wanted a great deal in his thirty-six years on earth.

Pacing the floor in his bedroom, which was connected to Adele's by a small sitting area, Matt kept enumerating all the reasons he'd be glad when this assignment was over. Once his marriage to the princess was annulled, he wasn't making any stops—not even Paris—on his way back to the good old U.S.A. He'd had enough of foreign countries, of exotic Mediterranean islands and of billionaires, royalty and one brown-eyed princess in particular.

What was Adele doing next door? he wondered. Had

she already slipped into her gown and gone to bed? Was she sleeping soundly or was she as restless as he? Was she thinking about him the way he was thinking about her?

His cell phone's unique ring jerked him from his fanciful thoughts and brought him back to the moment. He picked up the phone from where he'd tossed it onto the bedside table, then when he looked at the digital readout, he groaned. Ellen Denby! God, help him. He should have forewarned her about his marriage plans, explained the situation to her and— The phone kept ringing.

Matt punched the talk button and said, ''Yeah, O'Brien here. And if you'll give me a minute, I can—''

''You can what?'' Ellen's normally deep, sultry voice was hard and cold. ''You can explain why you've lost your freaking mind?''

''I take it that King Leopold has been in touch with you.''

''Oh, most definitely. His Majesty is not a happy client. And you know what that means, don't you? If the client isn't happy, then I'm—''

''Then you're not happy, and if you aren't happy, then I'm a dead man. Right?''

''Close enough.''

With the cell phone plastered to his ear, Matt began pacing again. ''There's a logical explanation for—''

''Did you marry Princess Adele today in Golnar?'' Ellen asked.

Matt hesitated for a couple of seconds, then confessed, ''Yeah, we got married.''

''Would you mind telling me why? You told me there was nothing personal between the two of you. When did that change?''

''It didn't. Not exactly. This isn't a real marriage.'' Matt opened the French doors leading to the balcony. ''No, that's not quite right. The marriage is legal, it's just not...

We did it to buy more time for Pippin Ritter, the Dundee agents and Theo's friend Khalid to try to dig up some evidence against the duke.'' Matt walked outside and breathed in the night air, scented with a combination of the sea, autumn flowers and rich earth.

''Who is Khalid?''

''What?'' Of all the things he'd expected Ellen to ask, that hadn't been one of them.

''Theo's friend, Khalid. Who is he?''

''I don't know really. Some guy who's got ties to the underbelly of society. He's supposed to have connections to just about every rebel and terrorist organization in the world.''

''And his name is Khalid? First or last name?''

''Don't know. He's one mysterious dude. But kind of handy to have around when you're fighting off kidnappers,'' Matt said. ''What's with all the questions about Khalid? When I reported in after the shootings, I told you that a friend of Theo's took out one of the kidnappers and—''

''You're right. It's not important. I got sidetracked,'' Ellen said. ''Back to your marriage. You do realize that your actions reflect badly on the Dundee Agency, don't you?''

''We're trained to protect and ready to lay our lives on the line for a client. Right?''

''Right. But you're forgetting one thing—King Leopold is our client.''

''Look, Ellen, I need you to trust me on this one. Take my word for it—in the end what we're doing will benefit the king.''

''Officially you're fired,'' Ellen told him sternly, then in a softer voice said, ''Unofficially—good luck, Matt.''

''Thanks, boss lady.''

Matt ended the connection and dropped the phone into

his pants pocket. Just as he turned to go back inside the villa, he caught a glimpse of movement on the balcony directly in front of Adele's bedroom. He stopped dead still, took a step forward and peered into the semidarkness. His pistol was in his room. Should he make a move without it? Surely Theo's guards hadn't let someone get past them, had they?

"Who's there?" he called. "Come on out where I can see you."

From out of the shadows, her body silhouetted in the moonlight, Adele walked toward him. "It's only me. I...I couldn't sleep, so I—"

"Yeah, I couldn't sleep, either."

"You were talking to your employer, weren't you? Is she very angry with you for marrying me?"

Matt grinned. "Angry? Yeah, she was at first, but she's cooled off now. I think firing me made her feel better."

"She fired you? Oh, Matt, I'm so sorry, but I thought— Didn't you explain why we married, what we're trying to do?"

"I explained," Matt said. "And if this all turns out the way we hope it will, then I'm pretty sure I can get my job back."

Adele moved closer and closer. Matt was of two minds about what to do. One, he should take her in his arms and make mad, passionate love to her. Two, he should say good-night immediately and lock himself in his room until morning.

"I've been very selfish, haven't I?" Adele came up to him, only inches separating their bodies. "I didn't give a thought as to how marrying me might affect your life, your career. Matt, I'm so sorry. Please, forgive me." She lifted her hand to his face and caressed his cheek.

Holy Moses! Didn't she have any idea what looking at her in that lacy black peignoir set was doing to him? And listening to that soft, honeyed voice with just a hint of an accent? Did she have to touch him, too? Hell-fire, a man could resist only so much temptation.

"Look, Princess..." Matt began backing away from her. "This might not be such a good idea. You and me, alone in the moonlight. You wearing that—" he raked his gaze over her body from breasts to thighs "—that sexy getup."

She glanced down at herself. "I chose this from the four peignoir sets that Dia ordered for me because I thought it the least sexy, the least like something a bride would wear on her wedding night."

Matt groaned, then swallowed hard. "If that one's... What the hell do the other three look like?" He held up his hand. "No, don't tell me."

"This isn't my ideal wedding night, either," she said. "But it's preferable to any wedding night I would have had with Dedrick."

The very thought of the duke kissing Adele, touching her, making love to her turned Matt's stomach. In all honesty he didn't like the idea of any other man coming anywhere near his wife. "Just making sure old mule face never gets the chance to touch you is worth losing my job," Matt said quite honestly.

"Oh." Adele rushed to Matt, threw her arms around him and hugged him fiercely. "I'll never forget..." Tears misted her eyes. "You must know that I will always...always think of you as my hero. My wonderful, wonderful American protector."

When he gazed into her teary brown eyes, Matt realized he'd reached the limit of self-control. With her arms still holding him around the neck, he spanned her tiny waist, lifted her off her feet and brought their mouths together. She closed her eyes and parted her lips. Two seconds into the kiss and Matt knew he was a goner.

Still kissing her, his body took charge and dictated his

actions. Without a moment's hesitation, he swept her up into his arms, carried her into the villa and straight to his bed. In his eagerness, he practically ripped the lacy robe from her shoulders to expose the sheer gown beneath. Adele's hands worked frantically, unbuttoning Matt's shirt and spreading it apart before she flattened her palms against his chest and gently stroked. With all five senses he absorbed her. And she seemed as totally obsessed with discovering him through sight and touch, hearing, smell and taste. Their mouths mated, then broke apart, and moist lips traveled over throats, down necks, onto shoulders. Time stopped and the world faded away. Only the two of them and this night apart from reality existed. Nothing stood between them—not the past, not the future.

Aching with an unbearable need, Matt forced himself to slow down, to make certain that Adele was with him completely, without any reservations or doubts. She lay beneath him as he braced himself on his knees and lifted his head to stare into her eyes.

"Are you sure about this?" he asked gruffly. "You're not going to hate both of us in the morning, are you?"

A fragile smiled trembled on her lips as she gazed up at him. "Our making love won't change anything," she told him. "It can't. We have to accept the fact that whatever we have together...tonight, tomorrow...for however long it lasts, is as temporary as our marriage."

Maybe she was right—maybe making love wouldn't change a damn thing between them. Hadn't he had sex with other women and walked away without a backward glance? Why should it be any different with her?

"A brief affair," Matt said. "I scratch your itch, you scratch mine."

Adele shook her head disapprovingly, but her smile widened. "Always so crude." She caressed his face. "My big, rugged American lover."

"I think you like the fact that I'm different from all the other men you've known your whole life," Matt said.

Adele rose up enough so that her mouth was able to touch his chest. When she flicked each of his nipples in turn with the tip of her tongue, he groaned deep in his throat.

"I like that you're more man than gentleman," she told him. "For once in my life I'd like to be more woman than princess. Will you do that for me, Matt? Help me to be nothing more than a woman making love to a man?"

"I'll sure as hell try."

Adele gave herself over completely to the moment, to her passion for this man, who, although he was her husband, was still a stranger in so many ways. Would she have regrets tomorrow? No. No regrets, she promised herself. The only thing she would regret is if she did not explore this sizzling chemistry between Matt and her. It was unlike anything she had ever experienced. He was as alien to her as if he'd come from another planet, and yet she felt as if he were a part of her. An integral, life-sustaining part.

Matt removed his shoes, socks and slacks, then went to work removing her gown. She lifted up to accommodate him so that he was able to slide the lacy garment down over her body, over her hips and off. When he hovered above her, she reached up and yanked on his briefs. Together they removed the last barrier of clothing between their bodies. She knew he was eager to take her, that being a man he probably didn't need or want any preliminaries, so she braced herself. One glance at his sex and she shivered with a mixture of uncertainty and anticipation. He was big and hard and ready. She closed her eyes and sighed as he came down over her.

Quite unexpectedly he buried his face against her shoulder, pulled her into his arms and eased into a side-by-side position in the bed. He nuzzled her neck as one big hand skimmed her from shoulder to hip and then traveled up the front of her body from belly to breasts. While he spread tiny kisses up her neck and over her ear, he caressed one breast and then the other, taking his time to pinch and release each nipple several times. Pure sensation shot through her, from breasts to feminine core, spreading pleasure and longing to every cell. Of their own volition, her hands began their own exploration, examining his broad shoulders and hairy chest, loving the feel of him.

He didn't seem the least bit interested in rushing; rather he appeared to be totally absorbed in learning every inch of her body. How indescribably delicious. How incredibly wonderful.

When he kissed and licked a path between her breasts, Adele whimpered, longing for him to suckle her. But he moved ever downward, across her stomach, over her navel and into intimate regions no man had ever fully explored. Ever so gently he spread her legs and nuzzled the thatch of dark hair covering her mound. Adele shivered as the implication of what he was going to do became apparent to her. Before she could consent or protest, his tongue went into action, licking in a long, slow, deep motion that brought Adele's hips up off the bed. Matt put his hand beneath her and lifted her up and against his mouth for easier access.

She moaned and writhed beneath him while he pleasured her almost to the point of madness. As she coiled tighter and tighter, release only moments away, Adele forked her fingers through Matt's hair and held his head in place, encouraging him to delve deeper and harder and faster. His movements obliged her, and with one final stroke of his talented tongue, he pushed her over the edge, into the deep abyss of fulfillment.

While she cried out as wave after wave bombarded her, Matt rose up and over her, then took her mouth in a heated, tongue-thrusting kiss. As the aftershocks rocked through her, she tasted herself on his lips and it excited her anew. When he positioned himself between her legs and sought entrance, she welcomed him, wanting him, needing him.

"More," she whispered. "I want it all. All of you."

With one powerful lunge, he entered her, thrusting himself deeply into her wet, hot depths. Stunned by how completely he filled her, Adele groaned. Matt kissed her again as he waited, allowing her body time to accommodate his size. And then he moved, slowly at first, setting an even rhythm that her body picked up instantly. When he bent his head to reach one breast, Adele's nipples peaked almost painfully. But the moment he sucked, she cried out from the intensity of the feeling that rocketed through her.

She tensed, frightened by her own response, uncertain that she could bear any more. "Matt…?"

"Don't fight it, honey. Just let it happen. Remember, it's happening to me, too." Matt increased the tempo, lunging and withdrawing faster, building the urgency within both of them.

Trusting Matt with her whole heart, she accepted the earth-shattering sensations that tore her apart into a million fragments of pleasure. And only seconds afterward Matt came undone in her arms, his big, powerful body trembling with his release. As they shared this ultimate satisfaction, Adele realized something that she had refused to even consider. She had fallen in love with Matt O'Brien.

Adele awoke the next morning alone in Matt's bed, the sun shining through the open French doors and the sound of a child's laughter coming from outside the villa. Glancing around the room, she saw no sign of Matt, but when her gaze traveled to the French doors, she caught a glimpse of his back. The minute she pushed aside the covers she remembered she was naked. She eased out of bed carefully, dragging the top sheet with her. Her gown and robe lay on the floor where Matt had tossed them last night, so she gathered them up and hurriedly slipped into them.

Tiptoeing barefoot, she made her way across the room and crept up on Matt. She circled her arms around him from behind and hugged herself up against his back.

"Good morning, husband." How was it possible that being near him, touching him, felt so good, so right?

Matt glanced over his shoulder and grinned. Adele loved his cocky, boyish grin. Loved his sky-blue eyes, his thick, unruly black hair. She even loved the dark shadow of his beard stubble. Oh, God, she loved everything about this man.

"Good morning, yourself," Matt said. "Although if you'd slept another hour, it would be good afternoon."

"Is it that late?" She hugged him tightly. "I'm afraid I was exhausted. Someone kept me awake all night."

Matt reached out, grabbed her and pulled her around in front of him so they faced each other. "Yeah, I had that same problem. Some wild woman kept begging me to make love to her...over and over and over—"

Adele jabbed him playfully in the stomach, and he groaned as if she'd actually inflicted pain. "As I recall, some man woke me at dawn and ravished me."

Matt kissed her, then pulled back and looked directly into her eyes. "The yacht is ready and waiting. It's docked in Dareh. Theo said we can postpone returning to Orlantha for as long as we'd like. The yacht is at our disposal."

"He knows? Theo knows that you and I...that we—"

"Dia stormed your room this morning," Matt said, "wanting details of your wedding night, and she found your bed empty. She put two and two together and... She told Theo, and they thought we might want a real honeymoon.''

''Oh.'' Reality had intruded all too soon. She should have known it would, but some foolish part of her had hoped she could postpone the inevitable.

''I told Theo that honeymoon plans were the bride's prerogative in our case.''

''Thank you. I...''

Matt pulled her to him and hugged her with a gentle possessiveness that wrapped itself around her heart. ''Thank *you,* Adele,'' he whispered softly against her cheek. ''Thank you for last night.''

''That should be my line, shouldn't it?'' Lifting her head off his chest, she peeked up at him. ''I think it was rather obvious that I was the one who'd never done some of the things we did, and I was the one who didn't realize sex could be like that.''

''Yeah, I know. And that's one of the reasons I'm thanking you. For letting me be the man to show you...to teach you...to take you places you'd never been.''

Adele knew she was close to succumbing to her desires, to throwing caution to the wind and saying to hell with duty. Matt was far too tempting. It would be much too easy to sail off into the sunset on a fantasy honeymoon with him. But she could not allow herself the luxury. She was Princess Adele of Orlantha. Her country was in danger. It was her duty to save her people from the threat of a Royalist takeover.

Forcing herself to take control of her emotions, Adele eased out of Matt's arms. ''I'm not sure how I'll face Dia. She's such a romantic. She won't understand that last night was only sex.''

For a split second she thought she saw a glimmer of anger in Matt's eyes, but it had been only a glimmer. And she'd probably imagined it.

He grinned. "Yeah, but you and I know better, don't we, Princess? Nothing romantic about two people not being able to get enough of each other. Just good old-fashioned sex. It's not as if we're in love."

*But I am in love with you,* she wanted to shout. *I'm so in love with you that my heart is breaking, knowing we have no future together.*

"I'll tell Theo that we want to go straight to San Marino," Matt said. "I think a twenty-four-hour honeymoon aboard the *Goddess* will be enough to convince everyone that our marriage is real. Besides, I'm sure that satisfied look on your face will be enough to assure your father and everyone else that we're lovers."

When he turned to leave her, Adele grabbed Matt's arm. "Are you upset with me? Is there something I've said or done that—"

He jerked loose and grinned at her. "Sorry, was I being crude again? I forgot that you don't like me to be crude...except when I'm making love to you. You didn't seem to mind my being crude and vulgar last night. As a matter of fact, you seemed to like it a lot."

Rage flashed through her. She drew back her hand, but caught herself just before she slapped his face. "Why is it that we antagonize each other this way? We can't seem to get along, except..." Adele groaned. "The only place you and I seem to be compatible is in bed." Oh, no, had she actually said that? Had those words really come out of her mouth?

Matt laughed. "Yeah. Ain't life a bitch."

He left her standing on the balcony, her face warm with embarrassment and her heart aching.

# Chapter 14

Captain Ferrex, a tall, stalwart Brit with graying red hair and puppy-dog brown eyes, gave the newlyweds a tour of the *Goddess,* seemingly taking a great deal of pleasure in the fact that the Princess of Orlantha was honeymooning on his yacht. And because Matt was Adele's bridegroom, the captain showed him the greatest respect.

"The *Goddess* is a 150 foot Palmer Johnson. She is one of the finest yachts of this size ever built," the captain explained. "She is a lady of perfection, and Mr. Constantine makes sure she remains flawless."

Adele feigned interest, while Matt actually enjoyed the tour. Sailing around the Mediterranean might be everyday stuff to Her Highness, but it was something new for Matt, so he listened attentively as the captain gave them the grand tour. From the large crew quarters to the commercial-quality galley, from the four guest staterooms below to the two open-air dining decks, the *Goddess* was impressive. Add to that a huge skylounge and a large main salon with a complete entertainment system, and the *Goddess* was truly a home away from home for a billionaire like Theo.

Adele had been accustomed to luxury like this her entire life. She took for granted all the things money could buy, the things that Matt had dreamed of having when he'd been a dirt-poor kid in Louisville. Lordy, Lordy, what would Aunt Velma think of all this? he wondered.

"Being rich ain't all it's cracked up to be," he could hear his aunt saying. "Money can't buy happiness. It's what's in a person's heart that counts. Love and pride and honor are what's important. And helping your fellow man whenever you get the chance. Best you don't forget what I'm telling you, boy."

Yeah, he guessed Aunt Velma wouldn't be impressed with the *Goddess,* the Constantine villa on Golnar and the high-and-mighty Princess Adele. And don't forget the grand palace in Erembourg, he reminded himself. That place was something straight out of a fairy-tale book.

And guess who had grown up in that palace, surrounded by servants at her beck and call, with more money than most folks could spend in a lifetime—hell, in two lifetimes? What had ever made him think he could be more than a servant to Adele, a means to an end? She needed him to help her save her country. After that he was expendable. But, of course, she didn't mind fooling around with him, picking up some practical tips on lovemaking that she could use sometime in the future with a man worthy of being her real husband.

Matt figured his bad mood that evening during dinner was the direct result of him thinking far too much about what had happened between Adele and him last night. After a man had spent endless hours making love to a woman, it was kind of difficult to turn off his lascivious thoughts. One good taste of Adele had only whetted his appetite for more. But he'd be damned if he'd beg to be taken into her bed. No, the way he looked at it was if she wanted him, she'd have to do the begging. So when he walked his bride to the opulent owner's stateroom, he paused outside the open door. Adele glanced over her shoulder.

"Is something wrong?" she asked.

"Nope. Just waiting to see you safely to your room."

"My room? But this is our stateroom," Adele told him. "Your luggage was brought here along with mine."

Matt nodded, then followed her inside and scanned the room. Ignoring Adele he marched to the closets, opened them one by one until he found his black vinyl bag. He hoisted the bag over his shoulder and walked out of the stateroom.

"Matt?" Adele ran after him.

He paused. "Yeah?"

"Where are you going?"

"Below deck to one of the guest staterooms."

"Why?"

"I'd like to get a good night's sleep," Matt told her. "We'll arrive in San Marino tomorrow and then fly straight to Orlantha. I figure I'll need all my strength to face your father, and you will, too. So unless you *need* a repeat performance of last night's events, I suggest we sleep apart."

Adele's facial muscles tightened. She tilted her cute little nose in that haughty manner he'd once hated but now found endearing. "Then I'll see you in the morning." She hovered in the doorway.

"See you," he said, then added, "if you decide you can't make it through the night without me, you know where you can find me."

She gasped. Whistling, he walked away, leaving Her Highness to think about what he'd said.

* * *

Matt showered, dried off and went to bed with his hair slightly damp. He'd left his door unlocked. Just in case. Maybe Adele would figure out that she really couldn't make it through the night without him. He sure as hell knew he'd have a difficult time going to sleep when he had the hard-on from hell.

For over two hours Matt tossed and turned, got out of bed twice, tried every trick he knew to shut off his thoughts and get some rest. Nothing worked. If he hadn't been such a proud, stubborn fool, he could be above in the owner's stateroom right now, in bed with his bride. But oh, no, not Matt O'Brien. Adele had wounded his masculine pride this morning when she'd made light of their night together, so he had to prove a point. But he was the one paying the price for his decision. Adele was probably sleeping like a baby.

What was that noise? he wondered. Had someone tapped softly on his door, or was his imagination playing tricks on him? No, there it was again, that series of quiet little knocks. With the flip of a switch, Matt turned on the wall lamp at the right side of the bed.

"Matt?" Adele whispered.

"Yeah," he replied. "You've got the right room."

She eased open the door and peeped inside. Matt sat up in bed, letting the cover fall to his waist.

"I…I couldn't sleep," Adele said.

"So you thought you'd look me up so we could do what—talk? Play cards? Have a drink together?"

She walked into the stateroom and closed the door behind her. "You weren't asleep, were you?"

"I was until you woke me," he lied.

"I'm sorry, I thought that you…that we—"

"What's the matter, Princess, haven't you got the guts to tell me what you really want?" Matt chuckled. "I figured you'd be back for some more good loving. After all, when a lady's had a taste of Matt O'Brien's particular brand of rough, crude lovemaking, she's bound to want more."

Adele rushed across the room, flung off her robe to reveal she wore nothing underneath, then threw her arms around Matt as she tumbled into bed with him. "Oh, shut up, you crude American beast, and make love to me."

"Yes, ma'am!" Matt kicked the covers to the foot of the bed, then rolled Adele beneath him.

She kept her hold around his neck as she lifted her hips and rubbed her mound against his hard sex. "This is what you wanted, isn't it?" she asked. "You wanted me to come to you, to beg you to make love to me."

Matt kissed her, then lifted his head, stared into her big brown eyes and cupped her buttocks. When he lifted her to him and spread her thighs, her mouth opened on an expectant sigh.

"I didn't hear any begging," Matt said. "I believe you gave me an order." He thrust into her, imbedding himself to the hilt in her receptive body. He loved the sound of her breathy gasps. "You told me to shut up and make love to you, and that's just what I'm going to do."

Adele undulated up and down, sliding over him, arousing them both by her actions. "Less talk," she told him. "More foreplay."

Matt laughed. God help him, he was crazy about this woman. She represented everything he disliked and disapproved of. She was the last woman on earth he would have chosen to have an affair with, but now that he'd been with her, made love to her, seen her at her best and her worst, he wanted her desperately. If he wasn't very careful, Adele Reynard could easily become as essential to him as the air he breathed.

Matt gave his bride what she wanted. More foreplay. He didn't leave an inch of her body untouched, loving her more thoroughly than he'd ever loved another woman. And together they reached new heights, their bodies mating in perfect unison, their hearts and minds entwined.

They spent the night making love, the way couples do on their honeymoons. And though their honeymoon was far from real, Matt could no longer see the difference.

Midafternoon the following day, they arrived at the airport in San Marino, Italy, to find that a bomb threat had closed the airport temporarily, possibly for the rest of the day. Matt and Adele agreed they should rent a car and head for Orlantha as soon as possible. Matt drove the Mercedes; Adele read the map.

"I'm afraid I'm unaccustomed to having to find my way," she told him. "I always have other people to take care of those matters. I have drivers and guides, and at home there are always the private guards. Oh, Matt, I apologize if I'm causing a problem with my inability to read a map correctly."

"You're doing okay, honey," Matt said. "Besides, I think I've got a pretty good idea which route we need to take once we cross over the border into Orlantha."

"But one wrong turn and we'll be headed toward Berdina instead of Erembourg." Adele flung the map onto the floor and huffed loudly. "I'm totally useless outside my element."

"You could learn," Matt told her.

"Yes, I could, couldn't I?" She smiled at him. "I'm very bright, you know, and I learn quickly."

"Yeah, I'm sure you do, but you'll probably never need to learn how to take care of yourself. Once we eliminate your problems back home, you'll become queen and your life will move right along as planned."

"Yes, of course, you're right." She picked up the map, folded it neatly and placed it in her lap.

Some wild part of Matt's nature had the crazy urge to turn the car around, to take Adele to the nearest airport in Italy and book flights to the U.S. He'd take her back to Atlanta with him, show her what it was like to live the way real people did. In Atlanta he might have a chance to keep her in his life. Matt knew that back in Orlantha, once Dedrick and the Royalists were eliminated as a threat, he would lose Adele. She would become a queen, with no room in her life for an American bodyguard.

They crossed the border into Orlantha shortly before sunset and took the road around the mountains that would led directly into Erembourg. The mountain highway led them higher and higher around dangerous curves, often with deep ravines on either side. Traffic was light, allowing Matt to make good time, although he drove with care because he was unfamiliar with the road and because he was carrying precious cargo.

The headlights from a fast-approaching vehicle behind them hit the rearview mirror and momentarily blinded Matt. He cursed under his breath as he grabbed the mirror and readjusted it to lessen the reflected glare.

"I hate it when somebody does that," Matt said, as much to himself as to Adele.

"Does what?" she asked.

"Rides my bumper. If I made a sudden stop the car behind us would wind up in our trunk."

Suddenly the dark sedan shot out into the oncoming lane and pulled up beside Matt and Adele. Before Matt realized what was going on, the car slammed into the side of their rental vehicle, shoving them off the road.

Adele screamed.

"Hang on, honey!"

Matt struggled to maintain control of the Mercedes. The minute he managed to put their car back on the road—and say a quick prayer of thanks that they hadn't gone over the side of the mountain—Matt increased the car's speed and zoomed past their attacker.

''What happened?'' Adele asked. ''What's going on?''

''I think somebody sent a welcoming committee to meet us,'' Matt said.

''But why? I don't understand. If Dedrick believes my father will disown me and choose him to be his successor, then why come after us? And how did they know we'd be traveling by— They must have had someone watching us, keeping tabs on us since we left Golnar!''

The dark sedan caught up with them and rammed into the Mercedes's back end, jolting Matt and Adele. She screeched. Matt cursed and pressed the gas pedal flat on the floorboard, which zoomed their car out of reach. Matt took each curve at over a hundred miles an hour, and with each turn he prayed. The car behind them picked up speed, quickly closing in on them.

Up ahead lay a sharp curve, with deep drop-offs on either side. When the sedan caught up with them, Matt maneuvered the Mercedes back and forth from one lane to the other, all the while hoping he wouldn't meet any oncoming traffic. And then he saw the headlights coming straight at them.

Adele let out an earsplitting scream.

# Chapter 15

Matt swerved the Mercedes back into the right-hand lane just as the approaching vehicle reached them. But the driver of the dark sedan directly behind them didn't have that option. So when he swerved, his car skidded in the loose gravel on the shoulder. Apparently, he lost control. Matt watched in his rearview mirror as the dark sedan dove headfirst off the road, through the fenced barrier and into the deep ravine. A loud explosion rocked the mountainside and flames shot up from the ravine into the black evening sky.

Turned halfway around in her seat, Adele gasped, then cried out as she realized what had happened to their pursuers. "Shouldn't we stop?" she asked.

"No," Matt replied. "There's nothing we can do for them. And the people in the car we almost hit will notify the authorities. You don't want to wait around for the police to find out that Princess Adele was involved, do you?"

She shook her head. "No."

Matt slowed the Mercedes, and they drove in silence for several miles. Adele felt the overwhelming need for comfort, but she said nothing. Inside her head she was still screaming, still scared, still afraid they were going to die. She wanted to ask Matt again why the Royalists would have sent someone to kill them. Why would they need to kill her if they believed she would never ascend to the throne? Surely her father hadn't already forgiven her? No, that couldn't be the reason. It would take days, perhaps weeks for his rage to subside enough for him to forgive her.

Matt broke the silence. "Are you all right?"

"I'm not sure," she admitted.

"Still pretty shook up, I guess." He stole a quick glance at her, then reached out and grabbed her hand. "I'm not going to let anything bad happen to you, honey. I promise you that I'll—"

"We could have died."

Matt squeezed her hand. "But we didn't. We're both okay. I was concerned something like this might happen," Matt said. "As long as there was a possibility that you'd marry Dedrick, they preferred to keep you alive. But now they don't really need you."

"But why kill me, if they believe my father will disown me and choose Dedrick as—" Oh, my God! That was it! "Dedrick and anyone else close to my father would be concerned that if I return to the palace, I might be able to persuade my father to forgive me, perhaps even recognize my marriage to you.

"We have to get through to the palace and persuade my father to allow us to stay there. We'll be safe in the palace. No one would dare—"

"You won't be safe anywhere, not even the palace. I suspect that someone your father trusts isn't trustworthy, someone other than Dedrick. Lord Burhardt or Colonel Rickard or even Pippin Ritter.''

"Not Pippin."

"No, probably not. But we can't rule out anyone else. Not until we know for sure."

"And my father? Is he safe? They wouldn't kill him, would they?''

Matt remained silent for several minutes, then said, "The sooner we get the proof we need, the better for everyone involved."

King Leopold paced the floor in the grand hall outside his private office suite on the second floor of the palace. "The very nerve of the girl, bringing that man here. I told her that I would denounce her, denounce this marriage."

Queen Muriel watched her husband from the sidelines, wringing her hands and shaking her head. "Leo, please, calm yourself. See Adele. Speak to her. You must find a way to solve this problem. She is your only child."

The king stopped abruptly and glared at his wife. When he saw tears in her eyes, he went to her and pulled her into his arms. "Yes, yes, you're right, my dear. I will see Adele."

Muriel lifted her head and smiled at the king. "And her husband, too?''

Leopold growled his displeasure. "Yes, yes, and her husband, too. But only to tell them that I will never recognize their marriage. Believe me, I have every intention of lambasting that dishonest American gigolo. He passed himself off as a detective, as a bodyguard!''

"Don't upset yourself this way." Muriel patted Leopold's arm. "I really don't believe Mr. O'Brien is a gigolo. It's very possible that he truly loves Adele."

King Leopold harrumphed. "Tell Colonel Rickard that

I shall give my daughter and her husband an audience. And I wish Lord Burhardt to be present."

"And Dedrick?"

"Yes, Dedrick, also. Let's get this done. Today. I shall denounce Adele and arrange to make a public broadcast."

Muriel stroked her husband's chest. "Do not rush into making a public announcement. There are many things to consider. You should give yourself some time to weigh all your options."

"Are you saying that I shouldn't tell Dedrick that I am considering naming him my successor?"

"I'm sure the Duke of Roswald is quite aware that he's the most likely choice to succeed you if Adele is deemed unworthy to take her place as queen of Orlantha."

"She has proven herself unfit by defying my wishes, by marrying a man totally unsuited to be her consort."

"I shall inform Colonel Richard and Lord Burhardt of your wishes."

"Might as well send for Chancellor Dutetre and Vice Chancellor Ritter. We'll have the lot of them present. I should have the opinion of the council before I make a public broadcast."

"Yes, my darling, that's very wise of you."

Lisa Mercer ran into the entrance hall on the first floor where Adele and Matt waited for an audience with the king. She rushed straight to Adele, who opened her arms to her secretary and dear friend.

"Your Highness. I've been so worried." Lisa hugged Adele, then pulled away and bowed. "Is it true? Are you married to Mr. O'Brien? The palace is abuzz with the news."

Adele hated lying to dear Lisa, but she couldn't be honest with anyone, except Pippin, about her marriage to Matt.

"Yes, we're really married. Matt and I fell in love at first sight and—"

"There you are, you shameless creature you!" Dedrick Vardan, Duke of Roswald, entered the antechamber, Lord Burhardt and Colonel Richard on his heels. "If you had no regard for my feelings, surely you should have considered what betraying me would do to your poor father."

"Oh, put a sock in it, Dedrick," Adele said.

Matt chuckled. Lisa gasped, her eyes wide as saucers.

"Your Highness, it is good to see you home in Erembourg." Lord Burhardt bowed politely, then slanted his disapproving gaze toward Matt. "Naturally, His Majesty is upset about your sudden marriage. Colonel Rickard and I agree that annulment proceedings should be started immediately. It is the only sensible thing to do…the only way to assure your succession to the throne."

"An annulment is out of the question," Adele said.

"Is that so?" Chancellor Dutetre entered the anteroom, his presence quite commanding despite his short, squat stature. He rubbed his fingertips over his thick, gray mustache. "Then, Your Highness, you must know that your actions will put the government in a state of panic. If the king refuses to recognize your marriage, if he were to disown you—"

"We must do all within our power to prevent such a disaster." Pippin Ritter joined the growing crowd assembled in the grand entrance hall. He wore a gray sport coat, black trousers, a gray tie, white shirt and a sweater vest. The tip of his pipe peeked out from the top of his coat pocket, and a lock of his curly, brown hair rested in the center of his forehead. Adele smiled at her dear and trusted friend, but instead of returning her smile, he cast a warning glare at Matt.

"I suggest we all go into the throne room," Colonel

Rickard said. "King Leopold has summoned us and is no doubt awaiting our arrival."

Within five minutes the entire assembly stood before the king of Orlantha. Holding Matt's hand tightly, Adele led him straight past the others and up to the foot of the king's throne. She bowed. Matt bowed, although it was against his nature to kowtow to anybody.

"Father, I'd like to introduce my husband, Matthew O'Brien, of the United States of America."

Grunting, the king took inventory, checking Matt from head to toe. "Mr. O'Brien and I have already met."

"So you have. But he wasn't my husband then."

King Leopold narrowed his dark gaze and frowned at Matt. "What have you to say for yourself? I hired you to bring my daughter home so that she could marry her betrothed. What made you think that you had any right to—"

"Don't speak to him in such a manner." Adele climbed the steps and walked onto the raised dais where the king sat on his throne. "Father, I know I've disappointed you, but I am here to beg your forgiveness and plead with you to welcome my husband."

The king growled. "I will not forgive you. Did you think you could walk in here and wrap me around your little finger as you have done all your life? Not this time, Adele. You have gone too far. Tested my patience to the limit. I will not recognize this marriage of yours to a commoner. An American commoner."

"Please, Father, tell me what I must do to change your mind? I cannot bear that you are so angry with me."

"If you mean that, then you will allow Chancellor Dutetre to arrange a discreet annulment, and we will make a formal announcement that there was absolutely no truth to the rumors that you had married your bodyguard."

"No, Father. I can't—I won't dissolve my marriage to Matt."

The king surged to his feet, his face red, his jaw tense. "Then I shall denounce you and your marriage in a public broadcast." King Leopold cast his gaze on Dedrick. "And when I make my announcement, I shall name a new successor to the throne of Orlantha."

Although her father had reacted the way she had known he would, indeed the way she had hoped he would, hearing the king declare such a harsh penalty unnerved Adele. It wounded her deeply. But in her heart she knew that her father would never follow through with his threat. She just hoped that Dedrick and the Royalists believed that he would.

Queen Muriel instructed the household servants to prepare the princess's suite for her arrival. She issued orders for the palace staff to afford the princess's husband every courtesy. Since the fact that her father had all but disowned her was nothing more than unsubstantiated rumors to the servants, their demeanor toward Adele was the way it had always been. She remained their princess. Her orders were followed without question.

Adele hugged her stepmother. "Thank you for being so understanding."

Muriel caressed Adele's cheek. "We must allow your father to expel his rage, then in a few days we will talk to him again. You and I. And until then I will see to it that he doesn't make a public broadcast."

Pippin Ritter bowed to the queen. "You are most kind, Your Majesty. The council is very grateful to you for interceding on the princess's behalf."

"I understand," Queen Muriel replied. "We share a common goal. We both want to see Adele take her rightful place as queen of Orlantha."

The queen smiled at Adele and then at Matt before she left the princess's private quarters. The moment the door closed behind Queen Muriel, Pippin turned to Adele.

"The Dundee agents that Mr. O'Brien sent to us have compiled a list of suspected Royalists. If this list is correct, their number is small. But we have discovered that there are several influential people with connections to the Royalists. Unfortunately, we have not been able to identify them." Pippin looked at Matt. "Is there no word from your other source, this friend of Mr. Constantine's."

"No word yet," Matt said.

Pippin nodded. "Mr. Shea and Ms. Evans were able to gain the confidence of several Royalists. They were told that the ultimate goal is for Dedrick Vardan, as a distant cousin of both King Leopold and King Eduard of Balanchine, to become king of the two countries and reunite them under the sole rule of a monarch."

"This is what we've suspected all along," Adele said.

"Suspicion is all we have against Dedrick." Pippin slammed his fist into the palm of his other hand. "Why is it that we can't seem to find any proof against him? Time is running out." Pippin gazed longingly at Adele. "Look at what lengths you have gone to in order to buy us time. You've sacrificed yourself for the good of Orlantha. If only I had been with you…"

"But you weren't," Adele said. "And even if you had been, who would have believed that a marriage between the two of us was a love match? My father would have seen through the ruse immediately."

Pippin nodded. "Yes, of course, Your Highness. You're quite right."

"You should return to the council and reassure them that the queen will do all she can to control my father. I'm sure the entire council is trembling in fear, uncertain about the king's intentions."

Pippin kissed Adele's hand, then bowed and backed out of the room. Adele walked over to Matt and went straight into his open arms. She laid her head on his chest and hugged him. He held her tenderly in his embrace.

"Poor Pippin," she said.

"You were awfully blunt with him."

"I know, but I thought it best. I truly had no idea that he had personal feelings for me, beyond friendship."

Matt kissed the top of her head. "My naive little wife, don't you know that every man who comes within a mile of you wants to get into your pants?"

"Matt! You simply must stop speaking in such a manner. It isn't proper for the crown princess's husband to—"

Matt silenced her with a kiss.

"A public broadcast," Dedrick said. "You heard him say it. He's going to publicly denounce Adele and name me his successor."

"Do not celebrate a victory quite yet."

"But, my dear friend, what could possibly go wrong? Adele is adamant about not giving up her American lover...her husband." Dedrick chuckled. "And King Leopold is wise enough to know the man is totally unsuitable to become the prince consort. My God, he could never allow a child fathered by that man to ascend to the throne of Orlantha."

"Do not rule out the king's great affection for his daughter. He has doted on her since the day she was born."

"Then it will be your duty to see to it that Adele doesn't speak with her father again. At least not without our being present. We cannot allow her to have the opportunity to change his mind."

"I will do what I can to keep them apart, but Queen

Muriel is quite determined to do all she can to help the princess.''

"I believe it is too late for anyone to help Adele." Dedrick rubbed his hands together gleefully. "The stupid girl could have been my bride, and we could have ruled Orlantha and Balanchine together. Now she will spend her life in drudgery as the wife an American commoner."

"Unless an accident befalls her. Our men failed to kill the princess and her husband when they were en route from San Marino to Erembourg, but will not fail again. I will personally see to it!''

Dedrick snapped his head around and stared at his comrade. "Is there any need to dispose of the princess now, to soil our hands with such a nasty mess?''

"Perhaps not. Unless the king changes his mind.''

"Then for Adele's sake, let us hope he does not.''

# Chapter 16

Adele lay in Matt's arms in the large, ornate, four-poster bed sitting on a raised dais in her bedroom. Although Queen Muriel had assigned trusted palace guards to stand watch outside the entrance to the princess's suite, Matt kept his pistol in plain sight on a bedside table. He wasn't willing to take any chances, not where Adele's life was concerned. Their marriage might be only a temporary arrangement, but Matt was already thinking of her as his wife. He'd never felt as possessive and protective about a woman, not even when he'd been a green kid in love for the first time. Matt's eyelids flew open.

In love? No way. He was not in love with Adele. He had a severe case of lust, just as she did. Hadn't she said so back in Golnar? What they shared was just sex. The best damn sex he'd ever had. And she made no bones about it—it was the best she'd ever had, too. So why pretend it was something more? *Because, you blockhead, it is more and you know.* It felt like more every time he looked at her, every time he touched her. Okay, so maybe it was more than lust, but it wasn't love. Hell, it couldn't be love. Fate wouldn't have played a trick that cruel on him, to make him fall for a woman who could never be his.

Adele moaned in her sleep and cuddled closer. Matt rubbed his hand up and down her arm. Her skin was like smooth, flawless silk. She threw her arm over his chest and twined a strand of his chest hair around her index finger. His sex hardened instantly. They had made love before they'd gone to sleep, but he wanted her again. Now. Matt slipped the covers down to reveal her naked breasts. High, round and full, they tempted him beyond reason. He lowered his head and kissed the cleft between her breasts. She mumbled his name. Her eyelids flickered. He took one pebble-hard nipple into his mouth and suckled. Adele whimpered.

"Hmm. Are you trying to wake me?" she asked.

"I'm trying to do more than that," he told her, then laved her nipple with his tongue.

She opened her eyes and cupped his head with the palm of her hand. "So you are." She stretched like a cat curling about its master's leg. "And doing a wonderful job of it."

"Honey, you ain't seen nothing yet." He snapped back the covers, sending them to the foot of the bed, then lifted Adele and set her astride him. "You seem to enjoy being on top. Are you ready for another hard, fast ride?"

Adele lifted herself up just enough so that he could slip inside her. She lowered herself over him, taking him completely. They both sighed with pleasure as their bodies joined.

"How is it that we can want each other—need each other—again so soon?" Adele moved up and down, fitting herself to him, aligning her sensitive area where it would receive the most friction.

"Your guess is as good as mine." He caressed her hips, stroking from the side, across each buttock and then down to the top edge of her thighs. "We just can't seem to get enough of each other."

"This can't possibly last. Sooner or later it will burn itself out, won't it?"

"I don't know, honey. It's never been quite like this before. I haven't been this horny since I was a teenager."

"There you go again, using crude language, and I've told you over and over again that—"

"That you love it when I talk dirty to you." Matt bucked up, ramming into her to the hilt while he held her hips in place so she would keep all of him inside her.

Adele gasped. "Oh, Matt!"

He laughed, then growled when she set a steady pace. Later, when she rode him in a frenzy while he suckled her breasts, he groaned against her naked flesh. And when they came to that final moment together, exploding simultaneously, he roared like a mighty beast.

While the aftershocks rippled through them, Adele collapsed on top of him. Matt reached down and pulled the covers up over them. They fell asleep that way, with Adele lying on Matt, their bodies still joined.

Matt came awake with a start. What the hell had awakened him? Before he could figure it out, he realized Adele was lying on top of him, fast asleep. He kissed her forehead.

Something was ringing. The telephone? No, it was his cellular phone. He eased Adele off him and onto the bed, then slipped out of bed and walked over to the chair where he'd tossed his jacket last night. He pulled the phone from the pocket and put it to his ear.

"O'Brien here."

"Matt, it's Theo. I apologize for waking you at such an ungodly hour, but I have news from Khalid."

That bit of information jarred Matt into a fully awake state. "What? What's the news?"

"He has what you need," Theo said. "Proof that Dedrick Vardan is a member of the Royalists. And a bonus, also."

"What's the bonus?"

"It seems that someone the king trusts implicitly might also be a Royalist, one of the ringleaders within Orlantha."

"Who?"

"Khalid does not know. He needs a bit more time to discover this person's identity and to document the facts. But in the meantime, he is prepared to send the evidence against Dedrick by private courier, but he needs to know to whom his courier should deliver the package."

Adele rose from the bed, slipped on her robe and walked over to Matt. "Who are you talking to?"

"Theo," Matt replied. "Mr. Khalid has the proof that Dedrick is a Royalist."

Adele sighed, then smiled broadly. "Oh, Matt, so soon. When can he get the information to us?"

Matt told Theo, "I want the package delivered directly to me. Disguise it as a wedding gift."

"A good idea," Theo said. "Matt?"

"Yes?"

"How are you and Adele?"

Matt understood Theo's question. "We're okay. Enjoying our time together. But all good things must come to an end."

"Not always," Theo told him. "Sometimes a man gets lucky and he can hold on to what he wants most in this world."

"Yeah, sure." Matt changed the subject abruptly. "When can we expect the package from Mr. Khalid?"

"His courier is en route to Erembourg as we speak," Theo said. "So, I'd say you can enjoy reading those documents while you eat breakfast."

"Thanks," Matt said. "And thank Mr. Khalid, whoever the hell he really is."

Theo chuckled softly. "Dia sends her love to Adele. Someday, perhaps…ah, but then, someday is a long way off. Good luck, my friend. Take care of your woman."

Before Matt could reply, Theo ended the connection.

"Mr. Khalid is sending us the proof that Dedrick is a Royalist," Adele said. "When? Today?"

"This morning."

"Then we can take the proof to my father and—"

"And put an end to all this pretense."

The smile vanished from Adele's face. "Yes, once my father knows the truth about Dedrick, he can arrest him for treason and for trying to have us murdered."

"There's proof against someone else, too," Matt told her. "But Mr. Khalid needs more time to gather that proof. He will send it later, when he's gotten hold of it."

"Who is this evidence against?"

"I'm sure it's not Pippin, if that's what's worrying you."

"Theo didn't say who it is?"

Matt shook his head. "Mr. Khalid doesn't know, but he's promised us proof of the person's identity soon."

"It's Colonel Rickard," Adele said. "I've never really liked him."

"My money is on Burhardt. Of course, it could be your secretary Lisa Mercer or even the queen herself."

"No. It's not Lisa or Muriel. They both love me. They would never do anything—"

"And doesn't Lord Burhardt love the king? Isn't Colonel Rickard sworn to defend the royal family?"

"My father must be told about Dedrick immediately,

and we must warn him that there is a traitor among his
trusted friends. When we get the information about
Dedrick, we must speak to my father alone."

"That might be easier said than done."

Adele read over the information that a courier had hand
delivered directly to Matt less than thirty minutes ago. A
part of her felt such relief, knowing that the documentation
she held would prove to her father that Dedrick was a
member of the Royalists. His seal and his signature were
plainly visible on the document swearing his allegiance to
King Eduard and to Balanchine. And among the papers in
the package Matt pored over was a document signed by
King Eduard making Dedrick his heir, with the provision
that Dedrick was, at the time of Eduard's death, either the
prince consort or the king of Orlantha.

"How on earth did Mr. Khalid get copies of these documents?" Adele wondered aloud. "The originals must be
on file in Balanchine, in the king's palace."

"I don't care how he got hold of them," Matt said as
he opened a sealed envelope. "I have a pretty good idea,
but it really doesn't matter, does it?"

"No, it doesn't matter." Adele stared at the contents of
the envelope Matt held as he dumped them onto the table.
"What are those?"

"Photographs," Matt said.

"Of whom?"

Matt spread the snapshots out on the tabletop. Adele
hurried over to take a look.

She gasped. "My God, it's pictures of Dedrick with
King Eduard." Adele gathered up the photographs and returned them to the envelope. "We must take all of this to
my father immediately."

Matt grabbed her wrist. "Wait."

She stared at him quizzically. "Why wait?"

"Don't ask for an audience with His Majesty. It's best if we can figure out a way to speak to him without anyone else around. You know his daily routine. When and where our best chance is of waylaying your father when he doesn't have an entourage around him."

Adele smiled as she snapped her fingers. "I know the perfect time and place."

King Leopold stood beside his first wife's grave, knelt and placed a single white orchid atop the white marble monument. Every day when he was in Erembourg at the palace, the king visited Adele's mother's grave. Although many within the castle walls, including Queen Muriel, knew of His Majesty's daily pilgrimage, no one ever spoke of it nor did anyone ever accompany him.

"Father?"

The king's broad shoulders tensed. "Leave me. I wish to be alone."

"You must know that I would never intrude if it were not of the utmost importance," Adele said. "But we have something to show you, something—"

"We?" The king turned abruptly and glared at Matt. "You dare to bring that man onto this sacred ground?"

"Father, Matt and I have documented proof that Dedrick is a Royalist. Please, you must look at these papers. They will prove to you that I have been right all along about Dedrick."

The king stared at Adele, a frown marring his weary features. "Where did you get such proof? How do I know it is not a forgery?"

"Look for yourself," Matt said. "Study the documents and make your own decision."

The king walked over to a small gazebo and sat on the bench inside, then motioned to Adele. "Bring me the papers."

Adele smiled at Matt, who handed the package to her and waited where he stood, several feet from the gazebo, while Adele took the documents to her father. She sat down beside the king and handed him the folder of papers that would prove the ugly truth about Dedrick.

The moments ticked by slowly as Adele watched her father read and study the documents. He didn't say a word, didn't even grunt. But his frown deepened. When he finished his perusal of Mr. Khalid's explosive package, he placed all the papers back into the file and handed them to Adele.

"I could have Dedrick arrested today," King Leopold said, his voice amazingly calm. "But I want to wait until we have proof of who his accomplice is. If I act too hastily, we could let someone far more dangerous than Dedrick escape."

"Oh, Father, you believe—"

"I believe my own eyes. I should have believed my daughter." The king held up his hand and motioned for Matt to come forward. "How did you come to be in possession of this information?"

"A friend of Theo Constantine's—a Mr. Khalid—managed to acquire this documentation for us," Matt said. "He believes he can eventually find out the name of the traitor at your court."

"I dare not wait," the king said. "As long as we do not know the face of our enemy, Adele's life will be at risk, as well as the future of Orlantha. These people must be stopped. Dedrick and whoever is pulling his strings."

"But, Father—"

The king grasped Adele's shoulders. "I must ask you to perform a great service for your country."

"Anything," Adele replied.

"If there were any other way..." The king cupped Adele's face with his hands. "The only thing I love as much as I do Orlantha is you, my child. I cannot do this. I cannot bear to choose between your safety and the good of our country.''

"Then let me choose, Father. Let the decision be mine."

"There is one sure way to bring this rat out into the open, to make him expose himself, " King Leopold said. "If I publicly proclaim my acceptance of your marriage, the Royalists will know there is no peaceful way to put Dedrick on the throne."

"No," Matt said. "You can't expose Adele that way. What you're thinking would be too dangerous for her. I won't allow her to—"

"Excuse me," Adele said. "But neither of you will decide what I will or won't do. I make my own decisions." She looked from Matt to her father. "If you publicly accept my marriage to Matt, then the Royalists will have to attempt to kill me. This person who is in our confidence, this person we trust, will likely be the only one close enough to me to do the deed."

Matt jerked Adele up off the bench. "Dammit, you can't do this. It's far too dangerous."

"Yes, Matt, I can. And I will." She turned to her father. "Make the announcement today."

"A royal wedding will be expected." Tears glistened in King Leopold's eyes. "Since much of the wedding arrangements for your marriage to Dedrick is already underway, it would be no problem to move up the date. Three days from now."

"Three days doesn't give us much time," Adele said.

"What do you mean a royal wedding?" Matt asked.

"The people of Orlantha will expect to see their princess wed in the Erembourg Cathedral. If we do anything less, Dedrick and the Royalists will suspect something is wrong." The king stood, placed his arm around Adele's shoulder and said, "From now until the day of your wedding, I will keep you under heavy guard, but on the morning of your wedding, at the cathedral, we will make it appear that you are alone. I will let everyone know that you are not to be disturbed while you say your prayers before the services begin.''

"How can you use her as bait?'' Matt asked. "She's your daughter.''

"She is the future queen of Orlantha and thus must be willing to risk everything for the sake of her country.'' King Leopold clamped his hand down on Matt's shoulder. "You will help me keep her safe. I can see that you love her, so I trust you to protect her with your life.''

"Father, there's something Matt and I must tell you about our marriage, about why we—''

"I have only to look at the two of you together to know.'' The king squeezed Matt's shoulder. "You have the same look in your eyes that I once had whenever Adele's mother was anywhere near me. She was the center of my universe.''

"Father, really, we need to—''

"No time to talk about love,'' the king said. "Matthew is not the man I would have chosen for you. But your choice is far better than mine.'' The king shook his head sadly. "We have much to do. First a public announcement proclaiming my acceptance and approval of your marriage. And of course there is no need to wait to bestow a knighthood on Matthew. I'll do it at the same time I make the announcement about the royal wedding.''

"Knighthood?'' Matt said.

"Yes, yes, the prince consort should have a title of his own. I'll inform the printers that the wedding invitation should read Sir Matthew O'Brien.'' The king looked at Matt. "What is your full name?''

"Matthew Desmond O'Brien.''

"I like the sound of it,'' the king said. "Sir Matthew Desmond O'Brien.

# Chapter 17

He knew what must be done and knew that he alone could be the instrument of death. The princess had been heavily guarded night and day, and her husband had not left her side for a moment. Even if Dedrick had been allowed an audience with Her Highness, he could not do the deed himself. The future ruler of Orlantha and Balanchine must remain blameless. Although he longed to be at Dedrick's side to act as his counselor, his life could be sacrificed. For the cause. He would kill the princess today, on her wedding day, and go to his death, condemned as a murderer. But one day, when history recorded what he'd done, they would call him a patriot.

He inspected himself in the full-length mirror, checking every detail of his attire. After placing his hat on his head, he donned his white gloves, marched from his office and went outside to the waiting limousine that would take him to the Erembourg Cathedral. No one would question his desire to speak alone with the princess. No guard would dare deny him access to Her Highness.

Those few moments of prayer that tradition dictated for the princess would be her last moments on earth. Such a shame that her death was necessary. She would have been the perfect bride for Dedrick.

"Matt, will you stop pacing," Theo Constantine said. "You make me tired just watching you."

"Damn, Theo, I can't take much more of this." Matt swiped his hand across his mouth and chin. "Why the hell couldn't Khalid get us the information we needed about the identity of the Royalist leader who is a close confidant of the king when he got the info on Dedrick? And if he wasn't such a damn mystery man, you'd have some idea how to get in touch with him to ask him to hurry. Adele's life could depend on it."

"Despite what many believe, Khalid is only human. And it takes time to gather information and to unearth evidence that is kept hidden. He will contact me as soon as he has a name."

"Yeah, I know. But going through with this insane plan today wouldn't be necessary if we just had the guy's name and any kind of proof of what he's done."

"All precautions are being taken to protect Adele," Theo said. "In a few minutes you will join the king and then take your place in the room adjoining Adele's while she is alone for her prayers."

"I'd rather be in the room with her than in the alcove." Matt stuck his fingers inside his shirt and loosened his tie.

Theo placed his hand on Matt's shoulder. "He will not make his move until Adele is alone."

"If anything goes wrong…if she gets hurt…"

Theo straightened Matt's tie. "The palace guards are stationed throughout the cathedral, and your Dundee agents are posing as wedding guests. All that can be done will be done."

"How would you feel if Dia's life was on the line?"

"I would feel as you do, my friend." Theo patted Matt on the back. "But my wife is not a princess. She does not have the type of responsibilities that Adele does. The future of an entire nation does not depend upon Dia's actions."

"Screw responsibility. Screw Orlantha. If I had my way, I'd go get Adele and hightail it out of this one-horse country and take my wife back to the U.S.A. with me."

"Spoken like a man in love," Theo said. "But Adele knows she cannot leave Orlantha. Her destiny is to rule this country, to keep the joint government in place and to lead her people into the twenty-first century."

Matt shut his eyes for a moment as the rage inside him subsided, then he looked squarely at Theo. "I realize that I'm going to lose Adele to this damn country of hers. But I can accept that fact as long as she lives. If she were to…if anything goes wrong…"

The church bells chimed, announcing the hour of prayer before the princess's wedding. Matt's body tensed.

Theo glanced at his wristwatch. "It is time. As your best man, I will go now and tell the guards that you are not to be disturbed while you are praying."

Matt grasped Theo's arm. "I may be a little too busy to pray. How about saying a few for me?"

Theo nodded. "Gladly, my friend. Gladly."

Adele preened in the mirror, pretending to be interested in the elaborately detailed wedding gown she wore. A fantasy gown, with an Alençon lace bodice overlaying a corset that laced up the back, a tip-of-the-shoulder neckline and three-quarter-length, sheer lace, poet sleeves and a voluminous skirt of silk over layers of tulle. The translucent veil fell from the small gold-and-diamond crown atop her head.

Dia and Muriel hovered over her, spraying her with perfume, adjusting the ten-foot train attached to her dress and placing around her neck the diamond necklace that her mother had worn on her wedding day thirty years ago. Adele felt like such a fraud. This wedding would never happen. It was nothing more than a trap to capture a traitor—a traitor whose existence posed a constant threat to her and to Orlantha. Neither her stepmother nor her best friend knew that her second wedding to Matt was a ruse, and that when they left her alone in a few minutes, she would become the bait used to ensnare a Royalist ringleader.

Cathedral bells chimed.

"There are the bells." Muriel kissed Adele's cheek. "We will leave you now, my dearest girl, for your prayers."

"I'll check on the bridesmaids," Dia said. "And I will give Phila last-minute instructions along with the other flower girls."

"Is she upset that she has to share the honor this time?" Adele asked.

Dia smiled. "No, she's quite excited about this wedding being here at the cathedral, but she can't quite comprehend why you and Matt need to go through with a second ceremony."

"Duty," Adele said, with a tinge of sarcasm in her voice.

Dia took Adele's hand. "Is there something wrong? I know you so well. I sense that you aren't as happy as you should be."

"Nerves." Adele forced a smile. "Just nerves."

"Come, Dia," Muriel said. "We must leave her to her prayers now."

Dia hugged Adele and left with the queen. Adele took a deep breath and began her prayers in earnest. *Please, dear Lord, keep me safe. I am so afraid. I do not know who will come to kill me. Whoever he is, I beg you to foil his evil plans. And watch over Matt. My beloved Matt. If it is necessary, he will sacrifice himself for me, as he knows I will sacrifice myself for Orlantha. I beg You, do not let any harm come to him. Keep him safe so he may return to America and to his life there.*

The door to the private chamber on the third floor of the cathedral opened. Adele held her breath as she turned to face her visitor. Standing there in the open doorway was Colonel Rickard, a small, gold-studded, wooden box in his hands. He clicked his heels and bowed.

"Colonel, I am at prayers and am not to be disturbed," Adele said in her most haughty voice. Her heartbeat thundered in her ears. Was the colonel her assassin?

"Please, forgive me, Your Highness," the colonel said. "I am here representing the palace guard. As is customary, I have brought the royal emblem worn by every crown prince or princess on their wedding day. The tradition goes back over four hundred years."

Adele let out a sigh of relief. She had forgotten about the royal emblem, a large round broach with the Reynard coat of arms in the center and circled by emeralds, diamonds and rubies. She stood straight and tall while Colonel Rickard attached the broach to the purple sash that crisscrossed the bodice of her wedding dress and was already laden with medals and broaches.

The colonel kissed Adele's hand, bowed, clicked his heels and exited the chamber. Adele clutched her hands together in an effort to keep them from trembling. She knelt before the small altar by the windows, but before she could form a coherent thought, the door opened again and Queen Muriel entered.

*Please, God, no, don't let the traitor be my stepmother.*

*It would break my father's heart and he would die from disappointment.*

"I am so sorry to disturb you, but..."

Muriel hurried forward as Adele rose to her feet. That's when she noticed the silk pouch in Muriel's hand.

"I have something for you," the queen said.

A rush of adrenaline, produced by cold fear, surged through Adele's body. "A gift?"

"A very special present."

Adele's breath caught in her throat. Muriel undid the silk pouch and removed a small wooden soldier. Adele stared at the child's toy. Hand carved. Hand painted. Two hundred years old. Adele burst into laughter. Her stepmother stared at her in puzzlement.

"You are pleased?" the queen asked. "I was not sure that you would want me to be the one...since it is a mother's place...but since your mother is not—"

Still laughing, giddy with relief, Adele grabbed Muriel and hugged her, then kissed her on both cheeks. "It is most appropriate for the queen to give the soldier to the princess on her wedding day."

Muriel sighed. "Even your father had forgotten about this special tradition. He didn't even mention it to me. But every royal bride for the past two hundred years has been given King Alexandre's wooden soldier. As you know, it comes with a wish for the bride to produce a male heir." Muriel grasped Adele's hands. "I wish this for you with all my heart."

After Muriel left, Adele went down on her knees before the altar again, but she couldn't concentrate on prayers. Were there any other traditions she had forgotten? Everyone knew she was supposed to be left alone, left to her prayers, but tradition overruled all else, even prayers.

Adele prayed. And waited. What if he didn't show up? What if, for some reason, he knew a trap had been set?

Just when she had begun to think no one else was going to disturb her privacy, the door opened again, then shut behind her third visitor.

Matt waited behind the heavy purple curtains, in an alcove with a secret door that opened to a hidden passageway leading to the chamber assigned to the bridegroom. On the other side of the door, quiet and well hidden in the narrow passageway between the two chambers, the king, Chancellor Dutetre and five trusted palace guards waited. They would move only on his signal. Matt had been prepared to attack twice before—when Colonel Rickard made his appearance and then when Queen Muriel paid Adele a visit. Now, a third visitor had arrived. Matt listened as the man spoke to Adele.

"You look incredibly lovely, Your Highness," a familiar voice said. "I beg you to forgive me for intruding on your time of prayer, but there is an urgent matter I must attend to immediately."

"You are forgiven if you are here on state business," Adele said. "Please, tell me what is this urgent matter that could not wait until after my wedding?"

Matt heard the nervousness in Adele's voice. He realized that this time she had no doubt about the motive of her visitor. But Matt also knew that he couldn't make his move too soon. The timing must be perfect. There would probably be only seconds between failure and success. And as far as he was concerned, failure wasn't an option.

He drew his SIG Saur P229 from the shoulder holster he wore beneath his leather jacket. Since dressing for the wedding had been nothing but show, he had changed immediately after Theo had left him alone for the hour of prayer. Matt parted the curtains a fraction of an inch, just enough to gain him a clear view of Adele and her visitor.

"It is most unfortunate that you would not marry the

duke. Together you would have made a magnificent royal couple.''

''But Dedrick is not the man I love,'' Adele said, backing slowly away from the man holding a small handgun pointed directly at her. ''And even if I had cared for him, I could not have married him. The duke is a Royalist, a traitor to my country.''

''So you tried to convince your father, but he would not believe you, would he? I am very sorry that I must do this, Your Highness. I have known you since you were a young girl and thought that your betrothal to Dedrick would join Balanchine and Orlantha without the necessity of warfare, without anyone having to die.''

''You're going to kill me, Lord Burhardt? Is that your plan, to eliminate me in the hopes that my father will still name Dedrick as his successor?''

''There is no other way,'' Lord Burhardt said, aiming his pistol.

''You won't get away with this,'' Adele told him. ''The guards outside—''

''It is unfortunate that I, too, must sacrifice myself for the noble cause.''

''If you're caught, and you will be, then it's only a matter of time until Dedrick is found out.''

''No, we have taken every precaution to protect the duke. I am expendable. He is not. No one must ever suspect that he was involved in any way with your death, with the earlier attempt on your life or with the Royalists. Your father must see Dedrick as the only hope for Orlantha.''

Adele backed up against the huge arched window behind her. Lord Burhardt's trigger finger tightened on the pistol. Still hidden in the shadowy alcove, behind the purple curtains, Matt lifted his gun and aimed. The sound of a gunshot echoed in the hushed stillness within the chamber on the third floor of the cathedral. Adele slammed her hand over her mouth to stifle a scream. Lord Burhardt, his eyes frozen in surprise, dropped to the floor, the blood from a single bullet in the back of his head staining his white-blond hair.

Matt stepped over Burhardt's body as he made his way to Adele. She rushed into his arms and buried her face against his chest. Dry, heaving sobs racked her body. Surrounded by guards, King Leopold and Chancellor Dutetre stormed into the chamber just as the guards outside burst into the room.

"Are you all right?" the king asked Adele as he caressed her head. When she didn't reply, he asked Matt, "Is she…was she harmed?"

"She's unhurt," Matt said. "Just badly shaken."

The king grunted, then turned to the chancellor. "Make that phone call immediately. I want Dedrick Vardan placed under arrest. The duke will be charged with treason. And inform the police about what happened here."

"Yes, Your Majesty." The chancellor, flanked by two guards, exited the room.

"Bring Adele with you," the king told Matt, then issued an order to the guards. "Let no one enter this chamber until the police arrive." The king glanced at Lord Burhardt's body. "I trusted this man as my chief advisor and my friend." A lone tear trickled down the king's cheek.

Alone together in the chamber where he had prepared himself for his wedding to the princess, Matt and Adele spoke privately, while King Leopold waited just outside the door, pacing madly back and forth as Queen Muriel stood by helplessly.

"All's well that ends well," Matt said flippantly.

"I owe you so much." Adele gazed into Matt's eyes. "The country of Orlantha owes you a great deal."

"Hey, I got to be prince for a day, didn't I? And I'm now Sir Matthew. Pretty heady stuff for a poor boy from Kentucky."

The cathedral bells chimed. Matt stiffened. Adele sighed.

"The bells chime the hour of our wedding," she told him. "The service will begin at any moment."

"Then I guess you and your father should get down there and try to explain to your guests that the wedding has been called off due to the fact that the bridegroom's on his way to the airport to catch a flight back to America."

"You don't have to go."

"Sure I do. Nothing for me here. And I'm sure if the king will put in a good word for me, my boss will rehire me."

"Orlantha could use a man like you," Adele said. "I need a man like you."

"Nah, you don't need me. You've got a palace full of bodyguards."

"But if you leave, I won't have a husband."

"Look, just send the annulment papers to the Dundee Agency, and I'll sign whatever needs to be signed. Once that's done, you can start husband hunting. My guess is that this go-round your father will let you do the picking."

*I choose you, Matt O'Brien*, she wanted to shout at the top of her lungs. But what good would it do? Matt didn't want to stay in Orlantha. He didn't want to become her prince consort. All he wanted was to go home to America as quickly as he could.

"I'd ask you to come to Atlanta for a visit sometime." Matt shuffled his feet. "But I know you'll be pretty busy once your father turns things over to you. I guess it's best if we say goodbye now." He searched her face as if looking for the answer to some unasked question. "Yeah, a clean break is best.'' He lifted his hand and reached out, as if he were going to touch her, then dropped his hand to his side.

Adele straightened her shoulders and tilted her head in a regal pose. ''Yes, a clean break is best.'' She held out her hand to him. ''Thank you, Matt. If ever you… Orlantha shall always be in your debt.''

Without accepting her hand, almost as if he were afraid to touch her, Matt headed for the door, then paused, glanced over his shoulder and said, ''Good luck, Princess.''

She nodded but didn't try to speak. Emotion clogged her throat, rendering her temporarily mute. Matt opened the door, walked out and disappeared down the hallway. Adele stood very still. She could hear her heartbeat. Could hear her soft breathing. Could hear her heart breaking.

King Leopold rushed into the chamber. ''Where's Matthew going? He waved at me and said goodbye and told me to take good care of you.''

''He's going back to America.''

''What do you mean he's going—''

''We're having our marriage annulled,'' Adele said.

''You are confusing me, daughter. Explain yourself.''

''Come in and close the door, Father, and I'll tell you all about my marriage and why, in just a little while, you and I must face our guests and tell them that the wedding has been canceled. Permanently canceled.''

Matt made it all the way to the airport, but the minute he got out of the taxi, he knew he couldn't leave. Not without Adele. To hell with her becoming queen of Orlantha. If she loved him, she'd come back to America with him. But he hadn't even given her the chance to say no. He'd made all the decisions.

Yeah, but if he loved her, truly loved her, wouldn't he

be willing to stay in her country and make a few sacrifices to be with her? He shouldn't have run off the way he did. He should have stuck around and talked things out more thoroughly. Maybe they could have reached some sort of compromise.

"Hey, buddy, take me back to the cathedral," Matt said as he hopped into the cab he had just exited.

"Back to the cathedral?"

"Yeah, and step on it, will you?"

"Step on what, sir?"

"Just get me back to the cathedral as fast as you can."

On the fifteen-minute drive, Matt went over every possible scenario that could give Adele and him a happily-ever-after to their romance. He wasn't sure how they would work things out, but he knew one thing for certain—he loved Adele.

When the cab stopped in front of the cathedral, Matt paid the guy and gave him a big tip, then rushed past the guards at the door and hurried inside to the vestibule. He walked up to one of the palace guards standing just outside the entrance to the sanctuary.

"Where's the princess?" Matt asked.

"Sir Matthew?" The guard inspected Matt's appearance. "Her Highness is with the king. They entered the sanctuary only moments ago."

Matt opened the huge double doors leading into the sanctuary. He gazed down the long, wide center aisle to where Adele and her father stood before the altar and faced their guests.

"May we have your attention, please," Pippin Ritter said. "King Leopold wishes to make a brief statement."

Matt took several hesitant steps down the aisle. Suddenly Adele saw him. Their gazes met and locked. Adele moved from her father's side and walked several feet up the aisle. The wedding guests murmured and glanced around to see what had gained the princess's attention. King Leopold smiled broadly, then slapped Pippin on the back. Adele walked faster. Matt moved toward her. Then Adele and Matt ran to each other, meeting in the middle of the center aisle. Matt lifted Adele off her feet and swung her around and around. She squealed with delight. Then he eased her down the front of his body and set her on her feet. She threw her arms around his neck.

"I couldn't leave," he told her.

"I didn't want you to go."

"I guess I could get used to being Sir Matthew."

"Prince Matthew," Adele corrected.

"Yeah, Prince Matthew."

"We could postpone the wedding until you're sure."

"I'm sure," he told her. "I'm sure I love you, and if I can't spend the rest of my life with you, my life won't be worth living."

"Oh, Matt. I love you, too. So very much."

"Then what are we waiting for? Let's get this show on the road. The sooner we finish up with this royal wedding, the sooner we get another honeymoon."

Adele surveyed him from head to toe, but didn't say anything about him changing out of his jeans and leather bomber jacket. She took his arm and led him down the aisle. The crowded sanctuary stilled as King Leopold came forward and ceremoniously took Adele's hand and placed it in Matt's.

"Glad to see you came to your senses," the king whispered to Matt, then winked.

An hour later, when the endless wedding service finally did end, Sir Matthew—soon to become Prince Matthew when his wife was crowned queen—kissed his bride. The entire assembly came to their feet and applauded. Cheers rose to the rafters. And the church bells rang out as Adele and Matt, now husband and wife in every sense of the word, headed out of the church to the awaiting horse-drawn carriage. Happily-ever-after was only beginning for the royal couple.

# *Epilogue*

A year after the royal wedding made headline news around the world, the christening of the new crown prince was heralded as the happily-ever-after to a Cinderfella fairy-tale romance between Adele and Matt. Theo and Dia Constantine were godparents to young Alexandre Leopold Desmond Reynard-O'Brien, who had his father's wild black Irish hair and his mother's exotic dark eyes. The little prince seemed to know that this celebration was in his honor and therefore was on his best behavior.

At the grand reception at the Erembourg palace, Queen Adele and Prince Matthew greeted their guests—the wealthy, the famous, the royals of the world. And Grandfather Leopold took charge of his grandson, whisking away the child to the nursery while the party was still in full swing. An hour later Matt and Adele left Muriel in charge of their guests, and they slipped away in search of the missing twosome.

Softly singing a melody from his own childhood, King

Leopold sat in a wooden rocking chair, little Alex in his arms. Adele and Matt stood in the nursery doorway.

"One day, my little man, you will rule Orlantha," King Leopold said. "There have been many changes made to my country since I was a boy, and many more will be made before you sit on the throne. Your mother's marriage to your father marked the beginning of a new era. I plan to be around for many years to see all these changes, so I must take good care of myself. That is why I gave your mother my old job of running this country. You see, Alex, I want to live to see you grow into a fine man...a man as strong and brave and honorable as your father."

Adele squeezed Matt's hand. They smiled at each other, then turned and walked down the hall toward their private quarters adjacent to the nursery. Carrying an armful of toys, Alex's nanny, Mrs. Pearson, met them in the hallway. When she tried to curtsy, two teddy bears and a musical rattle fell to the floor. Matt picked up the items and laid them atop the heap.

"His Majesty requested I go to his quarters and get these new toys he ordered for Prince Alexandre." Mrs. Pearson tsk-tsked. "Wherever shall I put them? The nursery is running over with toys and stuffed animals as it is."

"I suggest you weed through the toys and remove some of them from time to time," Adele said. "I'll arrange to have them sent to the children's ward at the Erembourg Hospital."

Ms. Pearson smiled and bobbed her head, substituting the action for a bow. "Yes, Queen Adele."

Once Alex's nanny disappeared into the nursery, Matt took Adele inside their suite, closed the door and pulled her into his arms.

"Have I told you today how much I love you?"

Adele smiled. "I believe you told me this morning,

when we showered together. But I never tire of hearing those words.''

''And I never tire of saying them.''

''We are very fortunate,'' Adele said. ''I never dreamed that I could ever be this happy.''

''Neither did I, honey.'' Matt nuzzled Adele's neck. ''If anyone had told me a couple of years ago that I'd wind up married to the queen of Orlantha and actually like my job as prince consort, I wouldn't have believed them.''

Adele grasped Matt's hand and led him across the room to the bed. She yanked on his arms, toppling them both down on the satin coverlet.

''You enjoy being the prince consort because you've created your own niche, my love.'' Adele wrapped her arms around Matt's neck. ''You're the first prince consort who actually knew how to do anything other than play polo, give speeches and spend money. Your computer expertise has helped reorganize the way our government is run, and your security background has helped bring our military into the twenty-first century.''

''I do what I can.'' Matt kissed Adele.

Adele returned the kiss with equal passion, and within minutes the queen of Orlantha was participating in her favorite pastime—making love to her husband. Her prince.

\* \* \* \* \*

# Chapter 1

Nikos stared at the woman. She was the same and yet vastly different from the girl he had known fifteen years ago. If possible she was even more beautiful now than she had been then. But there was no mistaking those stunning azure blue eyes, that platinum blond hair, though cut quite short now, and that incredible, luscious body. And yet this woman bore only a superficial resemblance to her former self. Gone was the exuberant smile, the tender young features and the twinkle of naive mischief in her eyes. But the woman standing before him, glaring at him with stunned disbelief, took his breath away, just as her younger counterpart had done.

"It is you, isn't it?" Nikos said, certain and yet unable to believe that this moment was possible. He had put any hopes of ever seeing her again out of his mind long ago. She had become a sweet memory, one he allowed himself, on rare occasions, to bring to the forefront of his thoughts and savor. She had been relegated to the part of his soul that existed in a fictional land called *If Only*.

She simply continued staring at him, neither speaking nor moving.

"What's going on here?" Theo glanced back and forth from Nikos to Ellen. "Do you two know each other?"

"Yes, we do, don't we, Mary Ellen?" Nikos took a tentative step toward her, but stopped instantly when he saw the expression on her face. She looked at him as if she was afraid of him. But why would she fear him?

"How do you know Ms. Denby?" Theo asked.

Nikos kept his gaze riveted to Mary Ellen. God, she was exquisite. Like something from a man's most erotic fantasy. A thick shock of white-blond hair, but severely short, did nothing to diminish her ultra femininity. Her face was classically beautiful, her fair, flawless skin lightly tanned. Not even the Spartan khaki slacks and crisp white blouse she wore could disguise the voluptuous figure hidden beneath.

"Is that your last name, Denby?" Nikos asked.

As if snapping out of a trance, Ellen sighed heavily, lifting and dropping her shoulders in the process. She huffed loudly, then closed the door and moved toward Nikos.

"We never exchanged last names, did we? And by the way, no one has called me Mary Ellen in a long time. I'm simply Ellen now." She halted several feet from him, but kept her gaze fixed on his face. "Nikos Khalid? Is that your real name?"

"It will do for now," he replied.

"Will one of you please explain to me how it is that you know each other?" Theo moved between them, glaring first at Ellen and then at Nikos. "If there's some reason why the two of you can't work together, I want to know now."

Nikos laid his hand on Theo's shoulder and gently shoved him aside as he moved closer to Ellen. "Don't you remember her? I introduced you to her at a party you held here at the villa. You told me what a lucky devil I was to have found such a rare jewel.''

Theo jerked around and stared at Ellen. His gaze travelled over her from head to toe and then back up again. ''When did we meet?''

''Fifteen years ago,'' Ellen said. ''But only briefly. Obviously I didn't make much of an impression on you.''

''Ah, but you did,'' Nikos corrected. ''But I'm afraid Theo was slightly drunk that evening and when he drinks too much, he remembers very little the following day.'' Nikos squeezed Theo's shoulder. ''I met Mary Ellen in Dareh during the Summer Festival.''

''Fifteen years ago?'' Theo absorbed the information. Suddenly his eyes widened. ''This—this is the woman that you... My God!''

''Mr. Constantine, I see no reason why Mr. Khalid is needed here,'' Ellen said, her voice quite stern. ''The Dundee Agency is perfectly capable of handling the negotiations without any assistance.''

''Perhaps you are,'' Theo said. ''But Nikos is not here to assist you in negotiating. He's here because of his ties to...uh...to rebel factions worldwide. He has knowledge of and experience dealing with the Al'alim cult. I assure you that he will prove indispensable to us.''

''I see.'' Ellen looked at Nikos, her eyes questioning him, doubting him. ''And exactly what is it you do, Mr. Khalid, that has given you this vast experience with terrorists?''

''Theo, would you mind letting me speak to Ma...to Ellen alone?'' Nikos eyed the door, then noted the direction with a nod of his head.

''Yes. Certainly.'' Theo walked to the door, opened it, then glanced back and said, ''Ms. Denby, either work out your differences with Nikos here and now or bring in another agent to take your place. We have no time for old lovers to work through past mistakes. Not while my daughter's life is in imminent peril. Do I make myself clear?''

''Yes. You've made yourself quite clear,'' Ellen replied.

Theo left and closed the door behind him.

Nikos crossed his arms over his chest and smiled. ''You're still very beautiful, but you've changed dramatically. What happened to that sweet, wild, young thing who was filled with such *joie de vive?*''

''She grew up, learned from her mistakes and moved on.''

Not by word or action did Ellen show any emotion, but the coldness in her eyes spoke to him silently. She was angry with him. Angry and perhaps hurt. Was it possible that after all these years, she still resented the fact that he'd left her sleeping in their bed at the hotel, leaving her only a vague goodbye note? Surely she hadn't held on to that youthful rage for fifteen years.

''I've thought of you,'' he said. ''More often than I'd like to admit.''

''Save it, will you? Save all your pretty little speeches for a woman who's stupid enough to believe them.'' A tinge of color blushed her cheeks. ''I doubt you've given me a thought over the years. After all, I was nothing more to you than a two week fling with a silly little American virgin.''

''Such anger. Why? Unless—''

''You're right. I'm overreacting. I apologize. I haven't given you a thought in years, but I suppose seeing you again refreshed my memory and all that old anger resurfaced.''

''Ah, I see. Of course, you had every right to be angry. I was your first lover and I left you with nothing more than a brief note. Very ungentlemanly of me.'' Nikos reached out and took her hand in his.

Ellen shivered. "My first lover, but certainly not my last." She jerked her hand from his. "I should thank you for being the first. You taught me more than you'll ever know."

"Did I indeed?"

"Mr. Constantine is right. Unless you and I agree to forget we ever had a past association, we can't work together to save his daughter's life. And saving Phila Constantine and her nanny, Ms. Sheridan, is why I'm here in Golnar."

"If you have no problem with our working together, I don't."

"As long as you allow me and my agents to do our job, we will work with you, since that's what Mr. Constantine wants."

Nikos eyed Ellen suspiciously. "Do you hate me?"

She hesitated for a couple of seconds, then said, "No. I have no feelings of any kind for you."

"Setting me straight, are you, Ms. Denby?" Nikos's lips twitched. "You don't want me to have any misconceptions about our picking up where we left off fifteen years ago. Am I to assume you have a husband or a significant other in your life?"

"You can assume whatever the hell you want, Mr. Khalid."

Ellen turned, opened the door and walked out into the hall. Nikos followed her as she made her way to where Theo stood halfway down the corridor. He was deep in conversation with another man, a big, burly guy. With the build of a professional wrestler.

Ellen walked up to Theo and said, "Mr. Khalid and I are in agreement. We'll have no problems working together."

Theo glanced beyond Ellen and looked straight at Nikos. "Is that right?"

"I would never contradict a lady," Nikos said.

But the look in his eyes said his presence on this mission wouldn't make things easy for the lady in question....

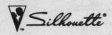

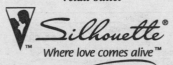

# $ Saving Money $ Has Never Been This Easy!

Just fill out and send in this form from any October, November and December 2002 books and we will send you a coupon booklet worth a total savings of $20.00 off future purchases of Harlequin and Silhouette books in 2003.

## Yes! It's that easy!

**I accept your incredible offer! Please send me a coupon booklet:**

Name (PLEASE PRINT)

Address _____ Apt. #

City _____ State/Prov. _____ Zip/Postal Code

**In a typical month, how many Harlequin and Silhouette novels do you read?**

❑ **0-2**     ❑ **3+**

097KJKDNC7                                    097KJKDNDP

**Please send this form to:**
In the U.S.: Harlequin Books, P.O. Box 9071, Buffalo, NY 14269-9071
In Canada: Harlequin Books, P.O. Box 609, Fort Erie, Ontario L2A 5X3

Allow 4-6 weeks for delivery. Limit one coupon booklet per household. Must be postmarked no later than January 15, 2003.

HARLEQUIN®
*Makes any time special* ®

*Silhouette*®
*Where love comes alive*™